LIFE IS STRANGE.
Steph's Story

T0347585

LIFE IS STRANGE

Steph's Story

ROSIEE THOR

TITAN BOOKS

Life is Strange: Steph's Story
Print edition ISBN: 9781789099614
E-book edition ISBN: 9781789099669

Published by Titan Books
A division of Titan Publishing Group Ltd
144 Southwark Street, London SE1 0UP
www.titanbooks.com

First edition: March 2023
10 9 8 7 6 5 4 3

This is a work of fiction. All of the characters, organizations, and events portrayed in this novel are either products of the author's imagination or are used fictitiously. Any resemblance to actual persons, living or dead (except for satirical purposes), is entirely coincidental.

A CIP catalogue record for this title is available from the British Library.

Printed and bound by CPI Group (UK) Ltd, Croydon, CR0 4YY.

For everyone who marches to
        the beat of their own drum
And for those who can't yet,
                but still want to

The Timeline – Author's Note

Life is Strange is a world of choices. Some are small and others are downright cosmic. None are inconsequential. Though Steph's life exists outside Arcadia Bay and Haven Springs, she is greatly impacted by events in both. *Steph's Story* occurs in a timeline where Arcadia Bay was destroyed but Chloe Price was not, one of many possibilities in the vast multiverse. Whether your choices mirrored these or not, I hope you choose to read *Steph's Story* with an open mind and continue to bring your creativity to the infinite universes of *Life is Strange*.

LIFE IS STRANGE.
Steph's Story

Spring

One

They say home is where the heart is, but I've never been in love. Sure, I've had my crushes—some attainable and others… not so much. My childhood bedroom used to be covered in posters of Kristen Stewart and Avril Lavigne. Not anymore.

I stand before the plain wooden door to my bedroom. Or what will become my bedroom the second I walk across the threshold.

> Changed my mind. You think Lia will notice if I sleep in her studio?

I tap out a text to Jordie, fingers too jittery to spell anything right. Luckily, autocorrect has my back. He replies almost immediately.

> I bet all the yarn in there would make a good nest

> Right??? COZY!

> So… that bad being back at your dad's?

My chest clenches and my throat closes up a bit. Dad's cleared a room for me in his new house. It's not really *new*. He's lived here since we moved to Seattle five years ago. I've managed to stay away as long as I can, between college dorms and couch surfing. But it's time to say goodbye to mooching off friends and hello to mooching off my father, since I've got my diploma and a knot the size of a small country under my shoulder blade.

Maybe I'll hang that on the wall. The diploma, not my shoulder knot.

No. I'm just being a baby

Well, grow up and then get
down here. I'm bored out of my skull

I tuck my phone into my back pocket and take a deep breath before turning the knob and letting the door swing open.

Dad's put in his best effort to make it feel like a real room. There's a plaid duvet covering the bed and it's not even an ugly color—blue and yellow, my favorites. Plus he's built an Ikea dresser and some shelves all by himself, like he doesn't realize I'm a lesbian.

"You got everything, Steph?" Dad calls up the stairs.

It's strange, hearing his voice. We've lived in the same city all this time, but I can count on one hand the number of times we've actually been in the same space. Mostly we email. It's not that we don't get along; it's just that we thrive in text format. Guess it would be weird to email him my response to such a simple question, though.

"Yep. I'm all set!" I glance down at my belongings. It's a meager showing. Just my trusty purple suitcase and backpack. Commence: the great unpacking.

It should take me a grand total of ten minutes to unload my clothes and toiletries and so on. I cut way back on all my stuff when I graduated. It just wasn't practical to be lugging around full-size shampoo bottles or my boxes full of vinyl. Only the essentials for me. The one exception I made was my art supplies.

They're the first thing I unpack—a sketchbook with a tattered cover and a plastic bag full of colored pencils at various lengths. My favorite color is near the end of its life—RIP Unmellow Yellow—so I'll need to scrounge up some more before starting the next issue of my zine. For now, I stow them in the top drawer of the desk and turn back to the rest of the room.

The walls are bare in this sanitized way that makes me nostalgic for DigiPen. Back in my dorm room there wasn't an inch of wall to be seen there behind all my posters, concert tickets, and concept art for my senior project—a fully realized tabletop RPG set underwater that culminated in a battle between mecha mermaids and an undead legion of shipwrecked sailors. It got a little overwhelming near the end there, but now I actually miss those drawings of zombie pirates.

Organized chaos. That's my jam.

> This room is huge

Jordie's reply takes a few seconds—he must have customers at the shop.

> Yipee!

> No, like too huge

> Cry me a fucking river

I groan. He's right, of course. Never thought I'd complain about having too much space, but it feels like this bedroom was put here specifically to mock me with its white walls, clean floor, and empty surfaces.

> What am I even gonna fill this place with? I don't have any stuff

Omg girl, buy some with your adult money

Lol what adult money?

Even if I had cash to burn, I'm not sure what I'd want to display. My life these days is mostly working at the board game café and figuring out whose couch I'll be crashing on. Now that I don't have to worry about the latter, it's like there's this void to fill. Like if I don't figure out who I am, I'll disappear against a backdrop of eggshell paint.

My gaze snags on some loose papers on the dresser by the window. On top is a brochure for a coding boot camp. Snore. If I wanted to sit behind a desk all day, I'd have actually applied for jobs in the video game industry with that fancy game-design degree of mine. Maybe someday I'll see the appeal, but for now I want to be on my feet in the world, not staring at a screen. Underneath the brochure is a flyer for the Oregon Shakespeare Festival down in Ashland. I know it's famous and a tech job might be fun, but I can't see myself going back to Oregon. Besides, I lost my taste for the bard after doing *The Tempest* back in high school.

Turns out storms really aren't my thing.

My phone buzzes, but it's not Jordie. I have a new email— from Dad. I roll my eyes, but it's not like I have room to judge since I considered doing the same thing just a few minutes ago. We really are hopeless at communication. Maybe we'll get better now that we're cohabitating.

The email is a forwarded job listing for an IT position at his work.

Thought of you, sweetie! Let me know if you apply and I'll put in a good word.

I sigh and type out a quick reply.

Thanks, Dad!

What I don't say is I'd rather eat my own hand than have him get me a job, especially one I don't want. You couldn't pay me to exchange the freedom of my hourly barista job for corporate IT. Not for all the health insurance and 401(k)s in the world. I'd much rather be slinging coffee beans on my feet all day than repeatedly telling people my dad's age to stop using Internet Explorer.

I check the time. Still a few hours before I need to be at my actual job, the one I got all by myself, thank you very much. But one more glance around this room that feels more hotel than home sends me out the door. I can always unpack later.

It takes me thirty minutes of fast walking downhill, across the Ballard Bridge, then through a sketchy parking lot to reach Save Point from my dad's house in Queen Anne. Not a bad commute to the board game café I've worked at for the past six months. I shove open the door with my shoulder and the electronic bell announces my arrival with the victory music from *Final Fantasy*.

Jordie Abdullah's round brown face covered in fresh black stubble pops up over the counter. He's wearing a rumpled button-up with a purple morning glory print under his apron and a pained expression. "Steph! Oh my god, I could *kiss* you!"

"Yeah, but you won't." I amble over and lean my elbows on the laminated menu.

"Ollie didn't show, and Amy couldn't find anyone else to take the shift, so I've been working a double."

"Wow, so we hate Ollie today, yeah?" I slip around the counter and grab an extra apron.

"Nah, he's out sick—time of the month." Jordie sighs and wrinkles his nose. "Can you cover for a sec? It's T-time, plus I have to pee."

"Release the river!" I shout in the deepest Treebeard impression I can manage as Jordie does a little skip over to the bathroom.

It's afternoon, so the shop isn't very crowded. A guy in a flat cap sits by himself, sipping a house coffee—or 'homebrew' as we call it at Save Point—while typing furiously on a laptop with a proudly displayed 'Plant Dad' sticker in the corner, and over by the window, a small group of teenagers are playing *Codenames*.

There will be a rush any minute with school letting out at three, so I set up the grinder and unload the dishwasher while I wait for Jordie. A John Mayer song plays over the speakers and I eye the store's tablet plugged into the wall. I may not be technically scheduled, but if I'm working, at least the music isn't going to suck. I sneak over and swipe to a different playlist.

'Cherry Lips' by Garbage blares from the speakers and I shimmy my shoulders to the beat. The techno intro is punctuated by a single rendition of victory music as the café door swings open and closed, and I turn to greet our new customer.

And there she is. A windblown white girl with long black hair, blunt-cut bangs, and an ear full of gold rings and studs stands opposite me, clutching a stack of loose papers to her chest.

I extract myself from my one-woman dance party and meet her at the counter. "Welcome to Save Point. What can I do ya for?"

The girl's gaze sweeps over and past me, her brown eyes lined with sharp black and purple liner. "Is Jordie in?" she asks.

"He's on break." I jam my thumb behind me toward the back of the store. Jordie hasn't been gone long, but I know it can be a bit of an ordeal to take his testosterone at work and I'm not about to be the asshole who interrupts his legally mandated fifteen minutes. "It'll probably be a bit if you want to wait."

She nods, glancing over at the empty tables, but doesn't move to sit.

"Can I make you something?" I gesture toward the espresso machine.

"Uh…" her eyes find the menu on the counter. "I'll have a cinnamon roll for initiative and… I guess an Eldritch Baja Blast?"

"Long or short rest?" I say, pointing to the ceramic mug and to-go cup on display. At the lost look on her face, I add, "For here or to go?"

"Here."

"On it!" I give her my best smile, and turn to make her drink—a pineapple and mango smoothie topped with blackberry cream. My gaze drifts from the blender full of fruit chunks to follow her movement as she sits on a stool at the bar, carefully guarding her papers like a windstorm might come along and blow them all into the air—which, to be fair, isn't outside the scope of normal for Seattle. "Whatcha got there?" I ask, nudging the papers with my pinky as I slide her cinnamon roll across the counter.

"What? Oh." She looks down at the stack in her arms as though she's only just remembered she's carrying them. "Flyers."

I start up the blender, letting the loud sound fill the space between us. Working here, I see all types of people—shy, loud, weird, rude—but I've never encountered this exact combination of nervous and cool. I can't tell if she's blowing me off because I'm obviously a nerd or if there's something else distracting her. It's strange to see someone so clearly confident in who they are be so uncomfortable in a space as normal as a coffee shop.

"They're for my band," she offers after the blender whirs to a stop and she holds up a flyer for me to see. "We're playing at Bar-None this weekend."

The page is filled with art deco lettering on a black background spelling out the words 'Vinyl Resting Place.' Beneath is a drawing of a drum kit with records instead of cymbals and a dark gold sound wave.

"Jordie said I could stick one of these in the window."

"Definitely!" I rustle in one of the drawers and pull out a roll of tape. "That's rad. I love music!"

"This your playlist?" she asks, pointing to the speakers while I make room by tearing down a poster for a haunted corn maze that definitely isn't still going in April.

"Oh, yeah. Just threw something fun on to liven up the place." I press a line of tape to her flyer and stick it to the window before turning back to find her gaze on me. I catch her eye and hold it for a beat too long. They're bright and brown like a whole planet lives inside her irises. Maybe I won't bother unpacking at Dad's house; I'll just move to whatever solar system she's hiding in there.

At that moment, the song changes and 'Rebel Girl' by Bikini Kill fills the room.

"I like it—old school."

Relief knocks my shoulders down a solid inch. I'm an equal opportunist when it comes to music, so it just as easily could have been Weird Al or the *Wicked* soundtrack. I don't get embarrassed by my taste in music as a rule. I like what I like, and if someone has a problem with it, that says more about them than me, but for some reason I really want this girl to think I have good taste. Whatever *good taste* is, anyway.

"Izzie!" Jordie returns quicker than expected. "You made it! Glad to see you found the place." He gestures to our surroundings with a flourish.

The girl's—Izzie's—demeanor changes immediately. Her shoulders straighten and her eyes brighten. Jordie reaches out to hug her, and for a second I wonder if there's something he forgot to tell me. Like that he's suddenly into girls. I give him a look, but all his focus is on Izzie.

"It's like a two-minute walk from my place. I'd have to be decapitated to get lost," says Izzie, pulling back.

"Could be cool, though, right? You could carry your head around under your arm and freak people out, headless-horseman style." I return to the counter and throw a mint sprig on Izzie's drink before sliding it over to her.

"Izzie, this is Steph. Steph, Izzie—she was the coolest French tutor I ever had."

"Did you have more than one French tutor?" Izzie's voice has lost some of its restraint and her lips upturn in a smile.

"Nope! Doesn't make you less cool!" Jordie tears a piece off Izzie's cinnamon roll, then says through a mouthful of pastry, "You two have that in common."

"He's right," I say, tipping my head just a bit closer to Izzie's and sliding forward on my elbows. "We are exceptionally cool."

Jordie leans in conspiratorially, a twinkle in his warm brown eyes that almost always precedes some mischief. "You're also both lesbians. Discuss!" He hops up and ducks behind the counter to clean the blender, leaving me face-to-face with Izzie.

"I, um…" Izzie glances up at me, expression entirely unreadable.

"Jordie!" I swear he is the worst wingman in the history of wingmen. Honestly, for a fellow queer person, Jordie should know better. Being into girls is the bare minimum requirement for my dating pool, and as much as I'm all about Izzie's vibe, if she's accepting girlfriend applications, it probably won't be from the barista at the game café. I know I should say something else to save Izzie from having to reject me here and now, but before I can think of a joke to cut the tension, she raises one eyebrow, the hint of a smirk on her lips.

"So, what kind of lesbian are you?" she asks.

"The kind that… likes… girls?"

She nods and sips her smoothie. "Same."

"Izzie's the rock-star kind of lesbian!" Jordie supplies helpfully. "Her band rocks—pun not intended."

"Liar!" I say at the exact same time Izzie says, "Yeah, right."

I catch her eye and scrunch my face in a way that is absolutely the least attractive I've ever looked, not counting the year I dressed up as a mayonnaise packet for Halloween.

Jordie just shrugs. "What can I say? I'm a pun gay." He turns his glittering gaze on me. "And Steph's a gamer gay. A *gay*mer, if you will."

"I absolutely will not," I mutter.

"Oh, come on, you're an amazing GM." Jordie elbows me, mistaking my objection to his pun for self-deprecation. "Really, you should see Steph in action. Last week she had us fighting these giant gargoyles in dense fog with an acid pit on one side of the battlefield and steep cliff on the other."

"Sounds harrowing," Izzie says.

I'm not into judgment from anyone as far as my hobbies go. If people think I'm a nerd because of it, well, they're right. I am a nerd and proud of it. Still, something about Izzie has me checking her expression for signs of disdain. Thankfully, I don't find any.

"Harrowing is right! Steph's got a gift—really makes you feel like you're there." Jordie taps a laminated copy of our events calendar on the bar. "We play every Friday night if you want to check it out."

"Oh, I don't really know how to play."

"Hey, newcomers are always welcome at my table!" I fish for a copy of the calendar behind the counter and pass it over. "Plus it's really not that hard. Rolling dice, a little basic math, a vivid imagination… I bet you'd have fun. Think about it."

"Trade you." Izzie slides one of her own flyers into my hand, smooth as can be. "Gig's on Saturday. Maybe you can add something new to that playlist of yours."

I fold the flyer and tuck it into my pocket, but all through the evening rush it lurks at the back of my mind. I don't forget, even as a classic Seattle spring rain pelts my face on the way home. And when I get there, I don't bother to finish unpacking. The last thing I do before flopping into bed is jam a thumbtack through the top of the flyer and pin it to my wall.

I knew it wouldn't stay empty for long.

Two

In the magical realm of Windmyre, I am the king of the castle. I'm also the evil advisor, the barmaid with a dark secret, the shopkeeper desperate to offload a cursed dagger, and the ice-blue dragon atop the mountain watching over it all. From behind my GM screen, I have total control—except when I don't.

"Natural twenty!" Jordie pumps his fist in the air.

With only two hit points left, the beholder they're fighting really doesn't stand a chance, but I'm not one to spoil the fun. Besides, I love the clickity-clackity of a satisfying dice roll.

"The beholder turns its massive eye on the great wizard Strive. You see yourself reflected in its iris, the same cerulean color of your skin. Your robes billow out behind you as you reach for the dagger at your waist and press the flat of the blade to your lips. Your whispered spell becomes a mote of flame that engulfs the monster before you." I point to Jordie's carefully organized dice tray replete with colorful hand-poured resin dice made for him by our friend Lia. "Roll your damage."

Jordie grabs a clear d10 with swirls of red and orange, and flips it onto the table. It lands with a gold number three facing up and Jordie's expression falters.

"Hey—you critted, though, so double the dice." Faye, one of our regular game-night attendees, nudges Jordie with an encouraging smile uncharacteristic of her stoic and stabby character, a rogue of many knives and few words.

"Okay, so six points of damage," Jordie says.

"As the flames dissipate, you feel a vibration through the chamber. The beholder falls to the ground, unmoving."

"Yes!"

There's a resounding cry of victory from the players, and several of them leap out of their seats. Jordie's grin is so wide it's in danger of falling off his face, and Faye is hugging Stephen, a new player who just started tonight. His character, a little bard girl named Osanna, fell in battle only moments before, but he's taking it like a champ.

This is the good stuff. This is why I play this game. Friends and strangers joining together to triumph over evil. Spellcasters aren't the only ones wielding magic in the café tonight. It's the people.

As if on cue, the *Final Fantasy* victory theme plays as the door to Save Point swings open. My heart jumps into my throat, eyes darting up to look for a flash of black hair, but it's not Izzie. I try not to let my disappointment show on my face as Pixie rushes in.

"Sorry I'm late!" Pixie crosses over to the table and pulls out a chair. Small and spritely, Pixie's name fits her perfectly. She's even wearing a T-shirt with a cartoon ghost holding a magic wand that says *Bippity-boppity-BOO* in curly purple letters that match her violet hijab. "Band practice ran long."

Pixie is without a doubt one of my coolest friends. She plays *Dungeons & Dragons* almost as well as she plays drums. We met during my sophomore year of college when I helped tech her graduation. Pixie's band, The High Seas, played a set, and it was the most piratey fun I've ever had. I've gone to every one of their gigs since and Pixie comes out for game night whenever she can. Even when The High Seas are on tour, we play an adventure over video chat so she can still get her RPG fix.

"I'd say no worries, but Osanna's down and we could use a healer," Faye says, jabbing her thumb at Stephen.

"Whomp whomp." Stephen's face splits into a goofy grin. "Can't believe I died my first time playing."

Pixie shoots me an appraising look. "*I* can—Steph, you've got to stop scaring off new players!"

"Hey, I just do what the dice tell me." I raise my hands and shrug. "Besides, she's not like *fully* dead."

Pixie plops a dice bag as big as her head onto the table and fishes out a couple d8s. "Mouser does a second-level cure wounds."

Exactly as I'd hoped. I rub my hands together and set the scene. "Mouser, you burst through the door just as the battle ends, red hair tangled with twigs and leaves in your rush to catch up. Seeing Osanna motionless on the ground and the crestfallen faces of your companions, you fall to your knees and grasp the bard's hand. A few whispered words pass your lips and light travels up Osanna's arm into her chest."

Pixie rolls her dice and I turn to Stephen, gesturing at the numbers faceup on the table. "Osanna, you feel warmth spread through your body. A weightlessness that had passed over you fizzles and you feel yourself falling into your own body. With a jolt, you return to life and the first thing you see is a smiling half orc in plate armor with a giant shimmering axe by her side."

Stephen's eyes shoot open and he turns to Pixie. "I sit up slowly and say, 'Thank you, thank you!'" He's adopted a slight German accent for Osanna, talking quickly.

"Don't mention it." Pixie waves him off, her own character voice for Mouser fairly low and even—not at all her usual buoyant way of speaking.

"I shall write about your greatness in my book!" Stephen says in his Osanna voice. "I am a storyteller, you see, and it would be a shame not to make a record of your heroic deeds."

Pixie just shrugs and grunts.

Jordie leans across the table to murmur, "That's a lovely sentiment, Osanna, but… Mouser can't read."

Pixie winks and her voice returns to normal. "Intelligence is my dump stat. Technically, there's not a mechanic for literacy, but I thought it made sense for my character."

"I help Osanna to her feet and give her back her violin bow," Faye says. "But I sort of twirl it, like I'm doing a knife trick," she adds as an afterthought.

"Make a dexterity check." Faye rolls a d20. It clacks across the table to land faceup on a natural one. "Yeah, you break it."

"Well… I guess that's as good a quest as any." Jordie turns to Stephen with a glint in his eye. "What do you say, shall we venture out to find you a new instrument?"

Stephen nods eagerly. "Sure, but first… I have this mending spell. Would that do anything?"

As Faye and Pixie lean in to look at Stephen's character sheet, I get up to stretch my legs. We've been playing for about an hour, so a break is in order, plus I'm starving. I duck behind the counter to grab a couple of day-old pastries for the group. We're lucky that our store manager, Amy, lets us use the space like this. Technically, Jordie and I are both working this evening, but no one comes in besides the usual crew and the occasional newbie. Still, they're all good sports about it and usually buy a drink or two so we can keep justifying it.

As I whip together a hot chocolate for Pixie and refills for the others, my eyes keep drifting toward the front door. It stays resolutely shut.

"Waiting for goth Godot?" Jordie sidles up next to me, eyes following my gaze to the door.

I shrug with my best effort to appear nonchalant. "I don't know what you're talking about."

"Oh, *come on*." Jordie grabs the plate of pastries and passes it across the counter to Pixie. "I may be useless at flirting, but I know chemistry when I see it."

"I don't know… I kind of thought she'd come. Like maybe we had a connection or something." I lean back against the sink. Cool metal bites into my skin where my T-shirt has ridden up, shocking me back to reality. "But it's a Friday night—probably she had something better to do."

"Better than fighting a beholder? I don't know, seems fake."

"It's fine," I say, the words bitter on my tongue.

The truth is, as much as I love playing this game, it's been a long time since I've had much to do on a Friday night besides this. I thought when I graduated from college my life would really kick-start. But classes and homework have just been replaced by working at the café and now a weekly routine of dinners with Dad. Even on the nights I hang with friends, we just do the same thing—on Sundays we chill at Lia's and watch *Game of Thrones*, on Thursdays we go to Jordie's for *Critical Role*, this awesome live stream where voice actors play *Dungeons & Dragons*, and then on Fridays we're here in the shop to play ourselves. I like all that stuff. I do. I just thought my life would have a little more adventure in it—*real* adventure, not only the kind in my imagination.

"Maybe it wasn't meant to be," I say. "Bad roll on the dice, you know?"

"Now that's some bullshit." Jordie whips around, planting the tip of his finger against my sternum. "You're the game master, Steph. You make the rules."

"In Windmyre, yeah. Not in real life."

"Why not?"

I swallow hard, thinking of all the things in the world I haven't been able to control: my parents' divorce, my mom running out of cash to keep me at Blackwell Academy, a literal storm ripping through my life and changing everything. But it's silly to compare Izzie to all those things. She's just a girl. She's not going to wreck me.

"Fuck it." I push off from the counter and land on the opposite side beside Jordie. "I'll just go to her gig tomorrow."

"Now that's the Steph I know!"

"But you have to come with me," I say quickly. "I don't want to look desperate."

Jordie's expression falters for a split second—but he recovers quickly. "Yeah... yeah okay. I was already planning to go with Ollie."

"Even better! You can be my entourage."

Jordie makes a guttural retching noise. "Please never call us that again."

"Fair enough."

I grab Jordie by the arm and lead him back out to the table where Pixie, Faye, and Stephen are already munching on muffins and croissants. I settle in behind the GM screen and glance down at my notes. I've prepared an adventure for them through a haunted crypt, where they'll eventually fight a lich, but suddenly I'm not feeling the dark and dreary labyrinth I've planned.

Instead, I close my notebook and look up at my players. "All right, I believe you wanted to look for a new instrument for Osanna."

Stephen nods vigorously, putting on his character voice as he replies, "Oh yes! The violin has such a lovely sound, but I think I'd like something a little louder for battle."

A grin spreads across my face, and the words flow like a wish. "You're familiar with fables of a nearby mountain where thunder caps its peak. A six-stringed instrument is rumored to be the cause, lightning sparking with every note. As you approach the trailhead, echoing down the rocky path you hear the striking minor chord of an electric guitar."

Three

There's this energy in the air at an indie concert like waiting for lightning to strike in a storm. It's not the same as the big stadium shows, where every single person there is the biggest fan ever and no one can afford seats within a mile of the stage. Here at Bar-None, people are packed along the walls, drinks in hand. Conversation fills the space as the audience buzzes with anticipation, cast in a purple glow from the stage lights. It feels like being underwater. It feels like standing at the top of the Space Needle. It feels like something great is about to happen.

So, of course, after about twelve seconds of being there, I spill the completely full drink Ollie just handed me down my shirt.

"Shit! Are you kidding me?" I groan. RIP pear cider. You would have been delicious.

"It'll dry? I guess?" Jordie offers. "Want me to get you another?"

"Nah. Don't bother." I hold the front of my Fleetwood Mac T-shirt away from my body, fanning it in a ludicrous attempt to dry it faster.

"Absolutely outstanding. Top-notch Steph content." Ollie brings his hand down on my shoulder, a smile creasing his face. "Oh my god, remember in school when you—"

"I was there, Oliver," I grumble.

Ollie's not even bothering to hide his obvious glee at my misfortune, blue eyes twinkling. He has this deceptive innocence to him. It's probably his dimples. Round-faced with curly hair and freckles, Ollie looks like a farm boy who's just found out he has magic powers pretty much all the time. It's deeply annoying and also adorable.

Already, he's turned to Jordie to regale him with my many embarrassing exploits from our college days. That's the problem with working alongside your old roommate. They know all your secrets. But maybe that's a perk, too, because as Jordie nods along eagerly, eyes fixed on Ollie, I can see the way Ollie leans in, the way his elbow brushes Jordie's.

I stifle a laugh. This diabolical genius made me spill my drink on purpose to get rid of me.

"I think I saw a merch vendor over by the stage. Maybe they have T-shirts." But neither of them are listening to me, too wrapped up in each other's company for little old Steph and her T-shirt emergency.

I squeeze through the crowd, pulling out my phone to shoot Ollie a few quick texts.

> Is this a date????

> Am I third wheeling your DATE??

> If you two wanted to be alone so badly, you could have told me to fuck off omg

It's hilarious and a little sad that, even after all these years, Ollie and I are still so bad at this. In the two years we roomed together, before he came out and switched to the boys' dorms, I walked in on him clearly making a move in our room too many times to count. Those memories are etched into my brain forever. At least this time they're both wearing clothes.

Thankfully, the merch booth in the far corner does, in fact, have T-shirts. They're sold out of my size, so I get a large with the same logo from the flyer and hand over a twenty.

"Is there… somewhere I can change?" I ask, looking around for a bathroom.

"Steph?" Izzie's voice is feather-soft, like sinking into a gigantic pillow. She stands off to the side, dark red electric guitar slung over her shoulder, wearing a leather jacket and black lipstick. Meanwhile, I'm wearing a pint of fermented fruit. Great.

"Hey! Izzie! Cool venue, very wet drinks," I manage. Totally normal. Nothing weird to see here.

Her lips twist into a smile, a little peak of red popping through as she catches her tongue between her teeth in a laugh. "I can see that."

"Yeah… about that." I hold up my new Vinyl Resting Place T-shirt.

"Follow me—you can change backstage."

Izzie's hand closes around my wrist to pull me forward and my brain stutters to a stop and all I can think about is her fingers on me. Can she feel my pulse jump beneath my skin?

We wind through a dark hallway into a back room that's more garage than greenroom. The walls are lined with boxes and kegs and the floor is cracked cement. Three other girls are clustered near the door. One carries an electric bass by the neck and another twirls drumsticks between her fingers.

"There you are. We're about to go on!" says the third, a redhead with a short bob and a tight tank top.

"Just a sec, okay? Steph needs a place to change."

I give them a little wave, but the rest of Vinyl Resting Place doesn't seem all that interested in me. That's fair.

"Here. For privacy." Izzie guides me around the back of a dark blue van parked in the greenroom, its bumper adorned with a dozen stickers touting various messages, from a rainbow 'Steer Queer' to 'I brake for Bigfoot.'

I give her a thumbs-up, and when she turns her back, I quickly strip out of my wet shirt and into the new one.

"Okay. All set," I say, a little breathless.

Izzie turns and looks me up and down. "Bit big."

I just shrug. "That's okay—I'll just wear it as pajamas."

"Dope." Izzie grins, wide and genuine.

"Maybe I'll dream of rock and roll."

"Izzie!" calls one of her bandmates. "Ditch the groupie and let's go."

"Coming!" she shouts back, but doesn't make a move to leave. Instead, she slides the guitar around so the strap holds it on like a backpack and takes a step toward me.

My breath hitches, and for a moment I think she's going to kiss me, which is wild. Cool rocker girls don't just take Steph Gingrich backstage to make out. And even if they did, Ollie and Jordie would never believe me.

But then Izzie takes a fistful of my T-shirt and twists a hairband around it so the fabric cinches in at my waist. Her fingers lightly brush my stomach as she tucks the knot up under the shirt. "There," she says when she's done, stepping back to examine her handiwork. "Very cute!"

As she joins her bandmates and heads toward the stage, I follow at a distance, absently brushing my hand against the hem of my shirt where her fingers ghosted against my skin. I don't even care when I can't find Jordie and Ollie in the crowd.

The lead singer's voice crackles over the speakers. "We're Vinyl Resting Place! Who's ready to rock and roll over in their graves?"

A cheer ripples out over the audience. I plant myself beside the stage, just a few feet from Izzie as her fingers fly across the strings to play the opening notes to their first song. I can't see the lead singer, or any of the undoubtedly cool lighting, but that's okay. The view's better from here anyway.

Live music is the closest thing to magic I've ever experienced. When I GM, magic can be destructive or illusory or even healing, but in the real world, music is everything. I bounce on my feet, dancing in my little scrap of space near the stage as Vinyl Resting Place play their set, notes lighting me up like fire.

If songs are spellwork, then Izzie is a sorceress. Her fingers dance across the strings, a mesmerizing melody spinning from her instrument. I am entranced, a willing victim of her witchcraft. It isn't until my phone buzzes in my pocket for what must be the ninth time in a row that I finally tear my eyes away to check the stream of texts from the group chat.

Jordie: Steph where are you???

Seriously, you okay? Did you get abducted by aliens?

Ollie: if so, bring us back a souvenir

also are the aliens hot

Jordie: Ollie's knee is hurting so I'm gonna take him home. Do you want a ride or are you good?

Ollie: wow ur not gonna offer me a ride?

Jordie: I literally said I was driving you home

Never mind I just got it. Oblivious ace strikes again

Ollie: u misspelled adorable

I bite back a grin. It's about time Jordie and Ollie found each other, and I can't help but feel overcome with hope at their relationship finally blossoming. Maybe it's a sign.

Get a ROOM

But really, I'll be fine. You kids have fun

I tuck my phone away and turn back to the stage as the song ends with an explosive chord and a cymbal crash.

"Thank you!" shouts the lead singer. "We're Vinyl Resting Place—and we've been great."

There's a collective chuckle from the audience as three of the four band members unplug their instruments and head my way. Izzie stands alone, looking over her shoulder, eyes wide and brow pinched. For a second, I think she's about to play a solo or something, but then she unplugs her guitar and follows the others.

"You were amazing!" I shout over the noise of the crowd dispersing.

Izzie catches my eye and smiles weakly. "Hey! Thanks." Her gaze bounces from me to the rest of her band, disappearing into the shadowy hallway toward the greenroom. "I have to take care of something first but… don't go anywhere, okay? Meet me in like fifteen?"

I nod vigorously. Way too much. Like, my neck hurts from all the nodding.

"Cool." She flashes me a smile before vanishing, too.

I lean against the wall to wait and scroll social media, but I'm barely looking. A few texts from Jordie trickle in and I do my best to answer, but all my attention is on that hallway, waiting for Izzie to reappear.

Did you know Oliver liked me???

Steph! What do I do if he kisses me?

LOL KISS HIM BACK

Right but I mean HOW?

Like... with your mouth?

How am I supposed to breathe?

I don't know if you know this, Jordie, but when you have your first kiss, you actually grow gills

...

Okay so like

Through my nose, huh

I am so stupid. Why does he like me???

Because you're stupid <3

It's gonna be okay man, just talk to Ollie about it

He knows you're ace and he's not a dick. You can figure it out together

Thanks, Steph <3

There's movement down the hall and I stand up straighter. Then I remember I'm the furthest thing from straight, so I contort my body into a casual lean that hopefully conveys that Steph Gingrich is a lesbian dreamboat, available for post-gig smooching, but the voice that carries up the hall toward me isn't Izzie's.

"The song just isn't our sound. If she doesn't get that, then she's not right for Vinyl Resting Place."

It's the lead singer, sporting short copper hair and a leather vest. The bassist and drummer flank her, nodding.

"Maybe it was harsh, but honestly she needed to hear it."

"It wasn't *that* harsh. We've been thinking it for weeks," the bassist says. "I'm just surprised she didn't see it coming."

I push off the wall. The drummer's shoulder bumps mine and she doesn't even bother to apologize. My mind races, but not as fast as my feet, which carry me back to the greenroom.

Izzie sits on the floor, guitar laid across her legs, shoulders slumped. She stares at a point across the room with unfocused eyes.

I want to sit down beside her, tell her she was brilliant, hold her hand through whatever she's dealing with. I remind myself I'm just Steph, some girl she met at a café. I'm not anyone to her. I'm not anyone to a lot of people. But then she says my name and I forget about everyone else.

"Steph? Shit, I forgot. I'll just… I'll get my stuff."

"Don't worry about it." I glance over my shoulder to check we're alone. "Are you okay?"

"Yeah! Totally fine." Her voice is too high, her smile too wide. Her eyes swim with unshed tears and she sniffles. "Damn it."

I shrug and lean against the doorframe. "Look, if you want to be fine, then we can do that. We can get a drink and celebrate an awesome gig, and maybe you give me your number."

"Yeah?"

"Yeah." I push off the wall and cross to her, sinking onto my knees. "But if you're not fine, we can also do this." I roll onto my hip and sit beside her, elbows knocking.

"What's… this?" she asks.

"We sit here and you tell me what happened. I tell you your bandmates are assholes and you're the real star. And then you still give me your number."

A laugh breaks through her chest, harsh and a little raw. "I think I'd like that. The second option, I mean."

"Great, because I have some choice expletives in mind and I'd really hate for them to go to waste."

Izzie is a pretty crier. Not in the way actresses are, where their face stays the same and they just shed a couple tears. Izzie is pretty when she cries because she *really* cries. Maybe it's the crying that's beautiful because she's not afraid to show how she feels. Or maybe it's the girl underneath the tears. Maybe I'd think Izzie was pretty no matter how red her face gets. She's hurt and she's angry and I don't know how to fix it, but then she's not asking me to.

"They just don't get it," Izzie says through a sigh. "They want our original music to be like… I don't know! Chill vibes only?"

"What does that even mean?" I make a face. "You're a rock band. That's not exactly easy listening."

"I think they mean they want our songs to feel… positive."

"So, no singing about your recent breakup or how much it sucks to be a hot single rock star."

"Are you trying to ask if I'm single?" Izzie elbows me in the ribs, but there's a smile on her lips that wasn't there before. Then she leans back against her van and her eyes flutter closed. "Here's the thing, they don't understand that my life isn't just rainbows and iced coffee, you know? I've seen some shit. And I don't just want to sing about love and partying. I want to sing about stuff that makes me angry and stuff that makes me sad, too."

"And they don't like that."

She shakes her head. "We were supposed to debut my new song tonight. We've been practicing it for weeks and I thought it was good. But I guess they all decided without me that Vinyl Resting Place doesn't need Izzie Margolis."

"That sucks." My eyes fall to her hand, palm up on her dark-wash jeans. It would be so easy to just… put mine in hers. Her skin looks soft and I want to trace my fingertip along the creases of her lifeline. And maybe that would make her feel better. Or maybe it would just make *me* feel better. So, instead, I look up at her face, at the smeared mascara along her cheekbones and the lipstick flaking off her lips, and I lean in to say, "Can I hear it?"

Izzie's chin dips to her chest and she rolls her lip between her teeth. "I mean… how? It's just me."

"Izzie, unplugged." I wave my hand before us as if pointing to her name in lights and she giggles. "I could probably do some bucket drumming, get a beat going."

"I'm not really a singer."

"So?" I rise to my feet and hold out my hand. "I'm not really a drummer." It's been years since I've picked up a set of drumsticks, but for Izzie I'm willing to put my muscle memory to the test.

We're both liars, as it turns out. The acoustics in the greenroom suck, but Izzie's voice carries anyway. Her song is raw and wounded, rising like a treacherous tide. I'm pulled under, breath catching in my throat as she sings.

> *"Chew me up and spit me out*
> *You'll still hear me scream and shout*
> *I reject your hetero-cis-pool*
> *The closet's full, we must come out!"*

I keep time, positioned behind the drum kit in Izzie's van. The drumsticks feel weighty in my hand, like each beat matters, just like each word.

> *"Don't eat that, pose, be quiet*
> *You can't make this body diet*
> *They won't teach you this in school*
> *The first Pride was a riot!"*

When she finishes, the last note tearing from her throat, she looks up. Her eyes are storms, cloudy and chaotic.

"Hell yes," I say in a soft exhale. "That was so good! Like, *so* good!" I'm almost shaking with the adrenaline, electric current spiking through my limbs.

"Yeah?" A blush creeps across Izzie's face. "I mean, yeah. I thought so, too."

"No offense or anything, but *why* are you playing literally anything else?" I extract myself from the drum kit, accidentally crashing into the hi-hat on my way. "And also, why aren't you the lead singer?"

"Because Astrid—"

"Astrid doesn't matter."

"She does if I want to stay in the band," Izzie grumbles.

I hop down from the van and clap a hand on Izzie's shoulder. "And why the hell would you want to do that? They clearly don't get you—your talent *or* your sound. They're just dragging you down."

"Is this your way of doing the 'you're better off without them' thing to make me feel better?" She narrows her eyes.

"Is it working?"

"I don't know." Izzie sets her guitar down on the bed of the van and turns to face me, hands on her hips. "Maybe you should try a little harder."

I cup my hands to my mouth and mimic the sounds of a rabid crowd. "Izzie! Encore, encore! You're the best rock star in the woooorld!"

Izzie grins and beckons with her hands for more.

"Yeah! Let's go, Izzie! Your sound is on fire! Can I have your autograph?" I travel around her in a circle, bowing and fanning her with my hands as if to say, *We are not worthy!* "The hottest one-woman band around!"

"Yeah, yeah, okay." Izzie waves me off, but she's grinning now too. "It's a nice dream, I guess."

"Why does it have to be a dream?"

"Well, I can't actually play all the instruments myself."

"What?" I deadpan. "Do you mean to tell me you *don't* have six extra arms ready to go?"

"I don't know if I'd need *six*," she says almost thoughtfully. "Could go for a simpler sound—guitar, vocals, and drums at least."

"That's not too bad. All you need is a drummer." I nudge her with my elbow, hoping she'll look my way again so I can drown in her big brown eyes.

And she does. Wide and full of mischief, her gaze catches mine, and she says, "No I don't. Already have one."

Four

Dad's garage is a lawless land, a graveyard for hobbies gone sour. There's a shelf full of action figures he started—and stopped—collecting the year I went to college and an old motorcycle he's definitely never ridden. I nearly trip over a literal bow and arrow on my way to the drum kit in the corner.

I swipe my finger through a thick layer of dust on the cymbals. Dad gave me this drum set for my fourteenth birthday. I can count on one hand the number of times I've practiced since then—such a noisy hobby. The last time I sat behind this drum set, I was in Arcadia Bay, in a house that isn't there anymore. Mom told me to keep it down, and I was only too happy to oblige. The gift was always more for Dad than for me, and he wasn't around to enjoy it.

I plop down on the seat and ghost my drumstick across the snare, eliciting a soft hiss. I *know* that I know how to do this, but without Izzie's eager face urging me on, I feel small and insignificant behind this mountain of rhythm I'm meant to climb. I set the sticks down on the floor tom and dig my phone from my pocket. There's only one person I trust to help me with this particular problem.

> Heyyyy little drummer girl

Pixie: Heyyyy

41

Pixie's reply comes immediately and I sigh in relief. I snap a picture of the drum set and send it to Pixie along with a caption.

> SOS

Have you never heard of a dust rag?

> Step one: cleaning. Got it

> But for real, what do I do? I haven't played in ages

Okay, for a start you should tune the toms and your snare

> You have to tune drums???

STEPH!

> Teach meeeee

Tradesies? I want to learn to be a game master!

> You've got yourself a deal!

I take Pixie's advice and clean the drum set first. It's grueling work, but when I finish, the drums are a shiny electric blue.

"Hey, sweetie. Find anything good?" Dad pokes his head into the garage, wearing a beanie and holding a green juice.

"Thought I might take her out of retirement," I say, clicking the hi-hat open and closed.

"I used to be in a band, you know." He descends the stairs and comes to stand in front of the drum kit, eyes a little glazed over behind his glasses. "Two, actually."

"The Kazoo Keepers don't count."

"We were very popular at office parties, I'll have you know." Dad crosses his arms and pouts, the corners of his mouth still turned up a bit, just like mine. All the years we spent apart after the divorce, and I'm still more like him inside and out than I ever was like Mom. "Okay, well, *outside* the office parties."

"That's more like it."

"So, what's the plan here? Please tell me you're not going to sell it."

"Nah. Had something a little more exciting in mind." With a snap of my wrist, I start a drum roll. The snare rattles and whines. Maybe I do have to tune these things. "I've joined a band!"

"That's great, sweetie!"

"Your turn." I point to the glass in his hand, sides stained green with spinach or kale. "What's up with the health potion?"

"Ah…" He looks from the glass to me and back again. "You know, antioxidants are —"

I shake my head. "Forget I asked."

"Oh, come on. It's not that bad. You wanna try one?"

"Absolutely not."

"More for me." He takes a sip and the twitch in his jaw says all too clearly he'd rather be drinking anything else. "You sticking around for dinner? I've got a colleague coming over I want you to meet."

"Is this a job interview?" I narrow my eyes and push off the stool. It wouldn't be the first time he's tried to lure me into something career-related — brochures left casually on my bookshelf and near weekly job listing emails.

Dad shakes his head. "No, no, nothing like that, she's —"

"Sorry, Dad. I can't tonight." I tuck the drumsticks into my back pocket and make for the garage door. "I've got band practice."

Izzie lives a few minutes away from Save Point in a light blue one-story house with a worn fence and overgrown hedges. She meets me on the porch stairs, barefoot and sporting a long-sleeve shirt made of sheer black lace over a tank top and big silver earrings in the shape of stars. She's holding a green notebook and an open can of root beer.

"Steph!" She waves me forward, leading me toward the front door. "What are you, a vampire waiting for an invitation?"

It takes me a second to follow, my body lagging behind my brain as I take in the space—her space. The walls are hung with all kinds of art—a grayscale oil painting of a sunflower, an old-school Rosie the Riveter poster that says, 'We Can Do It! We Just Don't Want To,' and abstract pink and blue blobs with the word 'gender' cut out from what looks like a bunch of different magazines pasted upside down over the top. On the far side is a double-stacked bookshelf full of tomes with cracked, unreadable spines bookended by a couple of glass whiskey bottles filled with swirling purple sparkles like a grown-up snow globe.

"So, this is my crib." Izzie poses with her hand on her hip, an over-wide smile plastered on her face like she's performing for a camera.

"Damn!" I peer around the corner into the kitchen where *matching* dishware is stacked in cabinets with glass doors. There's a breakfast nook in the corner with a little potted rosemary and two candlesticks in the window. "This is totally cute."

Izzie grimaces, eyes drifting to her phone.

"Sorry." My fingers worry the skin of my elbow. First time over and already I've found a way to accidentally insult her. Absolutely killing it. "Cute probably isn't what you were going for, huh?"

"What? Oh. No, cute is fine. It's a shared space, but my housemates have decent taste." She shrugs. "Besides, I can think of plenty of worse adjectives."

I raise my eyebrows. "She has vocab!"

"I contain multitudes." She lifts her phone and the sour expression returns. "Astrid just texted. She and the others are coming by to pick up their stuff later this afternoon. If we want to get any practice in before they whisk the drums away, we should do it now."

I nod and follow her through the kitchen and out a side door into the garage. Immediately, I can feel the Izzieness here. Power cords make a maze of the ground, leading from the wall to amps, speakers, and other electronics I don't know the names for. A dark red drum kit is nestled in the corner next to a large gold divider. It's pushed back to reveal the other half of the room—a queen-size bed against the wall with a purple bedspread and pillows that don't quite match, a desk littered with notebooks and gum wrappers folded into neat chains, and a large oak dresser with brass handles.

Izzie hurries to roll the divider back out. "Sorry—it's kind of a mess."

Even if it was, I wouldn't mind, but it's clear Izzie does. She's already picking up stray clutter—a water bottle, a guitar pick, a sports bra. I want to tell her to leave it. I like her mess. I want to see any part of her she'll show me. Instead, I climb behind the drum set and test the tension of the snare.

"Bouncy," I say, my drumstick ricocheting off the drum with a satisfying thump. "Way better than mine. I have to get it fixed up."

"Bring it over—once these are gone, we can tune yours. It'll be easier to have them here for practice anyway."

My heart jumps a little in my chest. We've only played together once and already Izzie's planning to do it again. Good. I'm glad she hasn't changed her mind. I adjust my grip on my sticks, determined to earn the faith she's placed in me.

There's a loud crackle as Izzie plugs her guitar into the amp followed by a melodious chord. She plays a couple more, testing each string and wiggling the tuning pins a bit, before hitting the strings with the flat of her hand and looking back to me, brown eyes smiling.

"Okay. Let's rock."

And… we do. Sort of. Izzie is even more magnetic with an electric guitar at full volume. Sunshine filters in through the garage door, bathing her in dappled light as she sings, and I'm mesmerized. It shows in my playing, for sure. I miss the hi-hat entirely a few times and my right foot pedals the kick drum shakily. Still, it's the most fun I've had in a long time, and when the song ends, I can't wait to play it again.

"Okay," Izzie says after the last chord has faded. "That's a start."

"I'm just stoked you said *start* and not *end*." I let out a nervous laugh and wipe a trickle of sweat already beading at my hairline. "I'm super out of practice." Anxiety rockets through me and my other foot jiggles, rattling the hi-hat.

Izzie slides her guitar onto its stand before closing the distance between us. With me sitting behind the drums, she towers over me—impressive, intimidating, intimate. Her gaze is steady, unlike my drumming, but as she catches my eye, I feel the energy inside me quiet. Her fingers close around the hi-hat and she silences the cymbals with a pinch.

"Slow down, roadrunner. It's a marathon, not a sprint," she says, leaning in.

Her eyes sparkle with reflections of the twinkle lights hung up around the garage. Every cell in my body screams that I should touch her. I could just… reach out, lace our fingers together, run my thumb across her knuckles atop the hi-hat.

There's a loud rumble as the garage door lurches to life and I tip back, spilling off my stool onto the hard cement.

"Oh, hey." Izzie's voice goes small and quiet.

"Hey, yourself." A voice I recognize—the singer from Vinyl Resting Place, Astrid.

When I recover, clambering over the knocked-over stool, I'm met by an army of scowls. Three girls stand at the lip of the garage. A blonde, a brunette, and a redhead walk into band practice. I don't know the rest of the joke, but the setup sure slaps.

"You look good," Astrid, the redhead, says to Izzie. "Better than you sound, at least."

A chuckle in three-part harmony echoes through the garage and I realize it's me — I'm the punch line.

Izzie doesn't join in.

"Steph, do you mind running to the kitchen to grab some sodas?" Her eyes meet mine imploringly.

I don't want to leave her with the mean girls. I fight the urge to stand my ground. Instead, I round my shoulders and bob my head. "Sure thing," I say, and head for the door, not because I want to escape, but because she asked me to.

The second I close the garage door, their voices become unintelligible. For all I know, they could be performing Shakespeare or reciting the digits of pi or shitting on my drumming. It doesn't really matter anyway. It's not their opinions I care about.

I trace my steps back to the kitchen to grab sodas from the fridge. There's a box of root beer on the bottom shelf with a sticky note that says 'Izzie' in sharpie. The whole fridge is organized that way, with stacks of tupperware labeled 'Mariana,' a carton of lactose-free milk labeled 'Bruce,' and a bowl with some kind of quinoa-based salad labeled 'free to a good home turns out I hate quinoa ~Saturn.'

"Uh, hi?"

A voice startles the root beers out of my hands. They tumble to the ground, bouncing and rolling across the hardwood.

"Hi," I say, looking up to see the owner of the voice is a short, rainbow-haired white person with dangly earrings spelling out 'they' and 'them' who, if I had to guess based on vibe alone, is probably Saturn.

"Hi," says probably Saturn again.

I'm tempted to say hi one more time, just to complete the greeting do-si-do we've found ourselves in, but instead I tuck my hair behind my ear and give a little wave. "Izzie asked me to grab sodas — I swear I'm not just some random girl raiding your fridge."

"Oh!" Their face relaxes immediately. "You're Steph."

"Guilty as charged!"

"Saturn. Izzie's told us all about you."

"Good things, I hope."

Saturn's lips curve into a grin. "Oh, very good things." They bend to pick up a couple of cans that have rolled to a stop at their feet, and set them on the counter. "Might as well grab new ones—these will probably explode." They cross over to the fridge, grabbing two for me and one for themself.

"Thanks." I motion to the fridge, balancing the cans in one hand. "Can you pass me three more?"

Saturn's eyebrows shoot up. "Thirsty?"

My cheeks flame and I shake my head. "Astrid and the others are here to pick up their stuff."

"Oh shit." Saturn's gaze bounces over to the garage door and back. "Give them the time bombs. They deserve it." They grab one of the cans from the counter and shake it more for good measure.

I grin, emboldened by Saturn's clearly correct opinion. "Yeah, they kind of suck, huh?"

"Honestly, I'd never say it to Izzie's face, but we're all pretty stoked to see the last of them. Their music is great, but their personalities?" Saturn makes a retching noise. "I thought they were annoying *before* Izzie and Astrid broke up, but the past few months have been hell."

"Oh," I say, because what else is there to say? "I guess intra-band dating can get messy."

"Sure. But this was definitely not your run-of-the-mill drama. Astrid is mean and she's not quiet about it. Girl likes to yell, and not in a fun way." Saturn plops into a chair at the breakfast nook and opens their root beer with a crackle. "I think Bruce was almost ready to tell them they had to practice somewhere else. He doesn't like to pull landlord on us—such a weird dynamic, since we all suffered through college together, but now he's got

this fancy tech job and makes more money than God—but like…
it's his house."

My eyes travel back to the garage door and I swallow with
difficulty. "Maybe I should… get back in there."

"Here." Saturn pushes the jostled root beer cans into my
arms. "Go armed."

I only catch the tail end of the Astrid show. They made quick
work of taking the drum set apart and loading the amps into Astrid's
car, so by the time I return, everything's pretty much done.

"Well… see you around, Izzie," Astrid says, twirling her
keys around her finger. "Good luck with… you know." She
gestures vaguely at the empty space left behind. Her eyes flit to
me once more before she piles into the car with her bandmates
and speeds away.

Izzie looks deflated, her shoulders concave, eyes hollow.

"You okay?" I ask, nudging her with my elbow. My hands are
still laden with root beer cans, otherwise I might be braver than I
have reason to be and hold her hand.

Izzie straightens up and clears her throat. "Guess that puts
an end to today."

"Says who?"

Izzie turns a bemused expression on me and says, "I don't
know about you, but without a drum set, what's the point?"

"Well, for starters, drumming isn't the only thing I can do."
I nod toward the open garage. The sun is still in the sky—it's
maybe four in the afternoon. "And we've got a lot of hours left in
the day. Pity to waste them."

"I'm listening," Izzie says. "What do you have in mind?"

"How do you feel about pizza and nerds?"

"The people or the candy?" Izzie takes a can of root beer
from my arms. "Never mind, I love both." She pulls the metal tab
before I can stop her and brown fizzy soda shoots up in a geyser
directly into her face.

"Uh… yeah… I meant to warn you…"

Izzie wipes her sleeve across her face and blinks rapidly. "I sure wish you had… shit… let me change first, okay? Don't want to be all gross."

"Yep. Take your time," I say, but they're not the words inside me, thundering against my ribs.

I want to tell her she could never be gross. I want to tell her she's beautiful, even when she's covered in sticky carbonated sugar water. I want to tell her to never change because I like her the way she is.

A shocked Jordie meets us at the door, a full two hours early for *Critical Role* night. It's our weekly nerd night where we crowd around Jordie's TV—since he has the biggest one—and watch the live stream. Jordie always makes geeky snacks and we play a custom sort of bingo with silly in-jokes and the names of spells in each square.

"We bring an offering!" I proclaim as I charge into his apartment, dual-wielding bags of barbecue potato chips.

"Damn right you do." Jordie tilts his head curiously as Izzie follows me inside.

"Don't mind me—had an exploding soda-can situation." Izzie gestures to her wet hair. "Hope it's okay that I'm crashing the party—Steph said you do this every week?"

Jordie and I face each other, finger guns at the ready, and say the show's tagline in unison, "Is it Thursday yet?"

"I'll take that as a yes."

"We only play once a week, so we have to get our fix somehow, am I right?" Jordie leads us into the kitchen, where he pops open the chips and begins pouring them into large metal bowls. "You really should play with us sometime."

My gaze snaps to Izzie, looking for a reaction, but she just reaches for a chip and shrugs evasively. Maybe she'd make a good rogue.

"Every Friday at the shop. Invite's open." I try not to want it too much, to bring Izzie into my world the way she's let me into hers. I know tabletop RPGs are cool, and I don't need her to think so too. But needing something isn't the same as wanting something.

Izzie gives me a thin smile. "Wish I could, but I've got something else on Fridays."

I steel myself for the disappointment that comes with a brush-off like that and try on a smile like an ill-fitting pair of jeans.

"Oh, of course!" Jordie smacks his forehead. "You've got Shabbat. I forgot!"

"Yeah. It's the one time I video call my parents every week, so I can't really skip it. Sort of an every-Friday-at-sundown kind of thing."

"And why would you want to?" Jordie turns to me, gesticulating enthusiastically as he explains. "I got the invite a couple times when we were still in college. You would not believe the challah Izzie's dad bakes. I still dream about the fluffy texture sometimes. It's like a cloud made of carbs."

"Okay, first of all, extremely rude of you to describe delicious bread without having any to offer me." I give Jordie a look of betrayal. "And second of all, the beauty of tabletop RPGs is you can play them on any day ending in Y. If you want to give it a go, we can play a short one-shot now before the show."

"Oh, yes please! I'll text Ollie—I bet he'd join in." Jordie snatches his phone from the counter, fingers flying across the screen.

I glance at Izzie. "What do you say?"

Izzie nods. "Yeah, okay. Why not?"

I set her up with a character sheet at the coffee table in the living room and immediately see the overwhelm in her eyes.

"Oh no—I'm having math homework flashbacks. Why is this so complicated?"

"Steph! Bless your heart, no!" Ollie exclaims from the entryway, where he's just arrived, carrying an entire watermelon.

"You're going to scare her off." He hands the watermelon unceremoniously to Jordie and crosses over to sit next to Izzie. "Okay, we're going to do this right. What's your star sign, favorite color, and your most played hype song? Also hi, I'm Ollie, I'll be your cruise director this evening."

"Capricorn, purple, 'Ever Fallen in Love' by Buzzcocks, and I'm Izzie—along for the ride, I guess."

Ollie looks Izzie up and down, eyes narrowed in concentration. "Okay, definitely a spellcaster, then."

"Warlock," I say confidently.

"Really? I figured bard," says Jordie.

"Oh, come on. Izzie's way too badass for bard, plus isn't purple like *the* warlock color?"

"Yeah, but she slays on guitar."

"You two, kitchen." Ollie points forcefully at the door. "Izzie can make her own decision without your commentary."

Jordie and I grumble as we get to our feet, but once we're safely in the kitchen, Jordie says, "Twenty bucks says she picks bard."

"You're on!"

We're both wrong. After much consideration, Izzie decides to be a cleric.

"There's no reason a healer can't be cool," she says with a shrug. "Can I buy a shield in the shape of a skull or something?"

"You can have a shield in whatever shape you want." I settle at the head of the coffee table and do what I do best—improvise. "You leave the temple in the dead of night. No one wakes to herald your departure. It's only you and your faith, a flickering warmth at your chest like a purring kitten held close. You take one look back the place you've called home all this time before taking your first step on the path to adventure."

I offer Izzie a set of dice. She takes them and her lips curve into a nervous smile. Maybe if the dice roll in my favor there will be room for me to come along on her adventure.

Five

I practice all weekend with Pixie. She runs me ragged doing drills over and over again, teaching me the names of different rhythms my body remembers better than my brain. It isn't exactly like riding a bike, but the longer I practice, the more muscle memory from teenhood returns. When Pixie goes home, I let the metronome be my teacher, drumming to its incessant steady ticking late into the night. The next morning, there's a pair of noise-canceling headphones sitting on the snare with a sticky note pasted to the outside of the box. *Don't permanently damage your hearing. Love, Dad.*

Once I start, I can't seem to stop. The rhythm lives in my bones even when I'm not behind the drums. At work, I drum on the counters with plastic forks, practicing along with whatever music's playing, and when I walk home at the end of the day, I move to an imaginary beat, thriving on the applause of an imaginary crowd.

Izzie gives me homework. She sends me playlists of artists I *need to know*, and playlists of songs she thinks we should cover, and playlists of songs that remind her of me. I listen to them all, but that last one is on repeat in my head even in silence. I try to dissect the meaning behind her choices—does 'Girls Like Girls' by Hayley Kiyoko remind her of me because I'm a lesbian or because she's a girl who likes me, also a girl? After running through the songs for the umpteenth time at work, Jordie tells me I have to play something else or he's going on strike.

"I love to stim to a song on repeat as much as the next person, but this is getting ridiculous," he says.

"It's okay, babe. I'll make you a playlist, too." Ollie presses his forehead to Jordie's and they both crack a grin.

"Oh, come on!" I protest. "Just because you two found each other doesn't mean the rest of us aren't allowed to have a moment of gay panic."

But, as Jordie and Ollie are quick to point out, it isn't just a momentary fixation. I spend my days waiting to spend my evenings with Izzie. I live for the hours spent in her garage learning about music theory and structure, puzzling through lyrics together, flat on our backs with a notepad between us.

That's where we are when she says it.

"We need a name."

I roll onto my side, face squishing into my arm. "What, you mean 'Izzie and Steph's family good-time band' isn't good enough?"

She hits my knee with hers playfully. "Very funny, but I think we might get sued by the creators of *Arrested Development*."

"What, scared of a little lawsuit action?"

"We need something that says queer punk band."

"And I'm guessing 'Queer Punk Band' is off the table?"

"Steph!" Izzie groans, but she's smiling.

I narrow my eyes in thought, trying not to stare at her lips or think about how soft they look. Instead, I throw myself into brainstorm mode. "Slam Punk, Punky Cold Medina, On Wednesdays We Wear Punk."

Izzie groans. "Okay, puns are not allowed."

"*Punk* Intended?"

Izzie throws a pillow at me.

"Okay, maybe if I understood the punk vibe a little better that would help," I say. "Don't get me wrong, I love the music, but I'm pretty new to the scene."

Izzie hoists herself up partway so she's leaning back on her elbows, long dark hair cascading down her back. "It's just that punk is so much more than a vibe, you know?"

I follow her lead, sitting up and crossing my legs. "Tell me," I say. I've spent days listening to every punk band she recommends. I know what the genre sounds like, I know the rhythms and foundations of the music, but none of that matters compared with what it means to Izzie.

"Punk isn't just a sound. It's an attitude, a lived experience. It's about being pushed around and oppressed, and rising up anyway. It's about being on the outside, about seeing injustice and *doing* something about it. It's about being angry and frightened, and shouting to be heard anyway."

I can't look away from this girl who feels like an epiphany. Izzie's eyes are glassy as she speaks. I want to reach out to her, a grounding touch to let her know I'm here, that I'm listening. My hand inches toward hers. It would be so easy to slot my fingers between hers and lace them together. All I have to do is be brave.

I chicken out at the last minute, instead bumping my pinky against hers. "Plus the black nail polish."

Izzie looks down at our hands, so close together, and for a breathless moment I think she's about to show me up, courage-wise. Her fingers curl toward mine, just slightly. But then, she nods and pushes up to her feet. "Yeah, we really need to get your look sorted out."

"What, you don't like the beanie?" I stand, too.

Izzie steps closer, and closer, and even closer, snaking her hand behind my head. The moment catches and snags, and I think if something doesn't happen soon I'm going to pass out.

"I love the beanie," she says, then tugs it from my head. "But maybe not for gigs."

"Gigs?" I raise my eyebrows.

"Yeah. If you—if you want to. I talked to some people I know who own a venue. It's not as big as Bar-None, but you know. We can start small… work our way up."

"Small or not, I'm absolutely gonna need a new look for when we play."

"Yeah?" She catches my eye and holds it.

"Yeah." I lead her past the room divider into the bedroom half of the garage and toward the dresser. "Make me over, Izzie Margolis."

Izzie has a lot of clothes. Way more than me—though that's not a very high bar, as I've been living out of my suitcase since graduation. It's nice not to have too many choices, but the high rate of laundry is less than ideal.

I run my fingers along the fabrics, stalling on a leather skirt. I hold it up to my body and show Izzie. "What d'you think?"

"Oh, definitely not."

"What? Don't think I'd look good in a mini?" I strike a model pose.

"You'd look good in anything."

She snatches the skirt from me, fingers brushing mine. She stills at the contact for a beat, eyes skating over my body, and do I detect a little wistful note in her tone? I let the hope blossom in my chest, and probably in my cheeks too.

"It's just that… you'll be behind the drum set with your legs…"

"What about my legs?" I take a step closer, unable to keep the smile off my face.

"They—they're good legs! I'm sure. I mean, I would assume." Izzie turns her back to me and rifles through a few drawers in the dresser. "It's just you might flash the audience."

"Okay, yeah. Let's not uh… expose ourselves onstage. Good call. So… got any leather pants?"

Izzie laughs at that. "What's with you and leather?"

"I don't know… feels… punky."

"There are definitely some vegan punks who would disagree." Izzie eyes me carefully, her gaze practically leaving scorch marks along my skin in its wake. "Besides, we don't want you to look like you're wearing a costume—it should feel natural, like an extension of your style, not an erasure."

"Okay, so what would you suggest?"

Izzie dresses me in ripped black jeans, a graphic tank, and a flannel tied around my waist. As a finishing touch, she fastens a couple of leather—or maybe pleather—bracelets around my wrist. Her fingers whisper over my pulse point, lingering.

"What do you think?" Izzie asks, turning me around to face a standing mirror in the corner.

"I like it," I say. Her hands drift to my hips, and I try and fail to stop myself from leaning into her touch. "Comfy—feels like me."

"Good. That's the whole point of punk, really. Being yourself in the face of compulsory conformity."

I grin at our reflections. Izzie's wearing red and black plaid pants with gold zippers and a black long-sleeve boat-neck top that hugs her body. A tattoo snakes up over her exposed collarbone, something viney. I wonder if it hurt like mine did. Ollie had to hold my hand the whole time, but by the end I had a black-lined swallow over my chest. I got it in college, after I decided I would never go home to Arcadia Bay again— the wings of the swallow carrying me wherever I needed to go. They've carried me here to Izzie's garage. Maybe they'll carry me further.

"We look cool together, huh?" I ask. "Like… like a real girl band."

"Yeah…" Something flicks across her gaze, unreadable and cloudy, and her eyes drift away from mine.

I feel the moment slipping away, just like her touch, and I cling to it for dear life. "What about like… eyeliner and stuff?" I ask.

"You want?" She gestures to her own meticulous cat-eye liner.

I shrug. "I've never really done much with makeup before, but it would be neat to try. You can…" I swallow. "You can maybe put it on me so I don't fuck it up?"

Izzie motions for me to sit, then pulls a basket of cosmetics from the top drawer and places it between us on the floor.

The thought of Izzie's hands on my face sends a shiver up my spine, and then her hands really *are* on my face. I freeze, afraid to so much as breathe the wrong way in case she stops. She rests the side of her pinky on my cheekbone as she swipes a brush across my face. My eyes flutter closed and I lean into the touch. I don't even care about the makeup. If we could stay like this forever, I would give up life's essentials like oxygen and coffee.

"What color do you want?"

Izzie's question is a feather-light breeze across my nose. She's so close. My heart hammers in my chest, a beat far steadier than my drumming, but I open my eyes and follow her gaze to the basket full of colorful eyeshadow pallets.

I swallow and do my best to sound normal—like I haven't been thinking about anything but eyeshadow. "Ohhh, so many to choose from!" I reach for the basket, sifting through the different options. "You've really got a whole rainbow here, huh? What is this, Target during June?"

Izzie rewards me with a laugh—a little guffaw that feeds my soul.

I don't need more than a few seconds to choose. I know what color I want—it's the same as the liner she wore the first time I met her, when she came into Save Point looking like a storm.

"Purple!" I hold up the pallet, a small plastic one with half a price tag still clinging to the back.

Izzie's expression falters. Her cheeks go slack and her eyes drift to the pallet in my hand. "No," she says quietly.

"Not purple?" I glance back at the basket, looking for another option. "Is it not my color or something?"

"N-no! Purple's fine. Just... not that one." She plucks the pallet from me and smoothes a thumb over the price sticker slowly, reverently. "It's really old," she says weakly.

She tears her eyes from it and places it on the nearby dresser before selecting a different purple. I want to ask, I want to *know*, what's so special about a cheap little drugstore eyeshadow pallet, but the words drown in my throat as Izzie instructs me to close my eyes and her hands return to my face. She swipes a thin brush over my eyelids, lingering on the corners. I wonder what she looks like when she's this focused. I wonder what she looks like when she's this focused *on me*.

The cool shock of liquid eyeliner hits my skin and I do my best to stay still as Izzie meticulously paints my skin.

Finally, she says, "Open," and holds a hand mirror up for me to see.

I look like an alternate-reality version of myself, with sleek black and purple angles lining my eyes. On the left side, she's drawn a little black star outlined in silver halfway between my lash line and my eyebrow. I look totally punk-concert-ready.

I cheat a glance at Izzie to find she's looking at me too. Her eyes are dark, the little flecks of gold in the irises hypnotic, like I'll be pulled in if I stare too long. And I do, I do, I do. There is a hitch in her breath as she inhales, and before my brain can catch up, before my silly little thoughts can stop me, I lean in and touch my lips to hers.

Kissing Izzie Margolis isn't like fireworks or lightning. It's quiet and calm and warm, like falling into a soft pillow. And I am, falling, so fast and hard. My hand finds her knee and I press up toward her, eager to touch her anywhere, everywhere. I want to run my fingers through her hair, brush my knuckles down her spine, press my forehead to hers and drown in the magnetic pull of her gaze. I never want this to end.

Izzie pulls away and my mind catches up. I've made a terrible error in judgment. I've misread the situation and ruined whatever good thing we had. I can probably kiss being in a band goodbye, and I definitely can't kiss anything else.

But then her eyes flutter open and her hand falls to mine on her knee. She doesn't push it away. She doesn't push *me* away. She just repositions, reaching up to brush my hair behind my ear, and says, "Thanks."

At the same time, I rush to say, "Sorry."

We both laugh awkwardly, and I rock back, clipping my shoulder on the corner of the dresser.

"I shouldn't have just—" I begin, but she cuts me off.

"No, I wanted you to."

"Okay good, cause I wanted to, too."

"I…" She hesitates, giving a one-armed shrug. "Do you remember at the café when I asked you what kind of lesbian you were?"

I nod. "Yeah, and I said the kind that likes girls."

"Right." She doesn't say anything else for a moment, fingers picking at the corner of the price sticker on that little purple eyeshadow pallet. "Well, I'm…"

I think for a moment she's about to tell me she's not a lesbian at all, that she was just kidding or experimenting, or the word 'lesbian' is actually French for one of those very yummy pastries with the flaky bits and the custard filling.

"I'm the kind that's trans," she says finally. Her eyes slide away from mine, down to the pallet in her hands. She peels a strip of the sticker off, worrying the residue away with her fingernails. "It's probably silly to keep it, but this was the first eyeshadow pallet I ever bought. I was twelve and my dad needed to pick up a few things at the store. He asked me if I wanted anything and I… I picked this." She slaps the pallet against her open palm, the sound hard and dull. "Drugstore makeup. It was $2.99. Dad didn't even blink. Just bought it for me."

I know better than to interrupt. Not while Izzie is letting me in like this. It's raw, I can tell, like she hasn't told this story a lot.

"It was the first time, you know? The first time someone accepted me for who I am. I didn't even use it." A laugh breaks from her throat, part joy, part heartache. "But it showed me it was safe to tell him when I was ready. It showed me maybe it would be safe to tell others, too. I hope… I hope it's okay that I'm telling *you*." Her eyes find mine again, bright and full of trust.

I remember, then, something my mother told me. *The truth is like a prayer. When you're honest with someone, you're asking for their grace and their integrity. And when they're honest with you, that's what you owe them in return.* I'd brushed her off back then. I wasn't much for prayer, anyway. Mom never made me go to church—she said faith was a choice I could make for myself. And I did. I decided it wasn't for me. But now, years after her death—knowing she died counting her rosary—I feel the weight of her words, like she's standing just behind me, reminding me how important it is to catch Izzie in her vulnerability and hold her close.

"Drugstore Makeup," I say slowly. "Has a nice ring to it."

"Huh?" Izzie's brows meet in a question.

"It means something to you—something really special and personal—but it's also punk. You, deciding to be brave with your dad, deciding to be yourself openly. And it's… part of our story now too." I reach out to hold the pallet with her, quieting her fingers as they try to rub the plastic clean. "What do you think? Band name?"

"You… you like it? You don't… care? About me being, trans?"

"Do I *care*?" I ask, incredulous, but the word feels different on my tongue, like it means more than I thought on the surface. "Of course I care," I say quietly. "I care because it's part of you, because it's your history. I care because… I care about you."

"You do." It isn't a question, but then she blinks and her voice goes quiet. "Like… in what way?"

"That depends." A sly smile sneaks onto my lips.

"On what?"

"Are you still the kind of lesbian who likes girls?"

A little laugh escapes her lips. "Definitely."

I can't wait to kiss her again. So I don't.

Summer

Six

As the blustery spring makes way for sunshine and blooming flowers, it feels like the world around me is smiling just like me. I play nothing but love songs at work in the weeks following our first kiss. Jordie has threatened to fight me in a Denny's parking lot multiple times, but no amount of physical—or emotional— warfare can dampen my mood, because I have a *girlfriend*.

Izzie isn't my first. I dated in college—not a lot, but enough— and even though I spent most of high school totally crushing on the beautiful but unavailable Rachel Amber, I definitely kissed my share of classmates back home in Arcadia Bay. But this just doesn't really compare to any of those experiences. There's something about not being students, about being adults, but there's also something about Izzie. Something special. Maybe it's the way she's so herself all the time, or maybe it's the way she strums her guitar, or maybe it's the way she marches into Save Point on a Thursday afternoon and declares in no uncertain terms, "Steph Gingrich, I'm taking you on a date tonight!"

It makes me utterly useless for the rest of the day. Poor Ollie has to pick up the slack while I play a game of mental dress-up, trying to decide what to wear.

"Oh my god, you *have* to talk to someone else about it," Ollie says as we round the three o'clock rush. "It's been years since I've thought this much about girl clothes."

"Hey, just 'cause I'm a girl—"

"Are you really about to lecture me about the gender binary?" He rolls his eyes, then tosses my phone to me from the back counter. "Text Lia if you're gonna be like this."

I stick my tongue out, but take his advice.

> Date noooooooooiiiight

Lia texts back immediately, like a true friend.

Omg what are you gonna wear??

> THANK YOU

> Ollie was making fun of me for caring about that

Ollie will make fun of anything

> True!!

> Anyway, I don't know. I feel like none of my clothes are really date material

You could always show up naked

> Dude!!!

What?! I bet Izzie would like it

I can practically imagine Lia's eyebrow wiggle, exaggerated to the point of comedy. I think she'd make an amazing actress, what with the faces she pulls, not to mention her absolutely stunning features. She has dark brown skin, long eyelashes, and cheekbones that could be considered a deadly weapon. But Lia was always more into the behind-the-scenes stuff like building sets. When we were in college, I used to spend hours in her dorm helping her sew or knit or bead costumes for the school's theater productions. Once, we were on such a tight deadline that we had to glue the seams closed instead of stitching them, and we forgot to open a window so we ended up high as a kite, giggling incessantly at four in the morning over a moldy muffin we found under her bed.

Lia was one of the first queer friends I met at DigiPen, besides Ollie. She walked into History 101 with a bi flag pin on her jean jacket and I knew immediately that we had to be friends. And, to our credit, we stayed friends, even after making out once. In our defense, we were being forced to watch M. Night Shyamalan's *The Last Airbender*, and the agony was simply too great to endure. Afterward, we agreed it was a necessary distraction, but would be a mistake to repeat, since Lia's poly and I'm more monogamous. Ever since, Lia's been my rock—my ride or die. It's only been a month since I met Izzie, but already I'm itching to introduce them.

> You really need to meet her...

> She should come with us to Pride!

> I'll ask her

> On my date tonight

> And I still don't know what to wear

> Your least holey jeans and the green flannel

> Makes your eyes pop

And NO BEANIE!!!

I'm gonna block you

You love me

I do, in fact, wear clothes on my date, but I *feel* naked without my beanie. It's too hot for it, as it turns out. June is approaching fast, and even the Pacific Northwest is feeling the heat of summer sneaking its way into the air. Soon, Dad will have all the windows open in the evenings with fans in front of them because he refuses to get air conditioning.

In true dad fashion, he insists on meeting Izzie, but at least he only manages one dad joke before we leave.

"Have her home by eleven!" he calls after us.

Izzie gives me a quizzical look, and I turn to raise my eyebrows as far as they'll go in his direction.

"In the morning, of course." And he waves like a proud papa seeing his daughter off on prom night.

"Sorry I didn't get you a corsage," Izzie mutters through a laugh.

"It's okay—maybe you'll still get lucky." I link our hands, smoothing my thumb along hers. "He's cringe, but… I get it. He wasn't there for shit like prom or anything, so he has to make up for it by being embarrassing now."

"Ah," Izzie says, squeezing my hand. "Child of divorce?"

"Yep. They split when I was eleven."

"Oof." Izzie lets out a long exhale. "That's rough."

I just shrug. It's too hard to explain that my parents' divorce is hardly the worst thing that's ever happened to me, so instead I ask, "What about you? Got any siblings or whatever?"

"What is this, first-date twenty questions?"

"Next, I'll ask about where you went to college and if you're looking for a serious relationship."

Izzie chuckles and squeezes my hand. "No siblings, my parents are still together but just as cringe, and as for the last one—"

"Oh my god, you don't have to answer. I was just kidding." Warmth sneaks into my cheeks and I'm sure I look beet-red, but I kind of want to know the answer anyway.

With a shrug, Izzie bites her bottom lip and says, "Maybe… if the right person came along." Then she turns to her van and opens the door for me. "Milady, your chariot awaits."

I climb up while she loops around the other side and I slide my phone from my pocket to see a few texts from my friends.

> **Lia:** Good luck babe!!

> **Ollie:** You got this!

> **Jordie:** We'll miss you for Critical Role night

I wince a little. I forgot to let Jordie know I wasn't coming for our Thursday-night hang, but I guess Ollie told him. I'm a little disappointed to miss it this week, but hopefully they'll understand.

Another couple of texts come in, buoying my spirits.

> **Jordie:** But have fun—don't do anything I wouldn't do!

> **Ollie:** Counterpoint, do literally everything Jordie wouldn't do!

It's the vote of confidence I need to reach across the space and slot my fingers together with Izzie's as she starts the van and backs out into the street.

Izzie drives with the windows down, inviting a breeze to

tangle her hair. It feels like laughter, like the wind is happy for us. She holds my hand the whole way. I never want to let go.

She finally does, though, just as we park outside a little bistro called Alberti's. It's not what I expect from Izzie. It feels so normal, so classic. I thought a date with a punk-rock goddess might involve more dancing in a dark corner of a club or looking at weird art or protesting the man. I feel a flicker of disappointment that Izzie doesn't want to bring me into her world, but I shove it down. This is Izzie, and I'd even be happy to watch sportsball as long I was doing it with her.

"Wow, so you're wining and dining me," I say as we get out of the van.

"Only the best for my girl!"

"Your girl?" I mean to tease her, but the words come out soft.

Izzie tucks her hair behind her ear and smiles up at me. "Yeah… if you want to be."

"Oh, I want!" and I pull her forward into the restaurant.

We're seated in a cozy corner of the restaurant. It's dark, lit with orange sconces and little tea candles on the table. It's supposed to be romantic, I think. And, hey, maybe it *is* romantic.

"My name is Randal and I'll be your server this evening. If I might draw your attention to our specials…"

The waiter tells us something about a bisque, maybe, and I think some type of fish, but his words slide right over me. It's like Izzie's presence is too loud for me to hear anything else. She's wearing a jean jacket over a black strappy dress with a silver ring at the center of her breastbone. I just want to hook my finger in it and pull her close. It's like a beacon—*Gondor calls for aid, and Rohan shall answer!* I inch my fingers toward hers on the table, my whole body thrumming with the overwhelming need to touch her, even just a little.

The moment our index fingers touch, Izzie's demeanor

changes. Something in her jaw twitches and her shoulders straighten before she draws back, placing her hand beneath the table.

"I'll be back with your waters in just a minute." The waiter smiles, but I barely notice.

"What… were the specials again?" I ask, scanning the menu, determined not to make a thing of whatever just happened.

But when Izzie doesn't respond, doesn't even look at me, I make a thing of it anyway.

"Okay, what's going on?" I whisper across the table. "One second you're calling me your girl and the next you're pushing my hand away?"

Izzie just stares unblinkingly at the place where the waiter used to stand.

"Earth to Izzie." I snap my fingers.

"I know him," she says, so quietly that if I didn't see her lips move, I might not believe the words really came from her. "From middle school." She blinks a couple of times. "Randy Hooper."

"Okay…"

"I don't… I don't think he recognized me."

That's when my brain catches up, putting the pieces together. "He doesn't know—about you being trans."

She shakes her head. "And if he's anything like he used to be, I don't want him to."

"We can go somewhere else, you know. We absolutely do not have to stay here." I bump her knee with mine under the table for reassurance.

She eyes me, rolling her lip between her teeth. "It's okay," she says finally. "I think I'd feel weirder if we just left. Like… like he'd be chasing us out of here, just like he used to chase people at recess."

"Are you sure?" I ask. Every instinct in my body says we should get up and leave, just book it out of here before he notices. The way Izzie's body has gone rigid, the way her shoulders cave inward, it's not the Izzie I'm used to. I don't like seeing her like this—afraid.

71

"Yeah. Yes. I'm sure." She rolls her shoulders back again and picks up the menu. "Just maybe... don't hold my hand where he can see?"

I find her fingers beneath the table and don't let go until we've finished our food and Randy brings the bill.

"Let me get it," I say, reaching for my pocket.

"No, no." Izzie waves me off. "I'm the one who asked you out."

I bite my lip. It's always weird, deciding who's going to pay when you're gay. For all the dates I've been on, we've always split the bill. It's safer that way, with no weird expectations or implications. I can tell it means something to Izzie, though, like she thinks this is her one chance.

"I don't want him recognizing your last name on your credit card," I say as quietly as I can. "You can get the next one, okay?"

"There's gonna be a next one?" she asks, eyes widening.

I grin and slide my card into the slot. "Course there is."

"Thank you." She exhales. "This isn't how I wanted it to go. It's our first real date and I should've, I don't know, picked somewhere better or more familiar or—"

I can't let her keep going on like that, so I lean in and touch her knee under the table. "This is *our* date—together. I want you to be safe. If you're not having a good time, then neither am I."

"Oh... guess it wasn't a very fun date, then." Her smile falters.

"I don't know... there's a lot of hours to go until eleven in the morning. There's still time to turn this around." I squeeze her hand under the table. "What do you say you let me take the reins for a bit?"

"What do you have in mind?"

A spark lights in her eye that wasn't there before and my chest swells. I want to make her feel like this all night, like she's special and worthy of a fun time without worry, without homophobia or transphobia. I want to hold her close and let our fingers bump in a shared popcorn bowl and kiss her again.

"Have you ever seen *Blade Runner*?" I ask.

"Please," Izzie says flatly. "Of course I have."

"Great. Then you won't mind when we don't actually watch it."

When we leave the restaurant, Izzie puts her hand back in mine, and though there's an evening chill in the air, I don't feel cold at all.

Seven

If Pride is an explosion of rainbows, then Pride with Izzie is the pot of gold at the end. It is a special kind of magic, watching her light up as we arrive at Volunteer Park. We are engulfed by expressions of queer joy. The word 'equality' is spelled out in colorful balloons and nearby the scent of soft pretzels fills the air. The sun is shining and there's even a disco ball at the entrance, but Izzie is still the brightest thing here. A smile bursts onto her face and her eyes twinkle as she takes it all in.

"You made it!"

Ollie and Jordie barrel toward us, bedecked in glitter paint. Ollie carries Jordie on his shoulders and Jordie wears the black, gray, white, and purple striped asexual flag around his neck like a cape. Their ensembles are nothing compared to Lia's intricate craftsmanship, though. She looks like a big gay maypole, strips of rainbow fabric twisted around her in overlapping patchwork, and strapped to her shoulders is a set of fairy wings made from translucent organza stretched in wire frame to look like stained glass. In her hair, worn naturally in springy black curls, she's twisted little pink, purple, and blue gemstones like a bisexual flag crown.

"Lia, holy shit!" I say, moving around to get a better look at her wings.

"The crafty bitch always shows us up," says Jordie with an eye roll.

"Yeah, I'm really putting that theater tech minor to good use," Lia mutters, reluctantly letting me get my grubby little hands all over her masterpiece.

"I wish I had half your skill with a bedazzler." I make my way around Lia's costume, eyeing what must be a few thousand tiny rhinestones along the wings. They catch the light and send rainbows skittering across the grass. "I don't even own a rainbow tank top, let alone a sparkle factory."

"Oh, we can dress you up," Lia begins, plucking at my green T-shirt. Then she spots Izzie and goes still. "Oh my god, Steph. Is this her?"

For a second, I think maybe they know each other. It's not all that uncommon in the lesbian community to accidentally date a friend's ex. The only thing more likely, actually, is to *purposefully* date a friend's ex. I just have to hope their breakup wasn't explosive or messy or—

"She's *stunning!*" Lia smacks me hard across the arm. "You're stunning," she says directly to Izzie.

Izzie may not be flashy like Lia, but she's still showing her pride. Little rainbow crystals hang from her ears, and she's painted her eyelids with little stripes of baby blue, pink, and white. It's elegant and subtle, and I love it.

"And I'm being so embarrassing, wow. I'm Lia—it's really nice to meet you."

Izzie takes her offered hand, and then Lia is grabbing mine too and jostling us forward. "Come on, we need to rainbowify you!"

"Oh, Lia, no we don't have to—" I start, but Lia raises her perfectly sculpted brows and fixes me with a capital-L *Look*.

"You're kidding, right? And deny me my greatest joy?" She clucks her tongue like a disappointed mother hen. "Nary a rainbow nor carabiner in sight! What are we going to do with you?"

"I mean…" I start, not wanting to be a bother, but Lia's eyes are already glittering with excitement. If Lia's offering her help, who am I to reject it? "Yeah, okay."

Lia marches us toward a blanket laid out on the grass and holds up a bag full of body paint. "You'll look great with a little lesbian flag on your face."

"I think you'd look great with a little *lesbian* on your face," Izzie murmurs before planting a kiss on my cheek.

We lie on the grass all afternoon, eating snow cones and listening to live music of varying quality. After a few hours, Jordie finally remembers to pass around the sunscreen. Ollie is already thoroughly burned, but we all lather it on anyway. Lia's partners, Rain and Wes, show up shortly after with a pack of bottled water and the largest collection of sour candy I've ever seen. We all squish together on the blanket to make room.

I've been to Pride a bunch of times, and every one is a little different. I've marched in the parades, I've listened to the charismatic speakers, I've looked at every vendor and informational booth. But my favorite thing about Pride is lazily sitting in the sun with my friends, just being queer and existing. I remember going to Portland Pride with my friends from Arcadia Bay and how exhilarating it was to just *be* with other queer people. There weren't many of us in my hometown who were out and proud, but I was lucky to have a friend in Chloe Price. I haven't seen her in years—not since I ran into her at a show for Pixie's band—but I hope she's well. I think she must be.

I smile into the memory of my rival in love. Back in our school days, we were both crushing on Rachel Amber. And who wasn't? She was gorgeous and funny and full of surprises. But in the end, neither of us really got the girl. In the end, the girl was a lot more complex than the love triangle we made for her. In the end, she didn't get to decide anything for herself because some asshole with a God complex chose for her. She never saw the end because she died for a man's sick idea of art.

I shiver and Izzie twines our fingers together.

"Okay?" she asks, concern etched into her brow.

"Yeah," I lie. "Just felt a chill for a second."

"Probably a sympathetic brain freeze," says Ollie through a mouthful of snow cone.

I nod and crack a smile. Today isn't for thinking about death. Today is for living, for rainbows, for kissing the girl beside me. I lean into Izzie and breathe her in. *I am happy.* I repeat it to myself until it's true. I hope somewhere Chloe is happy too. Me with Izzie, Chloe with Max.

I met Chloe's girlfriend a few years ago at a show. The High Seas were playing and I was helping to run things backstage. Max was cool—quiet and artsy, not at all the kind of girl I thought Chloe would go for. But… they worked. Max knows the Chloe of before. Before Rachel, before Chloe's dad died, before the storm. Chloe found love by looking to her past. But me? I'm fully focused on the future.

"Let's go on a food mission," I say. I need to move. I need to eat. I need to think about something else. I turn to the others. "Any requests?"

"Caaaaaake!" Jordie wails in an imitation of the current musical act's unfortunate falsetto.

"I'll see what we can do." I take Izzie's hand and begin the process of extracting us from the maze of other blankets spread across the lawn.

Izzie sighs, relief cascading across her shoulders as we step away from the crowded space. Maybe I wasn't the only one in need of an escape.

"Too much peopling?" I ask once we're out of earshot.

Izzie nods and leans into me as we walk, her head tilted slightly toward mine.

There's this period of time in any relationship—romantic, platonic, or otherwise—when you begin to learn the other person's non-verbal cues. The little glances that mean they're uncomfortable, the mannerisms that mean they're nervous, the silences that fill with unsaid anxieties. I realize with a jolt that I'm beginning to know Izzie's. We haven't been dating for long, but already I can tell that there's something hanging in the space between us, that if I stay quiet for long enough, she'll say it.

We get lemonades from a nearby food cart and clink our plastic cups together.

"Cheers!" I say, grinning.

"You look happy." Izzie takes a sip, rolling her straw between her teeth.

"Just thinking about last week, when the waiter came over and we stopped holding hands just in case." I twine my fingers with hers and look down at our clasped hands. "Fuck, it feels good not to worry about shit like that. Even just for one weekend."

Izzie nods and leans her head on my shoulder. "Yeah. One little oasis in the year when you don't have to feel like it's you versus the world."

I turn my head so I can see her face—calm and quiet, like all the thoughts that are normally storming in her brain have taken today off. Clear skies only.

"Hey." I tug on her waist. "Who says we can't take a little of the oasis with us?"

"You mean…"

I gesture at the vendor booths lining this side of the festival. "Let's each pick one thing, okay? That way we'll always have a little bit of Pride even when June is over."

We make our way through the stalls. There's jewelry, T-shirts, and all kinds of art. I can't even begin to decide what sort of thing I might want—really, I just want it all—and Izzie finally suggests that we should pick for each other instead.

"Ta-da!" she exclaims, presenting me with a large wooden block with the word 'pride' spelled out in sequins. It's sparkly and bright and so so Pride. "For your kitchen table, or something."

I take it and hold it up so sunlight bounces off the sequins. "I love it," I say, never mind that I don't have a kitchen table. Dad and I usually eat separately, but that's fine. I'll put it in my room and maybe that will liven the place up.

"My turn!" I grab her hand and we take off, continuing down the row of stalls. I consider a pair of rainbow earrings, but decide they aren't really right for Izzie, so I keep going until we find a booth with rainbow-painted wooden sculptures and accessories.

"What do you think of these?" I ask, but Izzie's expression has sort of glazed over.

"Sorry, what?"

I trace the curve of her jaw with my finger and I can see in her eyes that she wants to just skip back to gift giving, wall herself back up and forget whatever's bothering her. "Where'd you go?" I ask.

"Did you tell Lia?" Her eyes are unfocused as she crosses over to the table and picks up a barrette with a watercolor effect, swirling together the white, blue, and pink colors of the trans flag.

"That we're dating? Yeah. She knows."

She turns the barrette over in her hands, brushing her fingertips along the curl of the maple. "No, about me being trans."

"No. Why?"

"Oh, just… usually when people are that complimentary about my appearance it's because they're trying to like… I don't know, prove to me that they're not a transphobe. Like if they say the trans girl is pretty enough times it'll make up for their feminist activism starting and ending with people who have uteruses."

"Izzie…" I lightly cup her elbow and wait for her eyes to find mine. "I know there are people out there who absolutely do that. And I know that's probably really hard to swallow—dealing with that kind of stuff all the time is so shitty. But you also have to know—you *are* really pretty."

"Yeah?" She looks up at me through long dark lashes, eyes quivering like she doesn't quite believe me.

"I've always thought that, and I'll keep telling you so as long as you still want to hear it." I pass the vendor a crumpled twenty-dollar bill for the barrette, and brush Izzie's hair back into a half-up-half-down pony. "For example, I like your hair," I say, running my fingers through it. "And I don't know if you've noticed, but you have these incredible eyeballs—"

Izzie chokes on a laugh.

"I ruined it with the word 'eyeballs,' huh?"

"Little bit." But she smiles up at me anyway, and I see my opportunity for redemption.

"Oh—you've got something on your face." I point to my own, waving my finger around my mouth.

She wipes at her lip and says, "Did I get it?"

"Nah—here, let me." I swoop down to kiss her. "Got it."

"Are you sure? Maybe you should double-check." And she leans in for another.

Laughter bubbles up between us, and the moment feels so light and happy, like nothing can ruin it for us. The stark contrast between this and our date, when a homophobe seeing us share affection was dangerous, to this, where queer love is all around, makes me nearly burst, like skin alone cannot contain my euphoria.

But Izzie stalls halfway to my lips and rests back on her heels. Her spine goes rigid and her grip on my waist goes limp.

"Izzie! Didn't expect to see you here."

I turn around to see a familiar trio—a blonde, a brunette, and a redhead. The remaining members of Vinyl Resting Place bracket us.

"Why not? Still gay," Izzie growls under her breath. "Kicking me out of the band didn't change my sexuality."

Astrid raises one eyebrow, plucked to early 2000s levels of thin, just like my patience for her passive aggression. "Right," she sneers. "But you're not competing in Battle of the Bands, are you? There's no way you have a new band already."

I step forward, chin up, jaw hard. "Actually, she does."

The mean girls give me a once-over, recognition sparking all at once. "With the groupie?"

"Hey, I'm the first to admit I'm the number-one Izzie fan, but—"

"Leave it, Steph," Izzie mutters. "We're not playing. Just here to watch."

"Too bad," says Astrid as they back away. "Would've been fun to battle." She points at the stage where our friends are camped out.

"We'll see if you still think that when you lose!" I shout after them, but Izzie is tugging on my shirt, so I settle back and try to extinguish my anger. "Sorry," I say, though it doesn't really feel true.

"It's okay, just… you know, still raw." Izzie trails a hand along my side, a soothing motion. "Astrid's always known exactly how to hurt me. I was really looking forward to playing Battle of the Bands, and they know it."

"Fuck! I hate that they get to lord this over you. We should totally be playing. Imagine how good it would feel to beat them with that new song. The one they didn't want."

Izzie's nodding, but I can tell her head isn't here with me. "I don't know. It probably isn't good enough."

"Hey!" I shake her lightly by the shoulders. "It's a great song! And we're gonna practice a lot, okay? We'll get so good by this time next year, Vinyl Resting Place won't know what hit 'em."

"And you think we can beat them?"

She asks it so earnestly, so breathlessly, it takes everything in me not to just kiss her. I take her chin in my hand and I look directly into her warm brown eyes before I say, "I think we can win."

Eight

It's one thing to say we'll rock and another thing entirely to actually do it. I pace like I'm trying to hit a steps goal in the back room of Mug Shot, the boozy café we're playing for our first show. It's nowhere near as big as Bar-None. The stage is a little raised platform in the corner with barely enough room for my drum set and Izzie's amp. Tables and chairs fan out in a semicircle, full of friends and even some strangers. I can't decide which makes me more nervous.

"We've got this!" Izzie says, squeezing my shoulder a little too tight. "Remember, don't speed up."

"I am become a metronome!" I chant and rub my drumsticks together. I want to say more, or maybe I just want to avoid the audience longer, but then our name is announced and applause sweeps us forward onto the stage, where a big poster with our new logo is taped up like a banner: a red lipstick mark on a black background with vibrant violet text. I tried to get as close to the purple eyeshadow as I could with my colored pencils on short notice. I'll do another draft soon with better supplies, but for now, it's cool to see my art up there, like I get to have a contribution to the band beyond just keeping time.

I don't even make it all the way behind the drum set before I screw up, crashing into the ride cymbal headfirst. A loud clanging sound punctuates my entrance, but luckily I avoid any major injuries.

Jordie and Ollie are in the very front, both wearing matching grins. Jordie's sporting an 'I'm with the band' T-shirt and Ollie has a little red kiss mark on his cheek to match our new logo. We didn't have time to make merch for the gig, but I'm glad to see they made do anyway. A few rows behind them are Lia and Rain, and by the door my dad is craning his neck to see over the crowd. He's got one of those goofy proud dad smiles and he flashes me a thumbs up when I catch his eye.

"We're Drugstore Makeup!" Izzie says into the mic. Her amplified voice soothes my nerves. My heartbeat slows and I loosen my grip on the drumsticks. "Don't forget to tip your barista, and get ready to rock!"

And we *do*.

Playing with Izzie onstage is a totally different experience from practicing in her garage. It takes me a minute to adjust to the acoustics in the café. It's bigger and there are no sound-absorbing pads on the walls, but the energy of the audience is electrifying. As Izzie sings—and sometimes shouts—into the mic, people whoop and cheer. It's almost otherworldly, this collaborative moment between us all. It isn't just mine, it isn't just Izzie's, it's all of ours, together.

We play mostly covers—Gore Gore Girls, Paramore, Bikini Kill. Izzie insists we should fill our set list with mostly female vocalists, since they're so underrepresented in punk, but she makes an exception for Good Charlotte's 'Girls & Boys' because, as she explains to the audience, "if anyone's going to sing about how girls don't like boys, it should be lesbians."

For our last song, we play Izzie's 'Riot Pride.' Izzie thanks the audience and when she announces we're closing with an original, the crowd goes wild. How much of that is just Jordie and Ollie being the best groupies imaginable, I don't know, but I don't really care at this point. I'm having such a great time that even if some rando told us we sucked after the show, I don't think I'd believe them.

When it's over, I barely make it down from the stage before I'm engulfed by friends.

"Steph! That was so cool!" Jordie shouts into my ear at an entirely unnecessary volume. "Wait, is it supremely uncool to say so? I don't know the rules."

I shrug and grin into his embrace. "I don't know the rules either!"

"Great, okay, let's not tell anyone."

Ollie elbows in to get his turn, too. "Cannot believe you were this talented and you, what, *forgot* to tell me?"

"*Forgot?*" I hug him back. "I withhold that information on purpose—how else am I supposed to create a sense of mystery?"

"Drinkies?" Jordie suggests. "Our treat!"

"Don't you have the morning shift?" I ask. "Sure you want to stay out late?"

"He had some kind of vanilla coffee and kalua drink about an hour ago—I think it's gonna be a late night either way." Ollie pinches Jordie's cheek affectionately and adds, "This one's a little caf*fiend*!"

"Ohhh, that's a great name for a new drink at the café!"

While Jordie and Ollie argue about the recipe for their invention, I greet Lia and Rain, who've made their way over to squeeze me from both sides. Lia apologizes for Wes's absence, though it's not necessary. "They have a noise sensitivity. Rock concert isn't exactly their scene."

Rain scrunches up their face, little wrinkles rippling over their rosy brown skin. "They wanted to send flowers for you, but…" They trail off, exchanging a knowing glance with Lia.

Lia jumps in to finish for them. "It's not a ballet recital, you know?"

That certainly doesn't stop Dad from presenting me with a handful of wildflowers—lupines and poppies and Queen Anne's lace.

"I'm so proud of you, sweetie!" he says, squeezing my shoulder.

It's an awkward exchange. We're still not practiced at physical affection, or even just conversational affection. I almost expected him to slip out of the café before the end and email me his congratulations on a gig well played.

"Did you pick these?" I ask, half aghast, half impressed. The stems are untidy and the foliage still wild. A florist wouldn't be so sloppy, but honestly I'd prefer a collection of thoughtfully plucked weeds to any pristine store-bought bouquet. They're beautiful, if not exactly appropriate.

"You know me, I haven't been outside in a century." Dad laughs. It's our little joke that he's secretly a vampire, since he's such a hermit. "No, these are from Renee—you remember that coworker I was telling you about?"

"Hello!" A white woman about my dad's age with curly brown hair and treble-clef earrings waves at me over his shoulder. "When your dad told me you had a gig, I insisted on tagging along. Music is a joy to share, and your band has such a fun energy!"

"Thanks." I point to the flowers and nod. "For these—and for coming."

"You got plans after?" Dad asks eagerly. "Maybe we could get a bite—"

"Sorry." I glance at Jordie and Ollie, who are lurking nearby. "I think my friends want to get drinks somewhere. Rain check?"

"I told you, George. Leave the young people to their partying," Renee says, tugging on his arm.

I watch them go with narrowed eyes, suspicion sneaking into my chest but... no. My dad's too awkward to get a girlfriend. But then, I thought that about myself, too, and look at me! All girlfriended-up.

I scan the room for Izzie, but she's nowhere in sight. Maybe she's with some of her friends in the back room or outside. I definitely saw Saturn in the crowd with a few people, but there were plenty more I didn't recognize that have to be people Izzie knows.

"Well, since you just rocked, ready to roll?" Jordie asks with an exaggerated eyebrow wiggle.

"It's like you *try* to be cringe," Ollie groans.

I crane my neck to scan the dispersing crowd, but still don't see Izzie. "Hang on," I say. "I have to pack up first."

"We'll help!"

Jordie jumps into action, beginning to dismantle my drum set, and Ollie leans in to me to murmur, "It's okay—go find her. We got this."

I don't even get my thanks out before Ollie joins Jordie and they fumble their way through taking the drums apart. Even this silly little task is fun for them together. I love that for them—the simple joy of just doing mundane things with the person you care about the most. It's nice. It's… less familiar than I want it to be.

When I do find Izzie, she's already done packing up her guitar and is sitting inside the van with her legs propped up in the frame of the back door, notepad in hand.

"Whatcha writing?" I ask, tossing my drumsticks into the cup holder in front.

She doesn't respond right away, scribbling furiously.

"New song?"

"Same song." Her voice is clipped, her brow pinched in concentration.

"I thought it sounded good!" I place my fingers lightly on her knee.

"Yeah?" Her eyes flick up to mine, uncertainty embedded deep in her irises. "I think the third verse needs some work, and maybe we should add a guitar solo?"

I nod and smile. "Okay. Sure. That could be fun. Maybe we work on it tomorrow? My friends want to go out and celebrate."

"It's okay—you can go. I'll do this myself."

My chest constricts painfully. "Are you… sure? You're invited, you know. Plus I think I saw your housemates waiting out there for you."

She sets the pen down and sighs. "Yeah, okay. Guess I should check in with them."

"Do you want to invite them along maybe? We could all go out together."

"Nah." She swings her legs down from the van and lands beside me. "I wanna work on this some more."

She won't meet my eyes, and her avoidance hurts almost more than her words. "Did I… do something wrong? Do you not want me to hang out with your friends?" I ask, the words soft on my tongue. "I know I'm still new to this, but I will get better at drumming and stuff. I promise you can bring me to your cool punk parties and I'll be chill."

"What? Oh no, Steph. No, no." Her hand finds my waist and she pulls me closer. "You were great. I just… want to get this right. I feel like I'm in a creative groove and I don't want to lose that. I promise we'll hang with my friends another time, okay?"

"Are you sure?" My fingers seek hers, hoping that her touch will ground me, reassure me.

"Yeah. You go have fun." She gives my hand a perfunctory squeeze. It's almost enough.

Izzie makes good on her promise a few weeks later.

> Party at my place, 8pm!

Her text comes through while I'm still at Save Point, so I finish my shift and hurry home to scarf down some boxed mac and cheese, and change. I go against Lia's advice for tonight, wearing my *most* torn jeans and a tight T-shirt proclaiming my love for The Smashing Pumpkins. For a finishing touch, I throw on the leather bracelets Izzie dressed me in on the night of our first kiss. I forgot to give them back that night and I've just been hanging on to them ever since. I wonder if she's noticed.

87

Bruce, Izzie's housemate, greets me at the door when I arrive. He's a weird guy—very buttoned-up with a slightly too thin mustache. He's not usually home when I'm around, since he works more hours than he doesn't, but on the few occasions I've passed him in the kitchen or the living room, he's always been pleasant.

"Welcome to the party!" he shouts over the music and hands me an empty plastic cup and a sharpie. "Reduce! Reuse! Recycle!"

I give him an off-kilter salute and scribble my name on the outside of my cup before heading inside.

The living room has been transformed into a dance floor. Neon lights crisscross through the space and the seating has been carted off somewhere to make room for a DJ table, behind which Saturn is spinning tunes. I give them a quick wave before ducking into the kitchen to fill my cup.

"You made it!" Izzie captures my lips with hers. She tastes like sharp mint and raspberry. "Come on. Got people I want you to meet."

She drags me out to the backyard, fingers laced with mine, and over to a group clustered by the fence.

"Everyone, this is Steph." Izzie points at me with a big grin on her face. "Girlfriend, drummer, coffee connoisseur."

"Hey!" I nod to the group, eyes sweeping over them. There's about a dozen people out here enjoying the Seattle summer evening, not to mention the crowd inside. It strikes me all at once how many people Izzie must know. I'm pretty savvy when it comes to socializing, and even I couldn't come up with a guest list this extensive. There is so much of Izzie I still don't know, so much of her that exists outside of us, outside of me.

I glance over to see her expression awash with pride. Her eyes are trained on me, bright and brilliant, like she's actually excited to show me off, like I'm special. And, dammit, under her gaze, with her hand in mine, maybe I am.

"The myth! The legend!" A tall white guy with gauges

in his ears and a T-shirt that says 'Pro Union' reaches across the gap to shake my hand. "Heard you drummed up quite the audience for your first gig."

"Jerry, I swear to God." The girl beside him smacks his arm. "Ignore him. He makes puns instead of having a personality. I'm Ronnie—guitarist for Attack-o-Lanterns."

The rest of the group introduce themselves one by one. They all have names and bands, only half of which I remember an hour later once I've been thoroughly paraded around what seems like every person in Seattle.

Izzie pulls me onto the dance floor and tucks her face into the crook of my neck. The music is fast and hard, but Izzie's energy is quiet and soft as she leans into me. I run my fingers through her hair and sway to her beat. It's counterintuitive to all my drummer training, but I'd rather be attuned to Izzie's rhythm than Sum 41's. We stay like that for a few songs, wrapped up in each other, then Izzie slides from my grip and gestures to her empty cup. I can't hear her over the music, but I understand her meaning well enough.

After she slips away to the kitchen, I find myself shuffled into a conversation with Jerry, the guy from outside, who is patiently explaining to Bruce the many types of unions for which he is pro.

"All of them, really, man. Obviously I'm pro labor union, pro marital union…"

"Pro union army," I suggest.

"See, Steph gets it." Jerry gives my arm a soft punch.

Bruce shakes his head, eyes a little unfocused. "Okay, okay—I promise I'm not that dense, I just thought your shirt said Pro *Onion*."

"Oh man, yeah! I'm pro onion, too. Blooming, caramelized, satire publication…"

I'm ushered from conversation to conversation. Ronnie grabs me to talk about the best coffee in Seattle, a debate for which I'm highly qualified, and Saturn asks me to DJ while they take a bathroom break for "just a few minutes." It's way longer than that, and pretty soon I'm picking songs myself. I watch the room carefully, but people don't leave the dance floor. In fact, a few cheer me on and I feel somehow like maybe I actually belong here at this party, with this music, with these people.

When Saturn returns, I relinquish their seat and go in search of Izzie, following her path to the drinks station. It's been at least a half hour since she disappeared, and after a quick glance around, she's still nowhere to be seen—maybe she went back outside. I reach for a bottle of rum—the taste of Izzie's mojito still lingering on my lips—but my hand collides with someone else's.

"Good taste."

I look up to see a familiar face framed with cropped brown hair, an eyebrow piercing, and an expression verging on sour. It's one of the other girls from Vinyl Resting Place.

"Oh, hey—you're, uh…" I trail off, realizing I don't actually know her name.

"Bellamy," she supplies.

"Ah, I was close—I was gonna guess something starting with the letter B." It's way meaner than I intend and I wince immediately, an apology she doesn't really deserve but I probably owe suspended on my lips.

"That is fair, honestly," she says before I can take it back. "Sorry about all the drama—Astrid and Izzie have always been a bit radioactive and the blast radius is brutal."

"Yeah, sounds like it." I take the rum bottle from her when she's done, but don't pour. "Have you seen her?"

"Astrid? Are you kidding? She's not here. Tara and I got the invite from Mariana, but we're not stupid enough to bring Astrid."

"Oh, no, I meant Izzie." I cast my gaze about again.

"Think she went to the garage," Bellamy says with a shrug. "Hope you find her. See you around… Sophie?"

I don't bother correcting her. My heart beats high in my throat and my eyes flit to the garage. The house thrums with energy and loud bass, but my brain feels muffled. I put down the rum and instead fill my cup with tap water. Something tells me I'm going to want to err on the side of sober once I open the door.

Izzie's inside, lying on her back in the middle of her bed, knees tucked up to her chest. She rolls to the side when I move the divider.

"Found ya," I say, crossing over to put my cup down on the bedside table. "Does that mean it's my turn to hide?"

Izzie smiles, but it doesn't quite reach her eyes. "I wasn't hiding."

"You sure about that?" I settle onto the edge of the bed next to her and pull my legs up under me. "Maybe you should be a magician instead of a rock star—you've got the disappearing act down."

"I could get a rabbit."

I nod sagely. "Girls just wanna have bun."

She throws a pillow at me.

"But really, what's up?" I scoot closer, pulling her legs over my lap. "You just kind of left there. It's *your* party, you know."

Izzie blinks at me and I see it in her eyes for just a flash—the instinct to make a joke, to lie, to brush me off. It's what I would do in her shoes. No, that's not true—I wouldn't have left the party to begin with. I was having too much fun.

"Did you see Bellamy and Tara? Probably weird that they showed up, huh?" I ask, prompting.

"Oh… I mean, yeah, I guess." She sighs and lets her head fall back, hair splayed out around her like a crown. "I just don't really feel like being around people tonight."

"Weird day to throw a party, then."

"Well, it's not really for *me*."

"Huh?" I cock my head. "What do you mean?"

Izzie sits up and places a hand on my arm. "You wanted to party with my friends. You said so after our show."

"The party's… for me? To hang out with your friends?"

She shrugs but doesn't meet my eyes. "Yeah, sort of."

A hollow feeling fills my stomach. It *is* what I wanted. Izzie is this incredibly cool punk rocker and I wanted to see her world. I wanted to be deemed worthy of it. I wanted to belong there. But out in the garage where the music struggles through the soundproof walls, it feels like maybe Izzie's the one who doesn't really belong.

"Let me ask you something," I say, the words slow on my tongue as I wrap my head around this feeling of being just slightly askew. "All those people you introduced me to... do you actually like any of them?"

"What?" The word comes too quick, too hard.

"It's just... you invited a lot of people, and I *know* you're not friends with some of them. Like, come on, Bellamy and Tara?"

"You caught me, Steph." Izzie falls back onto the bed, her torso bouncing as a laugh breaks from her chest. "You sounded really excited to do the whole party thing, like you thought I had this alternative life to show you. I don't know, I liked that you saw me as some punk princess—punk-rock Barbie or whatever. But I don't really even know half the people here. Most of them are just people from bands I've played with, people I know from the scene because I gave them a bloody nose in a mosh pit. The only reason I know any of these people is because of Astrid and Vinyl Resting Place. Those girls—they *were* my friends. And without them, I don't really know how to be the girl you want me to be. I'm just Izzie."

There's absolutely nothing *just* about this girl before me. Izzie's eyes are closed, her mouth a little open. Her shirt is slipping down off one shoulder, revealing a bra strap cinched too tight, digging into her skin. She looks peaceful and serene. She isn't *just* Izzie because she is everything.

"Izzie," I say her name softly as I lie down next to her. The syllables catch in my throat, and all the other words I want to say dissolve on my tongue. There is only her.

"It's okay. You can go back in—enjoy the party." She pulls her hands back to her stomach, knotting her fingers together just above her navel where her shirt rides up. "I don't mind hanging by myself."

And maybe in another life I would do just that. Maybe I'd return to the noise and lights and crowd of bodies. I'd drink and I'd dance and I'd soak up the energy of these people I was so eager to meet. But it feels empty, knowing Izzie is here feeling friendless, feeling like a disappointment.

I curl my body to fit against hers and trail my fingers along the bare skin of her shoulder. "Not a chance," I whisper against her lips just before I kiss her. Tonight, I'm hosting a party for two.

Nine

Dad finally corners me for a family dinner in the most George Gingrich way possible. He sends me an e-vite. It's fireman themed, and I can't tell if he picked it to be funny or if he couldn't figure out how to select different options. He promises a home-cooked meal and suggests I bring Izzie. I show it to her, thinking we'll have a good laugh and I'll tell him we're too busy, but to my surprise she just says, "I'd love to," and doesn't even make a fire truck joke.

I write back:

Home-cooked?? By WHOMST?

Dad's email comes shortly after, as though he's been waiting for my reply.

Don't worry, I promise not to burn the salad.

And, to my surprise, he doesn't. I still remember the time we melted the waffle maker trying to make breakfast in bed on Mother's Day. Mom had to open all the windows and take the batteries out of the smoke alarm, muttering curses under her breath the whole time. Dad was banned from the kitchen after that. From what I can tell, he's mostly subsisted on takeout since the divorce, a lifestyle I'm more than happy to take advantage of while living with him.

Seeing him in the kitchen wearing an apron is almost enough to send me running back out the door. It's a fairly untouched space—the only appliance that gets any sort of regular traffic is the microwave above the stove. The light gray marble countertops are practically spotless and there's even a bowl of fake fruit on the center island. It looks straight out of a catalog. In fact, I bet he didn't change a thing from the day he moved in.

"Check me out, Steph! I'm boiling water!" Dad points to the burner where he is, in fact, successfully boiling water. With a flourish, he removes the lid from the pot and pours pasta from a cardboard box like he's been doing it for years.

"Next you'll tell me you've learned how to turn on the oven." I start to roll my eyes, but then a second head appears from behind him, curly hair pulled into a loose ponytail and sporting a painfully genuine smile. For a moment, my heart drops through the floor. A memory surfaces, gasping and flailing like a drowning victim, bursting to the surface of my brain. My parents, together, laughing over a pot of soup. Mom feeding him some with a big spoon, Dad yelping and frantically fanning his mouth when he burns it on the too-hot liquid. I can't even place the memory— maybe it's not even real—but it hits me like a sneaker wave, and I can barely stay afloat long enough for it to pass.

I blink, and the memory fades. In its wake, I see reality. Renee—the woman from the gig, his coworker.

Renee waves at me, an oven mitt that definitely doesn't belong to us covering her hand. "We've got homemade garlic bread baking!" She inhales deeply. "Smells amazing, right? Those cooking classes are really paying off."

When she returns to watching the oven, I mouth the words 'cooking classes' at Dad, trying to recapture our usual dynamic, but he's too busy to be mocked by his daughter, watching his pasta boil with an expression of shocked glee. Rude, really, as that's the number-one duty of a dad.

Izzie takes off her shoes behind me and nudges me forward.

"Where should I put these?" She holds up the box of pastries we picked up from Save Point.

I usher her over to the kitchen table, where there are already place settings laid out, dishes I don't think I've ever seen before with a gold floral pattern around the edges. I didn't know we had any matching dishware, let alone four sets. I've been washing the same ceramic plate and bowl every day, since Dad doesn't have very many and all of Mom's nice china was destroyed in the storm. In the center of the table is a bouquet of wildflowers—heather and a pretty dark dusty rose-colored flower I don't recognize.

"Hellebore," says Renee as she circles over to us to take Izzie's box of pastries. "It can be tough to find wildflowers this late in the summer, but I grow these specially in my yard so I can have beauty at my table through the year."

I didn't ask, and I'm about to say so when Dad interrupts my thoughts.

"Isn't it nice to have nature in the house?" he asks, leaving his pot of noodles unattended to step out from behind the counter and admire the centerpiece.

"If you can't go to nature, nature will come to you!" Renee smiles up at Dad, blue eyes twinkling with something oh so very much more than casual coworkerness. "I'm working on getting him to go outside at least once a day, but this little introvert is as stubborn as he is sweet."

Dad giggles—*giggles*—and that's about enough for me. I want to vomit, I want to yell, I want to stomp my foot and throw a tantrum like I'm twelve again. In some ways I never stopped being that kid whose dad left during the summer between sixth and seventh grade. It doesn't matter that Mom wanted him to, because I didn't.

Dad blinks down at me, waiting for a smile I can't give. I won't ruin tonight—not for him, not for Izzie, not even for Renee. I will swallow this feeling, wash it down with garlic bread, and hope it stays down.

"Izzie! Let me show you the rest of the house." I turn on my heel and grab her arm a little rougher than I mean to. I don't let go. She's the only thing grounding me right now and I'm afraid if I do, I'll be lost in a choppy sea. Or maybe even a storm.

I'm a terrible tour guide. I point and grunt like a Neanderthal, saying things like "bathroom" and "bedroom" and "hallway." My brain is moving through sludge, trying to process what just happened. Thankfully, Izzie seems to pick up on that and drags me into my room, sits me down on the bed, and kicks the door shut.

"Okay, you need to do some breathing." She places the heel of her hand on my back and rubs in slow circles.

I don't want her to see me like this, and I don't want to *be* like this. I want to be fun and breezy Steph. She's a guest here, but she's the one trying to make me feel at home.

"Good old oxygen will do wonders for you," she says into my ear.

I take a ragged breath and... well, she's not wrong. My head begins to clear almost instantly.

"You wanna talk about it?" she asks.

I shake my head. Talking about it implies there is anything to talk about. Dad got a girlfriend. So what? He's allowed. He's divorced. And besides that, Mom... well... she's not a factor.

She *should* be a factor.

"Talk to me about something else, then." Izzie kisses the top of my head, then pushes off the bed to examine my room.

It doesn't look that different from when I moved in. The Pride sign Izzie bought me is on top of my dresser. I've taped some drawings to the walls—sketches for the Drugstore Makeup logo, a new villain for the campaign I'm running, a rough doodle of Izzie I did while she was in the zone writing a new song last week. Her fingers trail over the portrait of her, then land on the Vinyl Resting Place poster—the one she gave me the first time we met.

"Well, this can go in the trash." She tugs it from its thumbtack, tearing the top. "Why do you even have this?"

"Oh, sorry," I say without thinking, the apology stumbling out of me before I have time to decide if it's warranted. "It was the first thing you ever gave me. Felt significant." I shrug.

Izzie stares down at the poster, a mix of emotions flashing across her eyes. I think at first she's going to tear it up or storm out, or something else equally dramatic, but then her shoulders fall and she sighs. "Guess I better give you some better stuff."

"I'm not really much for stuff these days, as you can tell." I gesture around at the room. My suitcase in the corner is propped open with a pile of clothes still lying in it and I've barely even attempted to fill the bookshelf.

"Yeah, why is that?" Izzie asks, plopping down on the bed beside me.

"I…" The truth fizzles on my tongue. Her fingers slide between mine and she gives my hand an encouraging squeeze, but I still can't give voice to the real reason this room is mostly empty, why I haven't unpacked. Maybe it's because I don't really know why myself. Instead, I shrug and say, "Stuff is just stuff, right?"

Izzie gives me a quizzical look. "I guess I just thought because you have so much personality it would show more in your space, but this room is like… it barely even scratches the surface of who you are! More like you're just staying here instead of actually *living* here."

And there it is. She's hit the nail on the head. I flop onto my back and stare up at the bare ceiling, suddenly very interested in the bumpy texture. It's like a topographical map with ridges and valleys and little towns near the ocean that can be swept away in a storm.

Tears prickle at the edge of my eyes, but I can't cry. Not in front of Izzie. Not about *this*. So, I plaster a smile onto my face, tugging Izzie down next to me, cushioning her fall with my arm.

"Okay, I'll play consumerist. What kind of stuff do you think I should get, Miss Interior Decorator?"

"Well, some more Pride shit for a start." She snuggles in close, her hair falling across my chest. "The home of Steph Gingrich should be colorful and loud."

"Describe it to me." My fingers trail down her arm, tracing a constellation of her freckles. "Paint me a word picture, Izzie Margolis."

Her hand finds purchase on my stomach and she whispers against my throat, each word a kiss. "Steph's house is a happy place. She has a lesbian flag hanging on the door and a welcome mat that says 'You're here. I'm queer.' Inside, there's a big comfy couch in the living room and a record player. She's got one of those antique arcade machines that only takes quarters—and she definitely collects when her friends come over to party."

Her hand inches up my body as she travels from the living room to the kitchen. "She has an espresso machine and too many mugs—all with cute little sayings on them like 'Tea Rex' or 'Live Laugh Lesbian.' On the kitchen table, she has a big centerpiece — not flowers. It's rainbow and it says Pride in rainbow letters, just in case anyone missed the other really subtle hints that she's gay."

"What about her bedroom?" I ask quietly as her hand finds my face and she strokes a finger along my jaw. "What does it look like in there?"

"Well… there's a big cozy throw rug on the ground. Purple. The kind that feels like a cloud on bare feet. And there's a desk where she can sketch, with all her colored pencils in a vase like a bouquet of flowers. The bookshelf is covered in little glass apothecary jars filled with dice. There's a basket for her drumsticks near the door, and a beanie on every surface."

Izzie nuzzles closer into the hollow of my throat, fingers trailing across my clavicles and sliding just under the edge of collar. "The bedside table has a vintage stained glass lamp and a book of Sappho's poetry. And the bed is made up with black and purple bedding, and… oh… what's this? There's a girl in there."

"Huh," I manage, my breath catching as her lips tickle my skin. "Tell me more about her. Is she hot?"

"You tell me." Izzie pushes herself up on her elbows and rolls above me, catching my gaze and holding it. Her voice is quiet, but her eyes are loud—like every time she looks at me, a party starts inside her irises.

I rise up to catch her mouth with mine, too overcome to think about this imaginary room. If Izzie's with me, I don't really care about my surroundings. I don't care about a lot of things— like the fact that my dad's finally moved on while I still can't, or the fact that the last time I had *stuff* in my room, it all got swept away by a storm.

Izzie pulls away and presses our foreheads together, breath heavy between us.

"Yeah, okay," I say, eyes still closed. "Pretty damn hot."

"More importantly…" Izzie eases off me and pulls me up with her. "This girl really likes you. She thinks you're cool and that you deserve to have stuff you like, even if you don't think so."

I blink my eyes open to see her smoothing out the wrinkles in her shirt and running a finger along her lipstick line. I want to pull her back down, wreck both our faces with smudged makeup and ruin her shirt, so when we finally feel like putting clothes on again she has to wear one of mine.

But Izzie's already opening the door and waving me forward. "Come on. I can smell meatballs."

I follow, pausing at the threshold to look back at my room, trying to see it through Izzie's eyes. The room she imagined for me seems so perfect, like she somehow knows me better than I know myself. Or maybe I'm just a fraud, pretending to be the kind of girl Izzie likes and sooner or later she'll realize I'm just like my room: a blank canvas.

*

I'm taking down a string of paper sunflowers at Save Point when the door swings open and the victory theme music nearly knocks me off my feet. It's nothing to the shock I feel when I turn around to see who's arrived.

Renee stands in the doorframe holding a bouquet of chrysanthemums and a card.

"Oh good, I caught you!" she says with a smile that lights up her eyes like she's genuinely glad to see me, like nothing could make her gladder. "This place is so fun! Very you."

I want to say she doesn't know me well enough to say that, but… she's not wrong. Instead, I head for the counter to take her order. The sooner I make her a drink, the sooner she'll leave. "What can I get started for you?"

"Hmm." Renee glances at the menu then back at me. "What do *you* like?"

I shrug and point to the list of lattes we offer. "The Vicious Mocha-ry is good or Expeditious Treat."

"What's your favorite?"

"Probably Tasha's Hideous Latte."

Renee nods. "Great, I'll have a Dexteritea for now, and I've got your next latte—as hideous as you want."

Something gums up inside me at the gesture. "Oh, that's really nice of you, but you don't have to—"

"Please." Renee holds up a hand. "I want to, if it's okay with you. And I'd really like to talk, but again, only if you do. There's no pressure."

But, of course, there *is* pressure, whether she means there to be or not. Dad isn't here in the coffee shop with us, and honestly if he was, maybe it would be easier to laugh this off and shoo her away. If there's one thing my dad and I can almost always agree on it, it's the value of *not* talking about our feelings.

"It's cool. We're not busy—you can take a break." Ollie gives me a thumbs-up and a smile.

I glower at him the whole time I'm making my latte, but he

doesn't seem to notice he's made it to my shit list. Without a good excuse to blow her off, I finally make my way over to Renee and sit down opposite her, spilling a little of my latte over the edge of the mug.

"So," I say, a little more brusquely than I intend. "What's up?"

Renee carefully removes the tea bag from her mug, squeezing out the excess water and depositing it on the saucer before she answers me. "First, I wanted to say thank you for welcoming me into your home the other night. I had such a lovely time, and it was great to get some face time with you and Izzie."

A knot pulls taut in my stomach at her words. Because I *wasn't* welcoming. I *wasn't* lovely. I was barely present at all, and if anyone was welcoming and lovely, it was her with her garlic bread and her floral arrangements. An apology sticks in my throat, even though it's not my fault. I didn't know she was going to be there. I didn't know that was even a possibility. I didn't know, and it's because Dad didn't tell me.

"I know it meant a lot to your dad, too," Renee continues, seemingly unaware of the impact her words are having on me. "He hasn't stopped talking about how proud he is of you."

"Really?" I look up from my mug. "That's, uh…" *surprising, doubtful, weird* "…nice."

Renee catches my eye and peers at me thoughtfully. "You and your dad don't talk much, do you?"

I shake my head, afraid if I tell her exactly how much, it will be some breach of the social contract between fathers and daughters who haven't had a substantive conversation since before the last *Game of Thrones* book came out. In fact, I could probably find a way to blame our strained relationship on media. Books and films are really the only things we have to enjoy together, and I bet without them we'd have to actually talk about shit.

"Well, I don't mean to meddle but I get the impression he wishes that was different."

My whole body tenses. "Yeah? Well maybe he should

try giving me a heads-up next time he decides to invite his girlfriend to dinner, instead of springing it on me like we live in a fucking haunted house." It's so much more than I mean to say, but the floodgates are open and I can't stop. "I didn't even know he was dating again. I didn't know he *wanted* to. So maybe instead of sending you here to make nice with me, he should do it himself."

"That is incredibly fair." Renee wears her surprise well, leaning back in her chair, brows raised, eyes wide. She takes a slow sip of her tea, wiping her mouth on a paper napkin before she speaks again. "I don't want to interfere with something that's not my business, so I'll just say this. I have a complex family dynamic myself and I know how strange it can be when someone new comes into the mix. I'm seeing your dad and I know that might be weird, but I hope we can get to know each other, too."

"Yeah, sure," I say, voice tight.

"We don't have to be best friends or anything," she adds quickly, sensing my hesitance. "I'm definitely too old for all that partying you kids do."

I *know* she's trying and I know I should try right back. Because that's what Dad would want me to do. But Dad's not here and he hasn't told me what he wants, so instead I do what I want. "I'm not a kid. And I'm not looking for a new mom."

"Of course not. You already have a mom and I would never try to replace her." She pushes the flowers and the card toward me on the table. "Think about it, okay?"

"Okay."

I do. I think about it as I pull shots and wash dishes and wipe down tables. I think about it as I lock up and trudge back up the hill to Dad's house. I think about it as I pass Dad's room and hear the sounds of the opening score for *Game of Thrones*. And maybe if I wasn't thinking about it so much, I would knock on the door with a bowl full of popcorn and watch TV with my dad. But I can't help but wonder if Dad told Renee about

Mom, if he's talked about Mom with Renee more than with me. So instead I drift into my own room and let the door click shut behind me.

I shiver a little and pull on a sweatshirt. Everyone in Westeros is always so worried about winter. Fools don't realize they have to contend with fall first.

Fall

Ten

Ask almost anyone from the Pacific Northwest what they like about living here and they'll tell you it's the mild winters, or the wildflowers in spring, or the summer hiking, but they're all lying. Fall is the season of Seattle. When the temperature drops, out come the cozy sweaters. Coffee-drinkers flock to cafés to get their pumpkin-flavored beverages… and scones… and muffins… and bread. The leaves begin changing color in October, a sunset of orange and yellow along every street.

There's plenty to like about fall, like how I can wear a beanie every day and no one bats an eye. And, of course, Halloween—the second gayest holiday after Pride month. But there are a lot of rainy days to get through before it's officially spooky season. One day in particular, actually.

October 11th begins as so many fall days do in Seattle: with gray skies. I muddle my way through my morning routine—trying to brush my teeth with the wrong end of the toothbrush *and* toasting my Pop-Tart on the bagel setting so all the icing melts off—but I still don't realize what day it is until Dad makes an appearance, expression serious, eyes searching.

"Wanna play hooky today and watch movies?" he asks. "I bought a jumbo pack of popcorn and I've got *The Lord of the Rings* queued up. All three. Extended editions. Make a day of it. What do you think?"

I freeze, hand halfway to my keys on the counter. There's an audible thunderclap overhead and a deluge of rain crashes down onto the roof, a whole percussion section on its own.

And maybe I should just stay home. My raincoat and boots will be a poor defense against the misery—both outside and inside. Dad's offered me such a tempting olive branch, and I know how the day will go. We'll fill up on junk food, swap trivia we both already know, and take turns shouting our favorite lines along with the actors. There will be a race to share the tidbit about Viggo Mortensen breaking his toe when he kicks the orc helmet, Dad will remind me to cover my eyes before Denethor eats those cursed cherry tomatoes—for a pretty violent movie, that's gotta be the most gruesome part—and we'll get misty-eyed at each of the many endings of *Return of the King*. We'll have fun. It will be a good day.

But there will still be the truth hanging over us, that Mom isn't here to enjoy it with us. And that even if she was, Dad would rather spend it with Renee.

We still haven't talked about it, the Renee of it all. I definitely won't be the one to bring it up. I wouldn't really know what to say if I did. I'm almost twenty-three, and that's old enough that I shouldn't care that my divorced dad has a new girlfriend. I'm not about to ruin this for him with my big feelings. Not today, anyway. Besides, that's just how we Gingriches do things. We wait until it's too late to do it in a normal way and just hope each other picks up on the context clues. It's worked for us so far, if by 'worked' you mean we know next to nothing about each other and still vastly prefer email to face-to-face.

And today promises to be full of face-to face.

"Nah," I say, averting my eyes. "I've gotta work. You have fun without me."

"Fool of a Took!" Dad shouts after me, and I almost want to turn around.

But I don't. I brace my shoulders against the storm and step out into the rain.

*

I try to drown out the storm the rest of the day, with music at the café and with drumming after work in Izzie's garage, but even noise-canceling headphones aren't enough. My rhythm becomes erratic and sloppy until I'm no longer keeping time, I'm chasing it. Memories of Arcadia Bay slip through the cracks with each thunderclap.

Wet wind whips my face as I run. I'm slow against such powerful gusts, and I can't even remember why I'm running. When I pause to look around, I barely recognize the street. I know it, but it's obscured by debris flying through the air. An entire bush is uprooted nearby and flies into the air, spinning and swirling toward a massive gray vortex moving toward me from the bay. For a moment, I just stand there, waiting to be swept away, too.

A hand lands on my shoulder and pulls me in the opposite direction.

"Come on! We have to get to the basement." Pleading eyes stare at me from a familiar brown face. Mikey's only sixteen, but he feels so much older than me in this moment, like he knows we will survive it.

And we do. We do. I remind myself of this until my heartbeat settles, until my drumsticks fall back under my control, the wood in my hands grounding me.

I'm behind the drums, in Izzie's garage. I'm not in Arcadia Bay.

No one is anymore, not really.

There's a ripple of static and then Izzie's hands are on my cymbals, quieting them with her fingertips. She moves her mouth, words lost to the ripping winds in my mind.

"What?" I say, but my own voice sounds so far away, I think if I close my eyes I'll find myself back in the basement with Mikey, rolling dice to keep our minds off the storm outside.

Izzie reaches over and pulls the headphones off my ears.

"What's going on with you?" she asks. "You sped up like triple time during the bridge and then you forgot about the kick."

"Guess I'm just off my game," I say, gritting my teeth. It's an understatement of epic proportions, but I'm not about to tell her that. Since our gig, she's been a real perfectionist at practice. I know she just wants us to be good, and I want us to be good, too. I want her to think we're good. I want her to think *I'm* good.

"Well, get it together. We've got two weeks to get this right before our next show." She turns back to her amp to fiddle with the dials, giving me a second to breathe.

But breath doesn't come. The rain takes this moment to double its intensity, hammering against the roof.

I hold the phone close to my face, finger jammed in my other ear, trying to hear if it's even ringing.

"Pick up, pick up, pick up," I chant.

Mikey's sitting opposite me, lying on the couch and staring at his phone, waiting for Drew to call back. It's been an hour, and still nothing from his brother. There's a shallow pool of water on the floor, so my boots splash a little as I pace back and forth. The only thing giving me hope is that I still have service. Which means Mom does too.

"Steph!" Mom's voice crackles to life on the speaker.

"Mom?" I yell, relief making jelly of my limbs.

"The whole town is rubble! It'll hit our house soon! I'm taking shelter but…" Her words grow steadier, louder, like it's this next bit that matters most. "I love you, okay?"

"Mom! Mom! I love you, too."

"Steph? Steph?" Izzie's tone matches my own, and I don't realize until she grasps my shoulders and hauls me back up, eyes wild with worry, that I must have collapsed. "Hey, are you okay?"

I gulp down oxygen and try to shake her off. "Yeah—yeah I'm—I'm…" But I can't even get the word out.

"What the fuck is going on with you?" Izzie asks, but her voice isn't angry so much as scared. There's a tremor in her words and her forehead pinches as she peers down at me. "Are you feeling okay?" She presses the back of her hand to my forehead to feel for fever.

And for all I know, I might have one. I feel hot and cold at the same time, hungry and nauseated, painfully alive and as numb as a ghost.

"When was the last time you ate?" Izzie asks. "Could be a blood sugar thing—or, I don't know, are you like, anemic or something?"

I shake my head, but the motion just makes me feel more out of sorts and dizzy. "I think I'm just tired," I say, trying to shrug it off. I push up to my feet and set my drumsticks on the snare. "Maybe I should walk home."

"In this rain?" Izzie gives me a withering look. "Absolutely not. You'll get soaked through."

"Okay, well you drive me, then." The words come out harsher than I intend, but I'm too tense to be polite. "I need to go home. I need to be there with her."

Izzie's gaze softens as she searches my face. I think for a minute she's going to ask me who I'm talking about and my stomach bottoms out. Because the home I'm talking about isn't the one at the top of the hill in Queen Anne. It's the one in Arcadia Bay, the one that's nothing more than a pile of splinters and shattered glass, roof shingles scattered around the street like flower petals.

But Izzie doesn't ask me anything. She just squeezes my arm and says, "I'll get my keys."

"Thank you," I whisper as she turns to go, but before she can so much as open the garage door, there's a loud click, and the amp, the space heater, the lights—they all go out, plunging us into darkness.

*

It's easier to grieve in the dark. No one can see if there are tears on my face, if my eyes slide out of focus, if my lip quivers each time thunder sounds overhead.

"You've got to be fucking kidding me," Izzie breathes beside me. "Guess practice is definitely over, then."

I can tell she's trying to joke—probably she's cracked a smile, but I can't see it in the dark.

"Sorry, Steph." She rubs a hand up my arm. "The streets are going to be a mess with the lights out—I think… I think we should stay put."

And she's right. Rational thought rushes back to me in a wave and I feel heat creep up my neck at the thought of my outburst. It's stupid to go home—yeah, Dad's there, but it's not like last time. This isn't the same kind of storm. Seattle's a rainy place. He'll be fine. I'll be fine. We'll all be fine.

I whip out my phone and turn on the flashlight. It's not much, but I can see Izzie's face in the ghostly glow, contorted halfway between concern and panic. With my other hand, I reach for her waist and give her a squeeze.

"You're totally right. Let's just… camp out here." I nod along with my words, trying to sell myself as much as her on the concept. "We can have a good old-fashioned slumber party."

"Yeah?" Izzie relaxes in my grip. "I never really had one of those growing up. You know, parents are sometimes weird about gender and sleepovers."

"Okay, well now we *have* to." I throw my hand up to cast the beam of light a little wider, revealing a path through all our stuff to the door. "We're gonna need a few things though—do you have any candles?"

A smile sneaks onto Izzie's face. She's still hesitant—probably totally weirded out by how I was acting before—but there's also a spark in her eye, illuminated by my flashlight, that makes me want to pull out all the stops. She deserves to know what it's like to stay up until a ridiculous hour, talking about silly shit and sharing secrets and eating the weirdest combinations of junk food imaginable. I'm going to make this the best slumber party ever—and maybe I'll even forget about the storm.

We cobble together a passable blanket fort in the garage, held up by my cymbals and a few dining room chairs. We fill the inside with throw pillows and the big comforter from Izzie's bed. We paint our nails in the light of a Lady Gaga votive candle, and after trying all the snacks, we determine that a BBQ potato chips sandwich with a peach gummy ring in the middle is the ultimate combo.

"What else do people do at sleepovers?" Izzie asks. She sits cross-legged, holding her newly painted toes—alternating black and purple. The light flickers over her face, an orange glow that matches our new culinary invention. "You said something about secrets?"

"Yeah, like sometimes you play games like truth or dare." I run my finger along the bottom of the chip bag, searching for crumbs.

"Okay!"

"Truth or dare?" I ask. Izzie's practically bouncing. It's cute. So cute. I hope she picks dare.

"Truth!"

I narrow my eyes in thought before asking, "Who was your cringiest childhood crush?"

"Noooooo." Izzie hides her face behind her hands. "What if I don't want to say?"

"You could always pick dare!" I waggle my eyebrows suggestively. "Or you could be like me and have no shame whatsoever."

"What do you mean? Who was *your* cringy childhood crush?"

"That is *so* not how the game works, but I'll give you this one as a freebie. You know *The Incredibles*?"

"Did you like Violet?" She flips her hair back. "She kind of looks like me. I could do a cosplay if you're into that."

"Oh, I'd be very into that—but no, not her."

"Okay, well, the mom is hot too. She has an absolute dump truck—"

"And also not the mom."

"Oh my god, who?"

"Edna Mode, fashion icon and short queen." I give a little flourish with my hand and say in my best Edna voice, "No capes!"

Izzie bursts out laughing. "Okay, taste. She's amazing."

"Your turn!"

"Ugh! Fine!" She gives me a sheepish look, a little embarrassed but mostly excited, like she's actually having a good time. "Sarah Michelle Gellar."

"Are you kidding? Buffy? That's not cringe—" I start to say, but Izzie holds up a finger to stop me.

"You didn't let me finish—Sarah Michelle Gellar, specifically as Daphne in the *Scooby-Doo* movies."

Now it's my turn to laugh. I flop back onto the pillows and throw my hands over my face. "Those purple outfits, though? Iconic."

"It sure was a look."

"I guess you're not super into femmes anymore, though?" I ask. I can't remember the last time I wore a dress, and Izzie or Lia always have to do my makeup for me. Anxiety pools in my stomach as I glance over at her, worried I'll see a lie behind her eyes when she reassures me.

Izzie tilts her head and lets out a hum. "I don't think I was every really into femmes, actually. It was more of a 'Do I want her or do I wanna *be* her?' thing, if that makes sense. Like, speaking of Buffy, Cordelia was a little bit of a trans awakening for me."

"Another amazing choice—although I was always more of a Willow girl myself."

"Okay, my turn—truth or dare?"

"Dare!" I sit up eagerly, but her face falls a little, clearly disappointed I didn't pick truth.

"Oh, okay, uh… what do I even dare you to do?"

"Something stupid, something gross, something sexy…" I shimmy my shoulders.

In the end, she dares me to eat a spoonful of mayonnaise—so something gross, for sure. We volley back and forth, her always picking truth, me always picking dare, until finally she groans and flops over on her stomach.

"When are you going to pick truth? I'm running out of weird stuff to make you eat."

"I'll pick truth when you pick dare," I say with a mischievous grin.

"Okay, fine! I'll pick dare, I promise—but it's your turn."

I cross my arms and pull my knees up to my chest. "Okay. Truth." The word rushes out of me, heavy and hard. Because I know what she's going to ask.

And sure enough: "Why don't you like storms?"

"It's not that I don't like storms, it's more that they don't like me," I say, but the attempt at humor falls flat and Izzie's silent patience weighs me down until I feel as though I'll never rise from the floor until I tell her. "There was a storm back home—in Arcadia Bay, where I'm from. And not like a little one—a really big one. Like apocalyptic. The whole town got destroyed. A lot of people died." And then, in a voice so small I almost don't believe it's my own, I add, "My mom died."

Usually when I tell people about my mom they say they're sorry. I hate it—it's not their fault she died, and honestly it's hard to tell if they're sorry it happened or if they're sorry they asked. But it's the only thing they can say, really. What else is there?

Izzie doesn't say anything, just moves closer until her body is pressed against mine. She wraps her arms around me and tucks her face into my neck. She holds me like I haven't been held in a long time. Maybe like I haven't been held ever.

"Today is the anniversary," I say after a long silence. "It was three years ago. Most of the time I can just, you know, not think about it, but sometimes it catches up to me. Especially when it rains."

"Thank you for telling me," Izzie says against the nape of my neck.

And it's so much better than sorry. To be thanked, like what I've said matters, like it's a part of me instead of some tragic backstory to be hidden away.

I turn over in her arms and press our noses together. "Your turn."

"Dare."

"I dare you to kiss me."

And she does. Her mouth is warm and her hands pull at my shirt, at my hair, at my heart. We tangle ourselves in each other until I forget the storm.

Eventually, Izzie blows out the candle and settles against me to sleep. I close my eyes and let the press of her body lull me toward slumber. My limbs are heavy, my mind heavier. But then she whispers my name, and when I don't respond, she rises up on her elbows and runs a hand down my side.

"Truth," she whispers, and she leans in close. "I love you."

I should feel happy, I think. I should feel light as air. I should feel like saying it back.

But the last person I said it to died right after, so I keep my eyes shut and let my breathing slow. Maybe in the morning, when the rain has stopped, I'll be able to tell Izzie how she makes me feel—maybe by then I'll know.

Eleven

Izzie doesn't say it again, content to believe I was asleep during her confession, I guess. The weeks before our Halloween show are swept away by a different kind of storm: a busy schedule.

It's the death of every TTRPG campaign, and as my calendar fills up with more gigs for Drugstore Makeup, I have room for little else. I have to cancel my sessions at Save Point three weeks in a row, and even Jordie has stopped checking if I'm coming over for *Critical Role* on Thursdays. He knows I can't, and I know I can't, but it still stings a little when his texts stop coming.

Izzie is ecstatic about the growing love for Drugstore Makeup, though. She sends me screenshots and pictures from forums and zines highlighting our "up-and-coming two-piece that embodies the spirit of 'be gay do crime.'" She is particularly gleeful at one that says of our sound "Move over gay pride and make room for gay wrath!"

But being in a punk band is a lot less sex, drugs, and rock and roll, and a lot more sitting in print shops, waiting for flyers, and arguing about what word rhymes best with 'carabiners.' We're unveiling three new original songs at our Halloween gig, and Izzie fiddles with the lyrics until the last minute—eventually surprising me by rhyming 'Stonewall' with 'blue balls' onstage. It makes me laugh so hard I nearly miss the crash with my drumstick.

I love that her brain works so fast like that, coming up with brilliant lyrics on the fly. I love a lot of things about her brain—

like how she has so much to write about. If I had to write a song on my own, it would probably be about cleaning the coffee grinder or rolling dice. Not exactly thought-provoking stuff. But not Izzie. She feels with her whole heart, every emotion under the sun. It kills me that her old band wanted her to hide that part of herself away.

And maybe… maybe this is what love is. Maybe it's wanting her to be exactly who she is because she's my person. Maybe it's not just a collection of things I love about her. Maybe it's her.

Or maybe I just wish it was.

We finish our set to an uproar of applause. I spot Jordie and Ollie near the front, dressed as Sherlock Holmes and John Watson, surrounded by what looks to be a group of pirates. Izzie grabs my hand as we descend the steps, engulfed by our friends who, despite our flakiness lately, showed up for us anyway.

"Girl, what are you supposed to be?" Ollie asks as he spins me around. "Izzie is obviously a vampire but…"

I glance down at my costume—a black bodysuit with pleather wings sewn along the arms and a big blue eyeball in the center. It's far from my best, but at least it's better than the mayonnaise year.

"I'm bat-an-eye," I say, fluttering my eyelashes rapidly.

Jordie groans. "That's bad, even for you."

"Careful or I'll tell everyone about your idea for an undead ice skater called the Zombini."

He whacks me on the arm. "I told you that under the influence of many beers."

"Speaking of, I would like to consume many beers." I let Jordie and Ollie lead me toward the bar, dragging Izzie along with me.

Attack-o-Lanterns take the stage after us while we form an oddball conga line to skirt around the crowd. The venue is packed. A few people wave or give a thumbs-up as we pass. I know they didn't all come out to see us—we're just one of half a dozen bands in the lineup—but it feels great to know that so many people heard our music.

I lean down to say as much to Izzie, pressing my lips to her ear, but her face goes rigid, her eyes trained on a zombie nurse. At first, I think she's just entranced by the general grossness of the costume—the bloodstains are really well done—but then I recognize the cropped red hair of her former bandmate, Astrid.

"Hey, Iz," she says. Then, to my surprise, she turns to me. "Steph, right? You were really good tonight."

"Oh, uh, thanks." I try to smile, but my fingers grip Izzie's wrist tight. And I wish I could leave it at that, but the last time we saw Astrid is burned into my brain—her cruel words, the way she practically taunted us—and I can't help but add, "You're not playing tonight?"

Astrid, to her credit, doesn't quite sneer in response. "They asked, but Bellamy had a prior engagement so we had to decline. It's nice that they gave the slot to someone who really needs it." She groans and puts her head in her hands. "Ugh. Sorry. I didn't come here to be an asshole."

"Why *did* you come here?" Izzie asks, fists clenched by her sides.

Astrid leans heavily into one hip and sighs. "I actually wanted to talk to you about something. Do you have a minute?"

I immediately step forward, ready to tell this girl that Izzie absolutely doesn't have a minute—not for her, anyway—but Izzie nods and pries my fingers from her arm. "Yeah, okay."

"You sure?" I murmur, trying to catch Izzie's eye.

She doesn't look at me. Instead, she says, "Yeah. I'll be back in a bit—get me a blackberry something or other."

And she walks off with Astrid toward the greenroom.

"Well, shit!" Ollie leans against the bar, eyebrows practically scratching his hairline. "You just gonna let that happen?"

"Izzie's an adult. She can handle herself." But as I drink my beer, I grit my teeth against the sour taste in my mouth.

*

All the ice in Izzie's blackberry mojito is melted before she returns to the main room. There's a new band onstage— Undeadicated—and Jordie and Ollie have forced me out into the crowd to dance. I wave my arms around and pump my fist into the air, trying to shed the discomfort of Astrid's presence, of Izzie's willingness to go with her. It's none of my business, I tell myself. In fact, now that we're done playing for the night, the only business I have is hanging with my friends and eating too much Halloween candy.

A hand lands on my hip, light and hesitant. I turn into Izzie's grip and throw my arms over her shoulders.

"You're back!" I shout. "Just in time—I was getting sick of being a third wheel."

Izzie doesn't join our dance huddle, though. She just tugs on my bodysuit and gestures with her head over to the door. "Can we talk?"

I can barely hear her over the music, but the shape of her lips is unmistakable. So is the crease in her forehead and the rise of her shoulders.

"Yeah, of course." I follow her to the fringes of the room, where she says… something I absolutely cannot hear over the music. "What?"

She groans and pushes open a door. Cold air catches us as we spill out onto the street, and the temperature whiplash hits me hard. So do the sounds. Inside was all rock and roll and partying, but outside it's eerily muffled. In the distance I can hear sirens and the loud exhale of a bus coming to a stop.

"That's better," Izzie says, but her voice is clipped like it's really, really not.

"What's up?" I try to pull her closer—for warmth, but also for comfort—but she dodges my fingers. "What did Asstrid want?" I emphasize the first half of her name for maximum rudeness.

Izzie doesn't reply, running her hands up and down her arms as she paces in front of me, eyes trained on the sidewalk.

"That bad? Ugh. I knew it." I throw my arms out a little more intensely than I intend and I stumble a little—I probably should have stopped after one drink, at least until Izzie got back. "I should have come with you. She is such a fucking jerk. Whatever she said, she's wrong, okay? You're an amazing musician and your songs are brilliant. She's just jealous she can't write anything as good."

"Yeah—I know." Izzie stops pacing now and looks up at me. "That's what she said, anyway. She actually... apologized?"

My eyebrows shoot up. "Like... sincerely?"

"Seemed so." Izzie shrugs. "She, uh... she asked me to come back. To Vinyl Resting Place, I mean."

"Oh." The word lands like a sprained ankle.

I can't find it in myself to be happy or sad. All I can feel is inevitability, because *of course*. This whole thing was too good to be true and I should have known. Izzie is so talented and I'm just... well, I'm me. I'm lucky it lasted as long as it did, this little adventure where I got to be a punk rocker. Where I got to be with Izzie. Where I got to be loved.

"Oh," I repeat, and it sounds even worse the second time. Jealousy makes a mess of my insides, twisting and tugging and turning my words to ash in my mouth.

"Say *something*, Steph. You have to do better than that."

I'm not better. I'm me. For this little scrap of time I got to be her version of that, but take away the drum set and the eyeliner and I'm still the same old Steph. I can't compare with Astrid and Vinyl Resting Place. I shouldn't try to compete—that will only end with me losing—so I swallow my pride and do my best to be supportive.

"I... I guess that's good?" I try on a smile, but it feels too small, too tight. "I'm... I'm happy for you, if you're happy."

"You're happy for me." Izzie's deadpan gives away nothing.

"This is what you want, right?" Images flash before my eyes of what could be—Izzie, headlining with Vinyl Resting Place at Pride, singing her songs with a full band behind her, winning the Battle of the Bands, going on tour, kissing Astrid beneath bright neon lights. It's what she's been working toward and I can't be the one who takes that from her.

"What I want?" Anger bleeds into her tone now, raw and red. "Fuck. You think that's what I want? To be begrudgingly let back into a group that didn't like me that much to begin with? You think I want to go back to that?"

I pluck at the arm of my bodysuit, letting the fabric snap back against my skin in rhythm with her words. "I mean… you want to win Battle of the Bands, right? I figure they're your best shot."

"Fucking hell, Steph. You are so dense sometimes." She drags her hands down her face, leaving behind trails of makeup—from sweat or tears, I can't tell. "If you don't want to play with me anymore you can just say it, okay. I won't force you—I *can't* force you."

"What?" I shake my head to clear it, deeply regretting that third drink. This conversation would be so much easier sober. "No, that's not what I mean at all. I love playing with you!"

"Uh-huh." She fixes me with an incinerating stare. "You love *playing* with me. I see how it is." She turns to go back inside, hair whipping me in the face as she leaves.

I lunge for her hand. "See how *what* is?" My heart beats into my throat, pounding against my words like a hammer.

When Izzie turns around, I see the tears. They trace a river of mascara down her cheeks. Her voice cracks a little over the words, but she says them anyway, and this time I can't pretend I'm asleep.

"I love you, Steph. I want to play *with you*. I want to win *with you*. I want to live my life *with you*. But if you don't want that, if you don't love me back, just say so, okay?"

I stand there, too quiet, too still. I know, in the vague sense, that my mouth is open, but no words are coming out. The response she wants hovers at the tip of my tongue. I could say it. I could say it and maybe I'd even mean it. *I love you, too*. It's not that hard to say. It should be easy, it should be *so* easy.

But as I try to form the words on my lips, it's Mom I'm talking to instead of Izzie, and she's going to die. I say them out loud, she dies. That's how it goes.

So maybe I should tell Izzie I'm sorry, I don't love her. I'll go back to my life, to my blank, boring walls, to my coffee-shop life where I'm Steph, the girl who used to be in a punk two-piece with this amazing rock star. I'll make espresso and zines and bad jokes, but I'll never again make music. I'll never make Izzie laugh, but I'll never make her cry either, and that might be worth it.

"Steph," Izzie says my name like a sigh.

And this is it. Either I want her or I don't, I love her or I don't. I have to say *something*.

Or, maybe I don't. Maybe I can just say nothing at all.

Izzie shakes her head and pulls her arm from my grasp. "Message received," she says, and then she's gone, along with my chance to decide for myself what kind of future I want.

Twelve

I'm dressed like a bat, but I make my way home more like a ghost. My feet brush the concrete, but I barely notice. Dad and Renee are on the couch watching *Hocus Pocus*. They ask me to join them, I think, but I just float upstairs and collapse on my bed without changing.

How long I lie there, I don't know. I keep waiting to feel something like relief or regret, but all I feel is numb. My phone buzzes with text messages from Jordie and Ollie, but my eyes blur over when I try to read them. Something about fighting a raccoon in an alley and ordering too much pizza. While they debate the virtue of artichoke as a pizza topping in our group chat, I roll over and stare at the wall.

The wall stares back. I still don't have enough stuff to cover it up. I could get one of those big wall hangings just to keep the white paint at bay, but then I'd have to pick something that feels important enough to cover that much space. Maybe I can fill more space with Pride merch or some *Critical Role* art. But when I close my eyes and try to imagine what this room could look like, decorated by me, all I can see is Izzie.

I want to play with you. I want to win with you. I want to live my life with you.

The room transforms before me—a purple throw rug, sapphic poetry on the nightstand, drumsticks piled in a neat basket by the door. It's the room Izzie described, the one she decorated with her mind for me. I want to be there. And I don't want to be there alone.

My eyes snap open. My brain is alert, focused, quiet—but for one word.

Izzie.

I don't think, I fly—down the stairs and out the door. It takes me about thirty minutes to walk from my place to hers, but it feels like hours. I'm drenched by the time I arrive on her doorstep, rain and sweat mingling for an altogether cold and clammy experience. But I don't care. I'd sit on a glacier or in a bucket of lava if it meant seeing Izzie again.

When I do, it takes my eyes a few seconds to adjust. She's washed her face of makeup, tired circles casting shadows beneath her eyes. I can't tell if she's been crying—but then I can't tell if I have either. Her hair is pulled back in a butterfly clip, but a few strands have broken free to frame her face. It takes everything in me not to grab her by the front of her dark red flannel pajamas and kiss her right there in the rain.

Instead, I say, "Hi."

Great. Good. Suave. Real substantive stuff.

Izzie doesn't say anything, which I choose to take as a good sign.

"I'm an idiot." Excellent. Really building on the momentum. I shake my head, scattering water everywhere. "What I mean to say is I'm not very good at this. I've never done it before and I kind of freaked out."

Izzie flinches as some of the water from my hair lands on her. Her face remains stoic and unreadable, but at least she's not slamming the door in my face.

"I just… I like you *so* much and when you said your old band wanted you back, I thought you were trying to like… soft dump me." I swallow hard, the unsettled feeling in my stomach rising with the memory. "And I got, I don't know, defensive. Like if you were going to hurt me anyway, I might as well make it easier and do it myself, you know?"

Izzie crosses her arms and looks just left of my shoes. "Save it, Steph. I'm really not in the mood for an explanation. You broke my heart, it's over, let's just… not do this, okay? It's gonna suck, whether I understand it or not, so no need to rehash your feelings for my benefit. "

I freeze, and maybe it's the cold catching up to me, or maybe it's the lifelessness in her voice. She's telling me to let it go, but me letting it go is how we got here in the first place, so I gather my courage and say, "You don't know how I'm feeling, Izzie. That's what I'm trying to say."

"Oh, I don't know how you're feeling?" She takes a step out onto the porch, bare feet gripping the welcome mat. "I told you I loved you, Steph. And you didn't say it back. I think it's pretty fucking obvious how you feel."

"That's it, though—you didn't give me a chance to explain."

"Fine. Fucking explain."

It's all so much. The harshness in her tone, the cold wind battering me from every angle, the unsaid words on the tip of my tongue. I wish I could just take her in my arms and show her how I feel with every touch, every kiss. But Izzie wants to hear me say it aloud, and even if it makes me want to curl into a ball and disassociate for hours, I have to do this for her. And for me, too.

"I want it," I say, hoping if I start there I'll find the finish line. "Everything—playing together in Drugstore Makeup, writing songs on the floor of your garage until three in the morning, slow-dancing to AC/DC like a couple of weirdos… I want it all. You said… you said you wanted a life together, and I think I do too."

"You think?" she asks, but the edge is gone from her voice, like maybe she believes me.

"I'm not great at talking about these things." I recall how I still haven't confronted Dad about Renee and about the six-month-old unanswered text message from Mikey sitting on my phone because if I think about him too much, then I'll think about Mom. "And it's not just a you thing—it's everyone. Maybe it's the dead mom trauma or maybe it's the whole broken-home divorce shit, but… You're important to me, Izzie. I care about you. I want you."

Izzie looks at me with hope in her eyes and it's enough to help me stick the landing, however clumsily.

"I may not express it the way you do, in exactly the words you do, but I… do." I run my tongue along my teeth, pleading with my mouth to cooperate. If I don't say it, she may not believe me, and I'm too far in to chicken out now. "I l-love you."

It comes out squeaky and small and not at all how love confessions should go, but at least I'm absolutely soaked through and standing in the rain. I *will* have my Mr. Darcy moment even if it all goes to shit after.

"Okay," Izzie says quietly. She takes another step and another and another until she's standing in the open with me, rain tearing through her pajamas. "Okay," she repeats.

Her hands settle on my hips and she kisses me. Her lips are soft and warm, if not wet with rainwater, and her touch is like an electric shock. I surge forward, crashing into her. It may not be a movie-worthy makeout, but I don't care. Everywhere we touch, I feel a little life come back to my skin, but even with Izzie's body pressed to mine, I can't help but shiver.

Izzie pulls away and I feel my entire body mourn the loss of her heat, but then she drags me forward toward the house. "Come on," she says with a little skip in her step. "You're soaked through and I'd be remiss if I didn't take this opportunity to get you out of this bodysuit."

It's not until I've been standing under a steady stream of hot water for at least five minutes that the feeling starts to come back to my limbs. I tried to get Izzie to hop in the shower with me, but it turns out standing in the rain without a jacket for almost an hour is my kryptonite. I don't melt like a witch or anything, but poor Izzie has to practically shuck the bodysuit off me and put me under the hot water like I'm a child who won't comply with bath time.

"You alive in there?" Izzie calls from outside the bathroom.

"I dunno," I shout back. "How do you feel about dating an undead girl?"

"It worked in *Carmilla*, so as long as you skew more vampire and less zombie, I think I'll manage."

"Not into rotting flesh?"

"You know, you'd think it would be that, but actually I'm more worried that my culinary skills won't be up to the challenge of aesthetically plating brains."

"Garnish with a little arugula and balsamic, maybe some parmesan…"

Izzie's laughter is like a balm to my soul through the closed door. "Okay, point taken. I'm going to make us some hot cocoa, but I've left some extra PJs by the door."

I take my time getting dressed, luxuriating a little in the feel of flannel across my skin. It's not until I've buttoned the last button and squeezed the water from my hair that I realize the feeling has returned to my flesh, but I still feel numb inside. I drum my fingers on the countertop and stare at my reflection. I look the same as I always do—a little soggy, but nothing else has changed. I don't know what I expected. It's not like saying the L word is that transformative, right? Maybe I don't feel different because saying it doesn't actually change me that much. I still feel how I feel.

I decide it's that, because the alternative is too much to process. It hangs in the back of my mind though, a gentle reminder that just because you say something out loud doesn't make it true.

Izzie's waiting for me at the kitchen table, two steaming mugs before her. She slides one toward me with an illustration of a possum on it.

"Feeling okay?" she asks.

I nod and take a seat across from her, silently lamenting that she's set us up opposite each other instead of somewhere I can more easily touch her.

She picks up her own mug, white with blue lettering that says 'I love you a latke.' "Warm?"

"Yeah… could be warmer, though." I give my eyebrows a suggestive bounce over my mug.

Izzie laughs, but doesn't move closer. "I thought we should probably talk more first."

I grunt noncommittally. The last thing I want to do right now is talk. I want to snuggle down next to Izzie, breathe in her scent, hold her so close I can feel her heartbeat. I don't want to waste time on words.

"It's just, not talking about what we were feeling is how we got into this situation to begin with, and I don't want to make that mistake again."

She's not *wrong*, so I nod and take a sip of my cocoa.

"Right, so…" At first I think she's going to ask me more about my mom or something, but instead, she says, "I definitely have abandonment issues. Or, I don't know, whatever it is when people constantly tell you that you're not enough or that you're too much and never just right."

"Ugh. What do they think life is, Goldilocks and the Three Bears?"

"Joke all you want, but yeah. That's exactly what life is." Izzie drops her eyes to her mug, watching the marshmallows melt into a white cream. "We're all looking for our perfect fit— whether that's a person or a place or a group or a goal—and I know I can't be that for every single person I meet. I've had enough therapy to know, intellectually, all I can do is be myself. But it's hard to look at the evidence and emotionally feel like myself is good enough. People always leave, one way or another. It's happened with the band, with my friends, with roommates… I guess I was just waiting for it to happen with you, too."

My chest feels torn in two, half heartbroken for her and the way she's been made to feel, half angry that she put that all on me, like she set me up to fail. "Okay, but that's—"

"Not fair, I know." Izzie knits her fingers together around the base of her mug, still staring into it like the marshmallow goo on top will somehow reveal the future. "I shouldn't have done that, and I'm sorry."

Her apology hits me like a freight train. It's unexpected and… unearned, I think. I'm the one who pretended not to hear her say, "I love you." I'm the one who couldn't say it back. "But… I'm the one who fucked up," I say quietly.

Izzie finally looks up. "We both fucked up, Steph. So, we both work to fix it, okay?" She lays her hand on top of the table, palm open. An invitation.

I've never RSVPed so fast.

I put my hand in hers and let her lead me to the garage, where we pile onto the bed and tangle our limbs and promise to try harder and do better.

We talk through the night. She tells me about her hopes, about her fears, about her absolutely unhinged love for peanut butter and pickle sandwiches. I hold her, lips pressed to her hair, while she cries as she recounts being left by a transphobic ex, as she explains how it felt to be rejected by her high school's cheer squad, as she worries over what to do when one of her housemates moves out and a new, unknown, person takes their spot.

And when the sun rises, dappling the blankets with patchy light, I don't want to go home.

So I stay.

Winter

Thirteen

I move in a few weeks later. It only takes one trip to get all my stuff from Dad's to Izzie's, though he certainly tries to stall me while I'm packing.

"It's the end of an era!" he writes in an email to which he has attached a baby picture of me and a screenshot of a frowny face emoji.

"If by era you mean eight months, then sure," I respond, and tack on a clown emoji for good measure.

The response comes immediately. A photo of a stack of DVDs—*Jurassic Park*, *National Treasure*, and, of course, *Blade Runner*.

I groan, but I can't help the smile spreading across my face.

"You know, not that much is going to change once I'm gone," I say as I hop down the stairs, two at a time. It's not like we've really *lived* together these past months anyway. Maybe we slept under the same roof, but the experience didn't really bring us any closer.

"Beg to differ!" Dad greets me in the hall, holding a can of orange soda with a crazy straw and a big bowl of popcorn. "For starters, I'll never have a reason to buy this toxic sludge again." He points to the soda.

"Elixir of the gods, I think you meant to say." I take the can and slurp a mouthful through the straw.

"So, what do you say, one last movie night with your old man?"

I raise an eyebrow. "You don't have to make it sound so funereal. You're not *that* old, and I'm only moving across the Ballard Bridge."

"So far! A whole ten-minute drive!" He presses the back of his hand to his forehead, feigning a swoon.

"However will you go on without me?"

He holds up *Jurassic Park* and says, "Life finds a way."

We settle in for an afternoon of dinosaurs and Laura Dern, which bleeds into an evening of Nic Cage being his Nic Cage-iest. Dad pauses the movie just as he says, "I'm going to steal the Declaration of Independence," and I let out a wail of protest.

"Oh, come on!" I shout, but my disapproval fades when I see Renee come through the front door carrying a pizza box.

"I'm not here to crash the party," she says preemptively. "Just thought you might be hungry after all that packing."

Dad leaps to his feet to help her with the box. "Ravenous."

"Suuuure. We all know who did most of the work." She winks at me and passes me a potted plant with fuzzy leaves and little blue flowers. "I thought this might be nice for your new place. It's an African violet, so make sure it you don't overwater it."

"Oh, wow. You really didn't have to." I run my fingers over the soft leaves. My stomach swoops low as I am reminded that I'll never have this kind of moment with Mom. She'll never help me move into a new place, never have an opinion about my girlfriend, never get me a housewarming gift to show me she approves. But somehow this little gesture from Renee feels like... not quite permission, but acknowledgment. Like I'm really doing this, like on some level Renee thinks it's the right move. It's almost enough. "Thanks," I say, surprised to find my throat tight, tears pinpricking my eyes.

Renee gives my shoulder a squeeze, then goes to help Dad in the kitchen, giving me time to get ahold of myself.

Once the pizza is on plates—real ones, not paper, thanks to Renee—she leaves us to finish our movie. We munch quietly on pineapple and pepperoni as Nic Cage plans and executes his heist. When the credits roll, Dad hits mute and turns to me.

"Do you like her?" he asks.

"Who, the blonde actress?" I point toward the TV.

Dad chuckles. "No, Renee."

"Oh." I chew slowly, buying myself time.

Do I like Renee? I don't really know Renee—except yes, yes I do. She showed up to my gig with a bouquet of flowers without ever meeting me. She came to me to talk about her and Dad without me ever asking. Tonight she brought me a potted plant and a pizza and didn't even stay to eat any, just to make my last night here with Dad fun. How weird is that, to do all those things for me? But then maybe they're not really for me. They're for Dad. And that's all I need to know.

There are dozens of things I could say—but instead, I just say, "She has really good taste in pizza."

"I'm a lucky guy." He holds up a slice to toast with mine.

I see this for the moment it is, the opportunity to actually say what's on my mind.

"Why didn't you just tell me about her?"

Dad sets his pizza down and looks anywhere but at me. His eyes skate over the stack of DVDs to his feet to mine. Finally, he clears his throat, and says, "I tried, sweetie."

"Bullshit."

"I did! I kept inviting you to meet her, but you were always busy, and I guess I figured maybe you didn't want to know."

I open my mouth to protest again, but a memory filters back—him asking me to have dinner with a coworker, me blowing him off to hang out with Izzie. I want to say if I'd known it was a *girlfriend* and not just someone from work, maybe I would've said yes, but I don't know if that's true.

Dad's eyes finally flick up to mine and there's a fatigue there I don't expect to see. "Sweetie, I know this might be hard for you because of how you feel about your mom, but—"

"You don't know anything about how I feel about Mom." The words leave my lips like the crack of a whip and I wish immediately I could take them back. I fight the urge to make myself smaller, to make myself uncomfortable instead of him. I am so used to shoving my feelings down for other people's benefit, but I don't want to do that anymore—at least not with Dad.

"You're right." Dad leans back into the sofa and draws his knees to his chest. "Your mom and I stopped having a relationship a long time before she died, so it's different, but that doesn't mean I don't miss her in my own way. Probably weird to talk about it with me, but… I hope you *do* talk about her."

I nod, the weight of tears heavy behind my eyes. I don't want to cry tonight. Not about this. Not in front of him. "Izzie," I say. She's the only person I've told about Mom—the only person I've had to.

"Good."

Quiet wraps around us, but the conversation doesn't feel over.

"Do you like her?" I ask, echoing his question from earlier.

Dad doesn't respond for a minute and I think maybe I just thought the question instead of asking.

"From what you tell me, Izzie is resourceful and resilient and she really cares about you. I don't think I could ask for much more for my daughter."

"So yeah? You like her?" I grip the carpet with my toes, waiting for his answer. My heart thunders against my ribcage like a percussive bass drum, punctuating our conversation. *Say yes, say yes*, I think over and over again.

"I don't know, Steph, and really I don't think it matters." He squeezes my shoulder and pulls me in for a side hug. "It's a lot more important that *you* like her. Anyone else's opinion is just that—an opinion."

It's not the answer I want. I almost press him on it, but he beats me to it.

"You *do* like her, don't you?" he asks with a chuckle. "I sure hope so, if you're moving in together. That's a big step!"

I match his laugh with mine, though it feels hollow. "Yeah, yeah, of course I do," I say a little too quickly. Because the thing is… I do like Izzie. I like her a lot. But what if it's not enough? What if I still let her down?

"Good. Okay, you up for *Blade Runner*?" He waves the Director's Cut in front of me.

I'm tempted, but it's getting late and I still have to unpack. "I don't know—why don't we save it for next time?"

"Next time." He nods, a grin sneaking out beneath his mustache. "Yeah. I like the sound of that."

I wrestle my feet into my shoes and double-check the hallway for any remaining boxes before giving him a wave. I shut the door behind me. It's closed, but not locked. I can come back any time.

As I drive away in Izzie's van, not even half full, and glance in the rearview mirror at the little white house on the hill, it still doesn't feel like home. But when Izzie greets me in the driveway of hers with a smile and open arms, I'm not totally sure this does either.

"Wait! You can't go in," Izzie says as I step toward the open front door.

I nearly drop the box I'm holding. If she's changed her mind about me moving in… but then I spot a strip of cloth in her hand and the wicked smile on her face.

"I did something. A surprise."

She steps up behind me to tie the cloth around my eyes, fingers ghosting against my hair.

"A blindfold, huh?" I lean back into her touch and waggle my eyebrows.

Izzie swats my arm and says, "Oh my god, Steph. It's not like that."

"Yeah but it could be, if you want…" I resist the urge to

needle her more and instead set the box down and let her lead me by the hand toward the house.

I only trip twice—once on the porch steps and once over my own shoelaces. Izzie stops to tie them for me, and there's something so oddly sweet about it that I wish more than anything I could take the blindfold off and kiss her.

Finally, she stops me and positions my shoulders.

"Okay, you ready?"

"As I'll ever be."

It takes a moment to adjust to the lighting. It's dark outside now, but I don't expect it to be inside as well. She flips a switch, and little twinkling lights come to life everywhere, speckles of gold running along the walls of the living room. She's cleared space on one of the bookshelves so there's an empty gap next to her poetry collection.

"I thought maybe we could put some of your zines here," she says, pointing to the shelf. "And—oh there's more!"

She tugs me forward through the kitchen, where she's placed a bottle of wine, and into the garage. She's moved the bed out from the wall to make room for a second bedside table. On it is a copy of Judith Butler's *Gender Trouble* and a greeting card that says 'Welcome homo.' In place of the usual pile of laundry, she's laid out a purple throw rug. Even her dresser has been condensed to make room for my clothes.

It's all so much like the room she once described for me, with all the little touches to make it feel like mine, too. It's a gesture I never would have thought to make. I take it in, running my fingers over the empty space I now have to fill.

"Do you like it?" she asks, voice tight and full of hope.

"You shouldn't have," I say. And really, I wish she hadn't. It is so much easier to fit myself into her life as is, to just slip through the cracks of this existing world she's built for herself. Instead, she's cleared all this space for me, and I don't know how to be big enough for it. I don't know how to put words to that feeling, so instead I throw on a smile. "You have been a busy worker bee!" I cross the room to tweak her nose and press a kiss to her cheek. "Why don't you open that bottle of wine I saw in the kitchen while I unload my stuff?"

"Are you sure? I can help." She follows me from the garage, bouncing a little on her toes.

I shrug her off. "Nah, don't worry about it. It won't take long. And then we can celebrate—maybe with the blindfold?"

She laughs at that and trots off to the kitchen for a bottle opener, leaving me to finish unpacking. True to my word, it doesn't take long. I only have a few boxes and my suitcase. I throw my zines in a pile on the bookshelf and fold my clothes into drawers, but when Izzie calls to me from the kitchen to ask if I'm ready, I glance down at a still partially full suitcase—art supplies and loose dice rattling around inside. It feels like it belongs to another version of Steph, the one who isn't in a punk band, who doesn't have a girlfriend, who still lives in Arcadia Bay GMing for Mikey and Chloe and Rachel, the Steph who still has a mom to come home to at the end of the day.

My hand snakes up over my heart, the muscles tight across my chest. I know that version of Steph is still in there somewhere, still a part of me, but I don't want to look at her—not yet. I shove the suitcase into a corner. For now, I'd rather drink wine with Izzie. The thing about baggage, though, is it's still heavy whether you unpack it or not.

Fourteen

We ring in the New Year in style. That is to say, dressed in sequins and playing for a crowd of at least two hundred. We debut our new song 'Compton Cafeteria' to an enthusiastic cheering section of friends and even some strangers. It's the most *on* I've felt behind the drums since our first gig. The applause sets me on fire as I hit the crash and ride simultaneously, ending our set with a flourish.

"Thank you so much!" Izzie shouts into the microphone.

I swoop up behind her, hands snaking around her hips, and I add, "Happy New Year!"

"Not for another hour and a half," says Brenna, the emcee for the night, as she takes the mic from Izzie. "We've still got lots of music for you tonight!"

I tug Izzie free from the amp and lead her offstage. Ollie and Jordie are waiting with drinks and a plate of garlic knots.

"My heroes!" I reach ravenously for the mound of garlicky goodness. "I haven't eaten since lunch."

Ollie offers the plate to Izzie, but she shakes her head. "Nah, I'm good. Too much adrenaline to eat."

"More for me," I say through a mouthful of bread.

There's some feedback on the mic and the emcee returns to announce the next band.

"Put your hands together—or hooks, if you've got 'em—for your favorite local pirates! The High Seas!"

I very nearly drop a mouthful of chewed garlic knot with the way my jaw hangs open. I turn around and, lo and behold, I see Tammi, Dex, Dwight, and Pixie take the stage. Last I heard from Pixie, they were still on tour, but that was months ago. I guess I've been pretty wrapped up in my own world lately, but still I feel bad that I didn't know they were back in town.

"Ahoy there!" Tammi says, waving at the crowd. She's wearing an eye patch and a big ruffled collar, with her natural black curls piled atop her head. "We're so thrilled to be back in our hometown, *Sea*-attle." She emphasizes the first syllable for puntastic effect. "Now, are you ready to rock this boat?"

And rock it they absolutely do.

Watching The High Seas do their thing is otherworldly. Tammi is a captivating singer. She makes the whole stage her instrument, dancing back and forth like she's a sound wave all on her own. Dwight produces some of the slickest guitar riffs I've heard, fingers flying across the bridge of his burnt-orange electric guitar. He's wearing a tricorn pirate hat over his platinum-blond dyed hair and his sunglasses reflect the light from the disco ball above the stage, casting little rainbow lights across his dark skin. Just behind him, Dex is tearing it up on the keyboard. He's changed his hair since the last time I saw him, vibrant purple on the left and dark red on the right. A stuffed parrot sits on his shoulder, bouncing up and down as his fingers travel across the keys. And then there's Pixie. She may be in the very back, but she's putting on a show just the same, a striped bandana tied over her hijab. She drums with such ferocity and spirit that I momentarily forget I'm in a room full of people and it isn't just me and the beat.

Ollie reaches over to rescue the plate of garlic knots from my limp arms and Jordie snaps a picture of my stunned face.

"Did you know they were going to be here?" I ask, when I regain control over my mouth.

"Yeah—didn't you check the flyer?" Izzie picks one up from a nearby table and hands it to me.

And there it is—their name next to ours.

"I can't believe we opened for The High Seas and no one told me."

"Mmm, but did no one tell you or is your reading comprehension just shit?" Ollie tweaks my nose affectionately. "I'm getting drinks. Who wants what?"

As Ollie trots off with Jordie in tow to get our first round, Izzie says, "I didn't know you were a fan of shanties."

"I mean, I love a good shanty, but that's not all—I know these guys!" I point unnecessarily at the stage. "Pixie, the drummer, she's basically my teacher. I can't wait for you to meet her!"

"Oh, that's cool!" But Izzie's expression has glazed over and she jabs a thumb at the greenroom. "I'm gonna go take a minute. Need to decompress."

"Okay…" I want to ask her to stay. I want to ask her why she doesn't. Instead, I just say, "Don't go too far, though. I want my midnight kiss!"

"Sure." She pecks me on the cheek, and then she's gone.

"Izzie pull her disappearing act again?" Jordie asks when they return. "I swear, that girl should have her own magic show."

I shrug it off, deciding that maybe if I don't talk about it, it won't bother me. I'm used to this habit of hers by now. At every gig we've had, she doesn't stick around to listen to the other acts or celebrate a gig well played. She goes back to the van instead, leaving me to find the fun for myself. I know it's probably just a difference in post-gig rituals, but it's still jarring.

I lose myself in the sound of my favorite pirate rockers. I sing along to their punkified version of 'Drunken Sailor' with half my usual gusto, and even their new song about some rich guy having a midlife crisis to become a pirate in the eighteenth century can't raise my spirits.

It's a quarter to midnight by the time The High Seas spill off the stage to uproarious applause. I join in, trying to hype myself up to greet them, but before I can so much as set down my drink, Pixie's making a beeline for me.

"Steph!" she calls out over the crowd, waving wildly in my direction. "It's so good to see you!"

"Ditto! You were great tonight!" I open my arms to receive hugs from everyone, which they provide all at once.

"Who cares about us—*you* were fantastic!" Tammi squeezes me even harder. "When Pix said you'd started playing again, I just knew you'd be great!"

"That's really nice of you," I say. "But do you think… Could I have a little air?"

"What, not into death by group hug?" Dwight asks and ruffles my hair.

I smooth it back down and grin. "That would be a sweet band name."

"Okay, speaking of sweet band names—Drugstore Makeup has a cool ring to it." Dex nudges me with his elbow.

"Thank you, thank you." I give a little bow.

Dwight looks around, craning his neck to see over the crowd. "Where's, uh… your vocalist. What's her name?"

"Izzie? Oh, she's… I don't know, actually." For a moment, surrounded by my fellow musicians appreciating my art, I'd forgotten to miss her.

"We're gonna grab drinks, but maybe when we get back you can introduce us?" Tammi gives me a wink. "And tell us what the deal is. You two looked pretty cozy up there."

She and Dwight disappear to the bar, while Dex seems to have found camaraderie with his fellow transmascs in Jordie and Ollie, leaving me alone with Pixie.

"If I'd known you were going to be here—" I begin, but Pixie cuts me off.

"You would've been soooooo nervous, right? Opening for your idols is a big deal."

I roll my eyes, but… she's right. "I cannot believe I didn't realize you were playing too. How come I didn't know you were back in town? I am so out of the loop."

"Good surprise?" She links our arms and gives me a bright smile.

I match it. "Good surprise."

"So… Izzie. What's going on there? Last I heard you were U-hauling big time."

My face must give away some of what I'm feeling because her eyebrows pinch together and she puts a hand on my arm.

"Oh, Steph. What's wrong?"

I try to shake it off, but… This isn't some random rocker I met after a show. It's Pixie! She's seen me at my weirdest, if not my worst, and maybe it'll help to say some of my worries out loud.

"I don't really know," I say, not knowing how to even start. "It's like… we play a great set, and I'm so energized and excited afterward, but she just melts away. She always goes somewhere to hide out until I'm ready to go home, and I just… Do you think it's something I did? Like was I actually bad up there? You can be honest, I can take it."

"Okay, first of all, you weren't bad. You're a good drummer, Steph!"

"I had a good teacher." I try to smile, but I know it doesn't really fit the moment. "Sorry. You know me. Relentlessly cheerful."

"Yeah, and I can see it's taking its toll." Pixie fixes me with a searching look, eyes wandering over the circles beneath my eyes and the worry lines on my forehead. "It's alright to be worried or confused or upset. You're allowed to feel things."

"Obviously," I say, but my shoulders inch higher and my chest gets tighter.

Pixie tugs the bandana off her head and adjusts her dusty rose hijab before continuing. "We all have different ways of handling the post-show adrenaline drop. For some of us, going to an after-party or vibing to someone else's music helps us feel the letdown more slowly. Others need some downtime." She nods at Dex, who has carved out a corner near the back wall to continue his conversation with Jordie and Ollie. "Maybe Izzie is one of those people who needs to be alone for a bit. Lots of musicians are like that after shows—Kurt Cobain, Freddie Mercury. Is she an introvert?"

"I actually don't know." I live with this girl, I play music with her all the time, I even sleep beside her, and I've never so much as thought about it. But it's there in the details. Her bedside table full of books by bell hooks and Rupi Kaur she'd rather read than go out to bars. Then there's the party she threw for me but didn't really want to attend herself. She doesn't even have that many friends besides her housemates—everyone else she knows are music industry people and half of them are her evil ex-bandmates. "Maybe you're right."

"Maybe." Pixie eyes me carefully before adding, "But maybe *you're* right. If you feel like something's wrong, don't wait to find out the hard way. It's almost midnight, so go get your kiss and then talk with her about it. The worst that can happen is she doesn't tell you."

I nod and take Pixie's verbal shove in the direction of the greenroom. But Pixie's wrong about that last bit. Really, the worst that can happen is that she *does* tell me and it's something I can't fix.

I find Izzie curled up in the back of the van, body circled around a notebook, a concentration line creasing her forehead.

"Heya." I hop up beside her as casually as I can manage. "Penny for your thoughts?"

"I heard they're discontinuing pennies—not worth the metal they're made of." Izzie closes her notebook and shoves it aside. "Might want to offer something else."

"Ah, but that will just make them more valuable. Scarcity mindset and all." Still, I fish in my pocket and pull out a hair tie and a stick of gum.

Izzie takes the hair tie, stretching it between her fingers to shoot it at me. "You drive a hard bargain, Gingrich."

"So, what's up with the isolation cave?" I ask. The words come out casual, but inside I'm a riot of nerves. I try to hold Pixie's advice close to my heart, but her calm keeps slipping away from me, replaced by prickling anxiety.

"Oh, you know." She waves a hand at her notebook. "Can't deny the muse when it strikes."

"New song?"

Izzie nods, but her eyes cheat down and to the side as her thumb brushes against the pages.

"Can I hear it?" I can feel Izzie tense beside me as soon as I ask, her shoulders jumping toward her ears. And, to be fair, I don't ask it out of a benign curiosity. The question is a challenge because, I realize with a devastating swoop of my stomach, I don't believe her.

"It's not really… ready yet," she says, still not looking at me.

I quirk an eyebrow. She's never shied away from collaborating with me on music, not even in the early stages of a song. I search inside myself for the bravery I found before coming in here, but it's gone.

There's a whoop and roar of "Happy New Year!" from the other room, muffled by the door. It must be midnight.

"Kiss?" She presses her nose to my cheek and tugs me toward her by the belt loops on my black jeans.

I lean into her. Even if I can't seem to say much of anything else tonight, at least my lips are good for something. Maybe I'll resolve to do better in 2017. Maybe, like most resolutions, I'll forget before the end of January.

Spring

Fifteen

For Izzie's birthday, I get her custom Drugstore Makeup guitar picks and make her a home-cooked meal of store-bought lasagna and apple pie. When I asked her what she wanted to do, she insisted on staying in. It's been a rough few months for a lot of reasons. Or maybe just for the one very orange, very angry, very presidential one. The year 2016 isn't something I'll miss, but I don't exactly have a lot of hope that 2017 will be much better.

The year is only fifteen days old, but already I'm sick of it. I spend most of my time at the café, working extra shifts. And Izzie spends most of hers on the phone with her mom and tucked behind her laptop, poring over spreadsheets.

"It *is* a big deal, Mom," I catch her saying into the speaker when I go to preheat the oven. "I don't want to argue about this anymore, okay? I love you, but you just don't get it."

"What doesn't she get?" I ask once she's hung up. "You having a quarter-life crisis?"

Izzie groans and drops her head against the chairback. "I'm having a crisis, alright. I don't know how she's *not*."

"That's a mood." I cross over to the oven and fiddle with the dial. "Is it a specific crisis or…?"

"She wants me to go to the Women's March next week." Izzie sighs and presses her fingers to her temples. "She's riled, I get it. And she should totally go. But I don't think she understands how scary it is for me. When people start talking about women's

149

rights and womanhood and feminism…"

"It gets really TERFy real fast."

"Exactly. I just can't be there when they start with the gender essentialism shit." She straightens up and looks back at her laptop. "Ugh. I can't concentrate. I'm gonna go play for a bit." There's a scraping sound as she pushes back her chair and heads for the garage, leaving her laptop behind.

"Dinner in like… I don't know, a lot of minutes!" I shout after her, searching on the lasagna box for the cook time.

I sit down at the kitchen table to wait for the oven to preheat, but as the minutes tick by, I get more and more antsy. I glance at the laptop across from me, drumming my fingers on the table, a nervous rhythm.

"Screw it," I mutter, and switch seats. It's weird how much Izzie's been glued to her computer lately. She does music stuff full-time—all the admin and bookings for our band, plus she teaches guitar lessons—and she generally prefers her notebook for writing songs. I can't help but think *something* is up and… maybe a little snooping won't be so bad.

The first thing I see is a spreadsheet. It's full of numbers and dollar amounts from gigs. There's a sheet with my name on it, too. It's got my rent and my cut of Drugstore Makeup profits listed by month. Maybe she's just keeping track of expenses? But then I see several entries for gigs we never played, dates I was working at the coffee shop. I peer closer, double-checking to make sure I'm not imagining it but… no. There are thousands of dollars and dozens of shows I wasn't even at. A low rumble of suspicion starts in my gut, winding its way up my throat.

Is this what she's been hiding? I was ready to let Pixie be right about Izzie, about her being an introvert, but maybe there's more to her secrecy than just a difference of social energy.

But, no. It doesn't do me any good to jump to conclusions. I minimize the window. Behind it is a browser with an advertisement for an open mic at a coffee shop dated for this afternoon and a bunch of Archive of Our Own tabs—all Willow/Tara. At least my girl's got good taste in fan fiction.

I resolve to ask Izzie about the spreadsheet over dinner and get on with the extremely taxing process of following the box instructions. But when I head out to the garage to fetch her, she's not there. And neither is her acoustic guitar. I double-check every room and even try calling her cell, but there's no answer.

I glance at her laptop and know instantly where she is.

It takes me all of three seconds to decide to follow her. I grab my keys and head out for the café, leaving dinner sitting on the table.

The coffee shop is only a few blocks away. Perkatory is cute, if a little run-down, with wood paneling and high ceilings. The acoustics are great—there's an older woman with long flowing gray hair playing the saw, of all things, and chanting in a deep, melodic tone. It's hypnotic, and I stand in the doorway, swaying to her song for a few moments before I snap back to reality. I scan the audience for Izzie, catching sight of her dark hair disappearing over at the other side of the stage just as the saw player's song ends.

"Great! Give it up for Lydia of Never Saw You Coming!" A barista hops up onstage, clad in an apron with little devil horns embroidered on the front. "Next, we've got Izzie Unplugged!"

My mouth falls open as Izzie takes the stage. She looks… different. Smoother, softer. She's in blue jeans and a loose green button-up I've never seen her wear before. She's even braided her hair to the side, like she's undercover as a country singer or something.

"Hey! I'm Izzie. I'm going to try out some new stuff today, if that's okay."

I blink up at her, absolutely baffled. Her voice is fluttery and nervous. I've never heard her sound nervous before a gig, and I've definitely never heard her ask permission from the audience to do anything.

"I wrote this song a few weeks ago and it's pretty fresh. No one's heard it before so… lucky you, I guess."

My chest tightens at that—*no one's heard it before.*

Izzie's fingers find their place on the frets and as she strikes the first chord, her eyes find me near the door. Her mouth opens, but no song comes out.

"Steph?" she calls after me, but I'm already gone.

There's really nothing like marching down the street in mid-January, wind whipping you into a frozen frenzy, as your girlfriend chases you down the street to make you feel like an idiot.

"Steph! Wait!"

Izzie's words sound far away, even though I'm only halfway down the block. I feel almost absent, like I'm watching the events unfold rather than living them, and just like a car crash on the side of the road, I can't look away.

"Hey!" Her hand slips around my wrist and she pulls me to a stop. "Why'd you run off?"

"Why?" I ask. "I think it's pretty clear what's going on here."

Izzie's gaze is soft and searching, not at all the defensive wall I expected to find. "Illuminate me, please, 'cause I have no idea."

"God, Izzie." I shake my head and gesture at her whole… situation. The outfit, the acoustic guitar, the coffee shop behind her. "Just… what is this? Are you soft-launching a solo career behind my back?" I can hear myself sounding paranoid, like I'm pulling at threads that weren't loose to begin with.

Izzie looks down at her outfit, then back at me. "No—Steph, no! We've talked about this. I don't want to play music with anyone else, and I definitely don't want to do it alone."

"Seemed like you were happy to do it alone back there."

Her fingers climb up my arm, seeking a better grip as if she's worried if she lets go, I'll dissolve into the wind. "Where is this coming from? I thought we were good."

"I thought we were too," I say, but the words feel false once I've said them. I try to remember the last time I felt like we were *good* and there's a smattering of memories and moments—onstage, playing music; at Pride, openly sharing our love; in the dark, playing truth or dare by the light of a candle. But there's this underlying discomfort I can't place, like I'm standing at the edge of a cliff and hoping I don't fall. "But that was before I found out you've been playing a bunch of gigs without me and writing songs you won't share with me. What's the deal? Do you like… want to do a softer sound? 'Cause we can do that. Just don't lie to me about this."

"Playing gigs without you?" Her brow furrows even deeper and confusion crosses her gaze—genuine or not I can't tell. "What are you talking about?"

"I saw the spreadsheet, okay? All those gigs you've been playing while I work the coffee shop?"

Her face goes slack, understanding finally dawning on her.

"Yeah. I know about all that." There's an edge to my voice, an almost smugness that I've caught her in this lie. And I'm not sure if it's cruel or not, but at least it's fair because now we both know. Or at least that's what I think.

"Oh my god, Steph. I haven't been playing without you—those were shows I turned down." She presses a hand to her temple and groans. "I've been keeping track of how much money we're skipping out on because of your work schedule, waiting for the numbers to make sense."

"Waiting for *what* to make sense?"

"To ask you to quit—your job, I mean. I figured if it started to add up, like if we could be making enough playing music during your work hours, then maybe you'd want to switch to full time."

"F-full time?" The words are a harsh exhale, like someone's hit me very hard on the back. "What, like… be a musician? Is that even an option?"

Izzie shrugs. "Yeah. It's not all glamorous stuff, like we might have to do some unplugged sets and a lot of covers, but it's all

153

exposure and could lead to more. I've even been setting aside a bit of money to get time in a studio so we can record some of our songs. We're missing out on a ton by not having records for sale at gigs, and like… it's not a lot of money, but it's stupid that we're not on Spotify. Plus, if we win Battle of the Bands at Pride, we'll be going on tour. A *real* tour. That's big stuff, and I want us to be ready."

"And today—the open mic?" My fists are still balled too tight, my heart racing too fast, but at least the pieces are beginning to fall into place. "The new song?"

Izzie's cheeks, already pink from the cold, flush a deeper shade. "I'm not used to writing without you," she says quietly, eyes downcast. "But I didn't want to spoil the surprise."

"Surprise?"

Izzie pulls her notebook from her back pocket and flips it open for me to see. Her sprawling handwriting fills the page, sections crossed out and rewritten with notations in the margins. At the top is the title.

'My Beanie Babe'
(Steph's Song)

"You… wrote me a song." It comes out flat, like all I can manage are the words, so I look up and try again. "You wrote me a song?"

Izzie shrugs. "Yeah. I mean. You could say that. It's really more about your choice in headwear, but—"

The rest of her words are lost against my lips. I apologize with my hand cupping her jaw, my arm around her waist, my breath tangling with hers. Relief floods my body everywhere she touches me, and I want to stay like this forever, not arguing, not worried, just feeling.

When she pulls away, I'm not ready, and I don't know how to form the word 'sorry' on my lips, so instead I say, "Okay."

"Okay?" She tilts her head.

I nod. "I'll put in my notice tomorrow."

Sixteen

Quitting is easier said than done. Jordie roasts me way more than the beans we use for coffee over it all.

"So you're telling me your solution to fighting with your girlfriend is to quit your job?" he says in a lull between customers.

"What? Who said *that*?" I ask while washing the same coffee grinder for the third time.

"You did! It's your MO." Jordie throws up his hands and crosses over to the sink to tick off my many offenses on his fingers. "First, you fought with Izzie, so you told her you loved her. Then you fought with Izzie, so you moved in with her. Now you fought with Izzie, so you're quitting your job. Before you know it, you're gonna be one of those people who has a baby instead of getting divorced."

I make a face. "Now *that's* some heterosexual nonsense."

"More like allosexual nonsense."

I shoot Jordie a disdainful look. "Who are you to talk, Mr. Also-in-a-relationship?"

"I love Ollie, but if we were fighting like you and Izzie, I'd be single again before you could blink." Jordie shrugs. "It's gotta be exhausting, right? Like I'm tired just thinking about being that anxiously attached."

"Okay, well no one asked you to think about it. A fun fact you might not know is that you can shut the hell up at any time," I grumble and turn to take my break.

Jordie catches me by the arm and says, "Hey, I didn't mean it like that. I know I get a little fatigued by relationship talk, but that doesn't mean I don't care. You're my friend, and I'm worried about you."

"Well, stop worrying."

Jordie surveys me with narrowed eyes. "Look, I'm not trying to argue with you—you're gonna do what you're gonna do—but... just think about whether you're doing this because you want to or because you're afraid if you don't you'll be single again."

"I'm not afraid to be single!"

"Fear or love, baby, don't say the answer."

"What is that, Justin Bieber?" I make a face.

"Oh my god, no. Jonathan Larson, you uncultured swine. Please, I thought you had a background in theater!"

I shrug. "Musicals were never really my thing."

For a second, Jordie looks like he might take this opportunity to educate me about musical theater, but instead he lowers his voice and just says, "Be careful, Steph."

"I'm going to be fine," I say, and I almost believe it. "Everything's going to be fine."

I head to Dad's that evening to finally fulfill my promise to watch *Blade Runner*, a six-pack of orange soda in hand as an offering. Renee's signature floral arrangement is in the hallway. So is the scent of freshly baked cookies. To my surprise, it isn't Renee in the kitchen, but Dad wielding a spatula and a bag of chocolate chips.

"Hey sweetie!" He points over to the counter. "Wanna lick the bowl?"

"You made these from scratch?" I eye the bowl carefully. "Do I dare?"

Dad mimes drumming with the spatula and sounds out the beats, "Ba da da da ba da da da ba da da da dum! Cooking lessons, remember? I'm practically Gordon Ramsay."

"Yeah and I'm Ringo Starr." I raise an eyebrow, but take a swipe of batter all the same. It tastes like a memory, too sweet and smooth.

Dad glances at the timer—there are still a few minutes left—and says, "So, what's new with my kid? How's the café?"

"Not a kid," I say defensively, focusing as hard as I can on cleaning this bowl instead of making eye contact. I'm not in the mood to be lectured about stability and retirement and health insurance.

"Right, sorry." He holds up his hands. "You are the master of your own fate, and all that."

There's a tense silence as I finish off the last of the batter and Dad watches the egg timer slowly tick forward. Finally, I say, "I put in my notice."

"You did, did you? Well, that's great, sweetie!"

"It is?" I don't even mean to ask it. The question just slips out.

"Well, sure. You're moving on. Growing up."

Growing up. A sick feeling settles in my stomach and I just *know* he thinks it's because I got some job he perceives as being somehow more adult, more responsible. It's almost enough to make me lie, but as I open my mouth, I can't seem to summon the energy.

"The band's really taking off. Izzie crunched the numbers, and we think we can really make it with Drugstore Makeup if we go all in. It's kind of a now-or-never thing and, well, I guess I'd rather try and fail than wonder what if." I feel the fight rising in me, the readiness to defend this choice I'm not even all that sure of myself. "We're not rushing into this, I promise. She has spreadsheets and everything."

Dad nods slowly and taps his fingers on the counter. "Izzie's a smart girl," he says slowly. "Real logical."

"Well, she's a Capricorn, so…"

"Right, and I'm a Wookie," he deadpans.

"It's an astrology thing."

"So I wasn't that far off with the *Star Wars* reference."

"Sure, whatever." I roll my eyes, a smile sneaking onto my lips.

"The point is, this is good. You're doing what you love with someone you love. Doesn't get much better than that. You have to do what makes you happy."

"Right…" I can't decide if I'm more thrown by his acceptance of my choice or by his characterization of it as something that will make me happy. 'Happy' doesn't feel like the word, exactly. Anxious, excited, a little bit terrified…

"I wish I'd done more of that, you know."

"More music?"

"Sure, but other things, too." Dad's gaze goes cloudy and distant, like he's not fully here with me anymore. "I spent a lot of time being unhappy for the sake of other people. Your mom did, too. We never should've gotten married in the first place, and we shouldn't have *stayed* married as long as we did. We both put our lives on hold because people told us it would be better for you if we stayed together."

I snort loudly. "That's a load of bullshit."

I remember the fun, and I remember the fights, but more than that, I remember the numb quiet of parents who just didn't love each other that much. It sucked having Dad live so far away up in Seattle while me and Mom still lived in Arcadia Bay, but it was way better than all living under one roof. Besides, if he'd stayed, he might be dead, too.

"What do you wish you'd done instead?" I ask, and it dawns on me how little I know my own dad—I know his hobbies, I know his favorite movies, but I don't really know *him*. There's this quality to dads, the way Hallmark and TV commercials mythologize them as types rather than people. They're grill-masters or lawn-tamers or thrill-seekers or nerd-fighters. But my dad's just a guy trying to live his life his way, and the realization is both sad and hopeful at the same time.

"I don't think I'd be that different—I'd still like what I

like and do what I do." He frowns, thoughtfully smoothing his mustache. "But there's one thing I'd be, and that's a better dad."

I open my mouth to argue, but he doesn't let me.

"I'm not saying I was a bad dad. I just think I would've been better at it if I'd spent more time living my life instead of trying to live the life your mom and I thought we were supposed to." He shrugs one shoulder. "Guess I wish I'd figured that out before you were all grown-up."

"I mean… I'm not *that* grown-up." I flick a little bit of cookie dough at him and it sticks to his shirt.

"Oh, well now you're definitely grounded."

"Daaaaaad," I whine. "You're totally ruining my life!"

The timer goes off, and Dad pulls a tray of chocolate chip cookies from the oven. "*Et voila!*"

I peer over at the perfectly golden-brown cookies and give an approving nod. "Maybe you would've been a baker."

He grins at that, and pats me on the shoulder. "That's what I'm talking about—it's good to chase your passions now. You'll have more time to enjoy them that way."

I nod as he plates up the cookies to take into the living room. My thoughts circle and spiral, a vortex of feelings. I came here, prepared to shoulder the weight of my dad's disapproval, but instead I'm left with all this unspent energy and nowhere to put it.

Seventeen

They say time flies when you're having fun and that's never been truer than when I'm playing music with Izzie. I work my last day at Save Point and almost immediately begin my life as a full-time musician with a gig that same night. We debut 'Beanie Babe' to an incredible audience, and we trade with Izzie's friend Jerry for time in his recording studio in exchange for help designing a new logo for his band.

"This is the place!" Jerry ushers us inside.

On the fourth floor of a high-rise, the elevator opens directly into his apartment. It's one of those places I've seen from the outside and wondered who the heck can even afford to live there. Jerry, apparently, is the answer. Izzie mentioned on the way over that he was wealthy, but I thought she meant that he was the type to fill up his whole gas tank or an extra-guac kind of guy. This is a whole other level.

"Woah," I say as we walk into a living room with a window as big as Izzie's van looking out on downtown Seattle.

"Wait 'til you see the studio." Jerry gestures us even deeper into his apartment. "First thing I did when I moved in was soundproof the extra bedroom and set up recording equipment."

It's a pretty big space for a recording studio inside someone's apartment. I really expected it to be more like a glorified closet. A full drum kit rests in one corner with a lineup of every electric instrument I can think of—guitar, bass, violin, and even a harp.

Microphones hang from the ceiling, and on the other side of a glass panel is a room full of equipment with blinking lights and buttons I desperately want to press.

"And your landlord let you do that?" Izzie asks.

"God, no. I didn't tell him."

"What about your security deposit?" I run my hands along the cushioned walls.

Jerry just shrugs. "I like to think of that as a premium for making my space the way I want it."

"Huh." I can't personally imagine thinking like that myself, but there's no need to share that with Jerry, especially as he's being incredibly generous to let us use his studio. "Cool if I set up?" I ask, pointing to the drum set.

Jerry gives me a thumbs-up and ducks into the other room to fiddle with some dials. While he and Izzie test the mics and levels on her guitar, I settle in behind the drum set. It's nicer than mine, for sure. He's got *more* cymbals. I didn't even realize there were more to have besides hi-hat, crash, and ride. I experimentally hit one of them squarely with my drumstick.

"Steph!" Izzie yelps. "We're trying to work here, could you cool it?"

"Sorry!" I wince and quiet the cymbal.

There's not much for me to do while they get things set up, so I lean back against the wall and twirl my drumsticks. I have to stop myself from accidentally hitting the kick drum multiple times as my leg bounces up and down, my body too full of jitters to stay still.

Finally, Izzie gives me a nod and Jerry's voice filters in through an intercom.

"Okay, ready when you are!"

I count us off and then we're full swing into 'Riot Pride.' The energy of the song rushes through my body and I feel like I'm floating. It's a transcendental feeling, playing music you love. I almost can't believe I get to do this for a living. Maybe if I'm lucky I'll get to keep doing it.

Izzie stops abruptly, and my drumming fills the space left by her silence. I follow suit a few beats later, coming out of the zone slow and heavy like I'm moving through glue.

"What's wrong?" I ask.

"I fucked up—gotta start over."

So we do. Three more times.

Finally, Jerry calls in to us through the intercom. "Hey, it's okay to play through the mistakes. If we can get a couple takes, we can edit them together in post so it'll be like you never screwed up."

"I just want to get it right," Izzie says, jaw tight.

We try one more time, but Izzie doesn't even make it to the chorus before she hits the wrong string. She lets out a loud groan and throws her pick on the floor.

"Maybe we should take a break?" I suggest. Izzie's dangerously close to the edge, and I don't want our trip to be wasted. If I can just get her to relax, maybe eat something, she'll rally and we'll get something usable.

Jerry nods and leads us into the kitchen—a room larger than the garage Izzie and I live in. I slide onto a stool at the center island and hand Izzie a granola bar from my backpack.

"Want anything to drink?" Jerry asks.

"Maybe some water?"

"Still or sparkling?"

The question is so absurd that I choke on my own tongue trying to answer.

"Still is fine," Izzie says, her voice faraway.

Jerry hands us both water bottles made of glass, then jabs his thumb over his shoulder. "I'll be in the sound booth. Come find me when you're ready to keep going."

I turn to Izzie as soon as he's gone. "You okay?"

Izzie nods and takes a sip of her water. "Yeah—I just really want to nail it."

"I get that."

"I feel like there's all this pressure," she continues. "We were about to make an album when I left Vinyl Resting Place. I really want ours to be good—better than theirs. Feels like they'll win if it's not, like Astrid will have been right to kick me out of the band."

"Okay, well first of all that's not true." I grab for her knee and turn her to face me. "Maybe she asked you to leave the band, but it was the right move. She was shitty to you, and you deserve to make the music you want to make."

"Right, but what if that music sucks?"

"It doesn't," I say emphatically. "I love our music. I love our sound. I love *us*. Other people will too."

Izzie's eyes swim with tears and she shakes her head. "What if they don't?"

I let out a long breath. It's an anxiety I can't soothe because it's one I share. People like us when they come to see us perform, but putting out recordings is a whole other deal. People on the internet will be able to hear us whenever they want, people from all over will have opinions about our songs. Maybe they'll be homophobic. Maybe they'll be mean. Maybe they won't listen at all. But none of them are in the room with us.

"You know, it's just me and Jerry here. If you fuck up, we're the only ones who will know."

Izzie nods—too quickly. She doesn't believe me.

"Let's get back to it," I say.

"You go ahead—give me a few to get it together." She doesn't look at me, eyes averted to the floor.

I want to wrap my arms around her waist and whisper affirmations into her hair, but that's not what she wants from me. Instead I just give a murmur of assent and head back toward the recording studio.

Jerry sits there with headphones covering his ears and I tap him on the shoulder to get his attention.

"Hey—Izzie's gonna be a minute." I sit down next to him and point to the computer screen in front of him. "What are you listening to?"

"Some of my own stuff—been messing around with editing some songs my band laid down last week." Jerry offers me his headset.

I pop the earphones over my ears and close my eyes. Something grungy while also techno crackles through my body, the rhythm strong with a synth melody over the top. "It's cool!" I say after a few minutes of bobbing my head along to the beat. "Not what I expected at all—in a good way, though."

Jerry laughs at that. "Yeah, I get that a lot. People always think I'm gonna suck."

"No—that's not what I—"

"It's cool. I'd probably think that about me too if I met myself. I know people usually think I'm just some rich poser or whatever, and you know what? Maybe I am. But like… so what?" He leans back in his chair and puts his feet up on the desk. "I'm not really in this to prove anything. I just want to make music and help other people make music."

I survey Jerry through new eyes. Maybe he is obnoxiously rich, and maybe he is kind of paying to play punk, but he's also being honest. It's something I'm growing to realize is hard to come by.

"How do you do that?" I ask after a few moments of silence. "Like… how do you get over the pressure?"

Jerry shrugs. "Guess I just don't take myself that seriously. They say you're your own worst critic, right? So if I'm easy on myself, then the rest of the world will be too."

"I'm not sure that's how it works." I glance toward the door, but still no Izzie. "Wish I could get Izzie to be kinder to herself."

"That's a losing battle. I've known Izzie for a minute and she's always been a perfectionist."

I nod and tip my chair back. "Yeah—I don't know what the deal is. Even when it's just us, she gets in her head. I wish she could see that without an audience we can be as messy as we need to be. Maybe it matters when we're onstage, but offstage?"

"Oh, Steph." Jerry sighs and gives me a pitying look. "Izzie always has an audience with you."

"What?" I start to ask, but just then Izzie appears in the doorway, looking weary but determined.

"Okay, let's try again," she says and enters the sound booth.

I stand to follow behind, but Jerry catches me by the arm.

"She's performing for you, whether you want her to or not. Remember that."

His words stick with me as I take my place behind the drums, adjusting the stool and testing my sticks against the snare. Izzie feels judged by me? I watch her plug her guitar into her amp and adjust her grip on the neck with ease. This all comes so naturally to her. I never could have imagined in a million years that I would be the source of her nerves, but her eyes cheat toward me, full of caution.

"Ready?" she asks.

I hold up my hand and beckon her toward me. "We're gonna do great, okay?"

Izzie just nods, and I can tell she's still anxious. Her lips curve down and her eyes are dim with worry. My stomach sinks. I wish she knew how beautiful and wondrous and talented she is. I wish she'd believe me if I told her.

"Hey," I say, quietly enough that Jerry can't hear. "I love you."

That gets a smile. "I love you, too."

When Jerry gives us a thumbs-up, we play and we don't stop until the song is over. And this time, we totally nail it.

Summer

Eighteen

We burst into this year's Pride festival like fireworks. Lia insisted on handcrafting our outfits for the stage, so we're rocking complementary ensembles that somehow balance punk with rainbows. Izzie's got a leather dress with rainbow fringe along the sides and I'm in a vest that matches.

"And now for the finishing touch!" Lia holds her makeup bag aloft like it's a holy relic. "In honor of Drugstore Makeup's triumphant performance to come, I have purchased some eponymous items."

"You make it sound so ominous," I say, but I crawl toward her across the grass.

"It can't be ominous. Not at Pride." Izzie tilts her head up and closes her eyes, letting the sun's rays bathe her in a glossy light. "I just love it here. It's like… everything else just melts away."

I reach over to squeeze her hand. She deserves this moment of peace so much. We all do.

"Well, I think you'll love this too." Lia pours her makeup bag out on the blanket and begins sorting tubes of lipstick. "Okay. Who wants to go first?"

Izzie slowly blinks her eyes open. "Go first for what?"

Lia's brown eyes dance, mischief in every crease of her smile. "I'm going to paint your lips rainbow!"

Izzie opens her mouth to interrupt, but she only gets a single syllable out before Lia cuts her off.

"No, I know. Not your style. But it's not for keepsies. We'll clean it off after and you can go back to your black lipstick if you want. But—hear me out, because when I thought of this I nearly exploded from cuteness—when I'm done, you each kiss each other to leave the lipstick mark, but instead of red like the logo, it's rainbow!"

"Okay, that *is* pretty cute," I admit. "Izzie?"

"You just want an excuse to kiss me."

I roll over to her side of the picnic blanket and plant a kiss on her jaw. "Don't need an excuse."

"Alright, alright."

Izzie and I sit patiently as Lia applies the cheap lipstick with an expensive brush. My knee brushes Izzie's and her hand finds my thigh, tracing little circles in the exposed skin. I'm grateful, and not just because of the June heat, that I chose to wear shorts today.

"All done!" Lia declares with a flourish.

I turn to Izzie, grinning, and walk my fingers up her body until I reach her face. Keeping her still with a hand on her cheek, I press my lips to the other. "Mwah!" I say as I release her. The rainbow kiss mark is vibrant against her skin, the pigments running together for a blended effect.

"It looks so good!" Ollie exclaims. "I want one too!"

I turn my gaze on him and raise my eyebrows.

"Ew, no, not from you." Ollie points to Jordie, who is innocently enjoying a snow cone, entirely unaware of our shenanigans. "Lia, get him!"

"With pleasure." Lia takes her tubes of lipstick and trots over to Jordie who, to his credit, just shrugs and goes along with it, no questions asked.

"Your turn," Izzie says softly.

I present my cheek, but she just brushes a thumb over the skin and turns her fond gaze on my body. "You know, I've been thinking…"

"Yeah?"

"About our sound—Drugstore Makeup, I mean." She trails her fingers up my arm, nails lightly scraping against my skin. "I know we're supposed to be this band that's all about queer rage, but, I don't know, it feels like rage is just so normal these days. Sometimes I worry it's the only thing I'll ever feel again—and then there are these moments, like this, that remind me I can feel joy too."

I understand exactly what she means. I remember the way she cried on election night, the way I cried, too. And every day since then has felt like wading through waist-deep water, trying to move forward against a current that wants to sweep us away and pretend we never existed.

"There's so much to be angry about, and I know that means I should have plenty of writing material to draw on but I just... I feel like the punk thing to do right now is to write about queer joy, too. I want to sing about lying in the sun with you and holding your hand and marking your skin with my rainbow lips."

And I want that too. I want to hold on to times like these and immortalize them in a song. I want to have that for when the world is terrible, and I think, even if just for a moment, that this is what love must feel like.

I lean up to kiss her, but before our lips collide, a hand comes down between us.

"Hey!" Lia shouts. "No mouth kissing!"

"Wow. Homophobic."

"No. Mouth. Kissing," Lia repeats. "Not until you do the thing. Otherwise I'll have to redo your makeup."

"Fine, fine!" Izzie rises up to her knees and leans over to kiss my shoulder, leaving behind a beautiful rainbow mark in the shape of her mouth.

"Thank you!" Lia points to her bag. "I've got makeup wipes in there, and then you two can go to town."

We fall over each other, trying to get to the makeup wipes quickly. Our bodies collide and we spill into a mess on the ground, laughing. I cradle Izzie in my arms and press our noses together.

Izzie ghosts her lips over mine, whispering into the corner of my mouth just before she kisses me, "I think this is going to make a great song."

The bliss of the afternoon doesn't last long. As time ticks on and the Battle of the Bands draws closer, Izzie grows more and more tense. I notice it in her body first, the way her shoulders pinch and her jaw tightens. Then she stops partaking in the conversation, and her gaze travels away from us to stare off into the distance.

"Okay, time to get ready," I say, a full hour before we originally intended to head backstage. I help Izzie up to standing.

"Woo! Break a leg!" Jordie says.

"Are you supposed to say that to musicians?" Ollie points up at us. "Or is that just for theater people?"

"Figuratively!" Jordie amends.

With a wave and a smile, I take off, steering Izzie by her shoulders through the crowd. I stop to get a couple of burritos — it's unlikely Izzie will eat before we play, but just in case, I'd rather have food available than not. I plop hers down in the driver's-side cup holder when we get to the van, then dig ravenously into mine.

"And here we have the Steph in her natural habitat. See how she devours her prey with an exacting chomp!" A voice drifts over from the van parked beside ours, and when I look up, I see Tammi with her arms hitched up by her sides, prowling toward me with exaggerated leg movements like some kind of cryptid. Behind her, Dwight and Pixie laugh while Dex rolls his eyes.

"Hey!" I say through a mouthful of beans and cheese. "I didn't know you were playing!"

All four members of The High Seas circle around me as I climb out of the van. Dwight gives me a playful jab on the arm and Pixie squeezes me tight.

"Battle of the Bands!" Dwight pumps his fist in the air. "Course we're playing!"

"Big prize," I say, nodding.

Dex shrugs. "Big audience."

"Big fun!" Pixie nudges me in the side, smile wide.

In the lead up to Pride, Izzie's put the pressure on. Winning is a big deal—the tour, the exposure, the record deal. It would be our big break. She's put so much effort into Drugstore Makeup that I want it for her almost as badly as she wants it herself. It would prove that it was worth it, it would prove that songs like ours matter.

"You're not nervous?" I ask, glancing back at Izzie, who's curled up in the van, hunched over her notebook with a line like a coin slot in the center of her forehead.

"Oh, we want to win as much as anyone," Tammi says. "But it's easy to get tunnel vision about that and forget to actually enjoy the experience." She flings an arm over my shoulder and points to the stage. "Just think about it. You're going to play on that stage, for all those very cool people—" she shifts her arm to gesture at the park, filling with more and more blankets and rainbow-clad attendees "—in a lineup with other very cool people." She motions to herself and the other members of The High Seas.

"Did you just call yourself cool?" I ask, eyebrow raised.

"Hell yeah, I did."

"Come on, have a drink with us." Dwight kicks open a blue and white cooler.

I look over at Izzie, but she's in her own world, so I pluck a ginger ale from the ice chest and settle in as my friends regale me with stories from their tour. It isn't lost on me that maybe someday that will be me and Izzie, and if things go well tonight, that future could come sooner than I think. I hope I'll be ready for it when it does.

*

The sky is just beginning to darken over the Pride festival and the lights from the stage are bright. Behind it, musicians mill about. Some have noise-canceling headphones on and pace back and forth. Others do warm-up vocal drills. There's a group of bass players—including Dwight—playing hacky sack, and a couple of drummers are horsing around, pretending their drumsticks are lightsabers.

"Are you ready to rooooock?" I call as I clamber back into Izzie's van, energized well beyond a normal sugar high. "Izzie?"

I look around, but she's not here. That's odd—but her guitar and notebook are still lying on the back seat, so she can't have gone far. I climb over the seats and land in the passenger side to grab my drumsticks from the cup holder. I see her burrito, still untouched, beside them. Then my eyes drift up to look out the front window and there she is—and she's not alone.

Izzie is leaning against the front bumper of the van, arms crossed. She doesn't look happy, she doesn't look angry, she just looks kind of empty as she stares. I follow her line of sight and see three girls I recognize. Vinyl Resting Place. That can't be good.

I open the door and leap down onto the grass.

"Hey," I say.

Izzie shifts her gaze to me and echoes my greeting. "Hey."

"What's going on?" I nod in the direction of her former bandmates' retreating backs. "Everything okay?"

Izzie shrugs. "Yeah, I think so. I guess."

"What'd they want?"

"They…" Her forehead wrinkles and her mouth twitches into a smile, of all things. "They wanted to wish me luck."

"Peace at last?" I raise my eyebrows and reach for her, fingers forming a loose cup around her elbow.

"Maybe." She leans into me, inhaling deeply and letting out a long sigh as my arms close around her. "Still want to pummel the shit out of them onstage, though."

"That's the spirit!" I cackle and drag her back toward the van.

"Come on—let's check the lineup."

We find our name on the list posted by the stairs leading up to the stage. We're second to last, which Izzie says is great placement.

"Anywhere in the middle is bad," she says. "Too easy for the judges to forget you. First or last is obviously best, but I'll take it!" And her face lights up, excitement in her eyes for the first time in hours. "Even better, we're after Vinyl Resting Place."

"Hell yeah!" I punch my fist into my open palm. "We'll show them how it's done!"

Izzie catches my fists in her palms and presses a kiss to my cheek. "I love you," she says quietly. "Thanks for doing this with me."

My chest swells and I pull her closer, sinking my fingers into her hair. I brush my lips against hers and whisper, "I wouldn't do it with anyone else."

Nineteen

When we take the stage, a roar of applause greets us. The crowd has had plenty of time to get fatigued—we're the eleventh band in a lineup of twelve to play—but they're still just as loud for us as they were for The High Seas who opened the show two hours ago.

I settle in behind the drum set. For a show like this, it doesn't make sense for us all to bring our own drum kits, so I'm using the same one as everyone else. I adjust the seat and give a quick drumroll before Izzie grabs the mic to introduce us.

"Hello, Seattle!" Her voice carries on the large speakers and there's a cheer in response. "I'm Izzie and this is my girlfriend, Steph. We're Drugstore Makeup. Hope you like our sound!"

We kick things off with 'Riot Pride.' It's such a strong anthem of a song, and I love that it's what brought us together in the first place. That it's the song that made Vinyl Resting Place kick her out is just an added perk. They've got to be kicking themselves backstage as they hear us absolutely killing it with the song they rejected.

"Thank you!" Izzie takes the mic in both hands and leans a little closer to the audience. "That was our song, 'Riot Pride.' I'm so grateful to be out here with you tonight—something that wouldn't have been possible without Marsha P. Johnson and the Stonewall riots. Let's give it up for everyone who's fought for queer rights. We owe them big time."

The crowd loves that, shouting out other names, too.

"Stormé DeLarverie!"

"Sylvia Rivera!"

"Harvey Milk!"

"Let's all remember to support a queer future, too. Battle of the Bands is benefitting the LGBTQIA youth shelter, so if you're able, please help us fundraise for them and help homeless queer kids find their footing."

Next up, we mellow things out a bit with 'Beanie Babe.' With time for only three songs, we had to be strategic, and this is the best way to show our range.

"I wrote this song for my girlfriend," Izzie says and the crowd erupts in cheers.

Someone near the front yells, "We love lesbians!"

I chuckle and pull my own mic closer to my lips. "So do we!"

When we reach the final echo of the chorus, I quiet my cymbals and let Izzie's voice stand alone. I bask a little in the emotion of her tone, knowing it's for me when her voice breaks just a little on the last note.

"Love you, Steph," she says into the mic.

"Kiss her!" someone yells. Others echo the sentiment and soon it becomes a chant.

I don't need to be told twice, so I stand up and lean over the drum kit, lips puckered. Izzie jogs back and plants one on me. It's quick and perfunctory—not at all the kind of kiss that Pride deserves—so I grab for her and pull her closer.

"Give me a second, guys. Gotta do this right," I say into the mic, then I step out from behind the drums, twirl Izzie into a little dip, and find her mouth with mine.

The cheer we get is enough to blow the roof off the stage.

"We got this," I whisper as I pull Izzie back up and send her back toward the front.

"Happy Pride Seattle!" Izzie's voice is strong as she returns to the mic. "Real quick, thank you guys so much for coming out tonight to support the LGBTQIA Youth Shelter!"

"Also?" I chime in, heart pounding with fondness for this audience, this event, this moment in time. "I just want to say, holy shit, you all have made this the best Pride ever. Literally ever."

"We have one more! This song is called 'Compton Cafeteria'!"

I count us in, "One, two, three, four!"

I grin the whole way through the song. It's one Izzie wrote early on, building on the same emotions from 'Riot Pride.' She said she wanted to highlight more moments of queer history other than Stonewall, to honor everyone who made living her life in the open possible. I can't think of a better message to end with—I love this song and I love this stage. The adrenaline pumping through my veins feels like lightning, like I could light up a whole city with the static charge.

> *Rainbow flags and marketing*
> *They want our supper? Make them sing!*
> *It's about making money fast*
> *But not the story of our past*
> *Corporations wanna join?*
> *It started in the Tenderloin!"*

Izzie's voice falters a little when she hits the last chorus, sliding a bit before hitting the final note—maybe it's emotion, maybe it's just exhaustion—but the audience chimes in to sing the last lines with her, fists pumping in the air. I can't see much from behind the drums, but I catch sight of Ollie on Jordie's shoulders, holding up a big glittery sign with *Drugstore Makeup* written on it, and it nearly brings a tear to my eye to know our friends are out there cheering us on. I feel like I'm a million miles in the air, floating up in the sky with the stars.

Honestly, I don't even care if we win. But I know Izzie does, so I squeeze her hand as we go backstage, listening to the final band, and then wait for the judges to make their decision.

"You were so good!" Pixie squeals when she sees us. "That

second song—*so* sweet!"

Tammi nods her agreement. "Yeah, that one's new, right? I don't think I've heard you play it before."

"It's on the EP," Izzie says shortly.

I nudge her, trying to bring her into the moment. I can feel the tension wound through every part of her body just in her grip. I know she doesn't mean to be rude. Probably. She's met The High Seas a couple of times now, and even if she's not usually up for our shenanigans, she and Dex at least get along.

"Well, you killed it," I say to change the subject. "Really set the tone—I feel like after your set the energy was just so…" I mime an explosion with my free hand.

"We're gonna party after this," Dwight says. "Win or lose, we figure tonight's worth celebrating. You in?"

"Hell yeah!" I knock elbows with him, grinning from ear to ear as I revel in this shared experience we get to have. How good it feels to be with friends.

The emcee, who's been killing time by plugging the fundraiser some more and telling some pretty bad jokes, clears their throat and their voice booms across the park.

"Alrighty, folks. We've got the results here. Are you ready?"

The crowd, both in front of and behind the stage, erupt in cheers. Izzie's hand goes rigid in mine, and I rub soothing circles against her palm. I can feel the held breath in her chest. I long for the exhale, one way or the other.

"Your winner of the 2017 Battle of the Bands—winning a fully funded West Coast tour, eight hours of studio recording time, a cover shoot and interview in *Sounds of the Sound*, and free ice cream from Molly Moon for a year—is…" They open a folded piece of paper, smile, then turn back to the mic. "The High Seas!"

Energy erupts around me. Pixie jumps up and down, catching Dwight's hands in hers while Tammi sends her fist into the air and shouts, "Yes!" Beside her, Dex just stares, eyes unfocused, at the stage, mouth open.

"You did it!" I shout, though my voice is totally drowned out by the audience's roar. I clap Dex on the shoulder and give him a little shove toward the others as they make their way onstage to give an encore.

As they strike up the first chords of their song 'Ghost,' I feel Izzie's hand slip from mine, limp and tired.

"Hey." I try to catch her arm, but she evades my grasp. "I'm sorry we didn't win."

"Yeah." Izzie's voice sounds so far away, like I've already lost her to whatever liminal space she disappears to after gigs. But this time it doesn't feel the same, like she's so much further out of reach. "Have fun tonight, okay? I'm gonna go home."

I don't watch my friends in their moment of triumph. Instead, I watch Izzie drive away. Tammi's voice, melodious and warm, wraps around me like a wind. I know Pixie dedicated the song to Chloe and Max, but right now it feels like it's for me.

> *"If you choose to go, I hope you know*
> *I'll love your ghost, I'll love your ghost."*

Twenty

Pride after dark is a kaleidoscope of colorful lights, glow sticks, and glitter. Dex has taped lime-green glow sticks along his body like an alien stick figure, and Tammi has built a crown out of his castoffs. Lia practically looks like a disco ball, the sequins in her dress catching every light.

I do my best to put Izzie out of my mind. It isn't my problem if she doesn't want to party with us, and besides, she told me to have fun. After a few drinks and some encouragement from Pixie, I join them in front of the stage, busting a move with the rest of them. Even Jordie is swaying back and forth arrhythmically next to Ollie while a Tegan and Sara song plays over the speakers.

The festival comes to a close too soon, but it's a public park so, as the emcee says, we don't have to go home, but we can't stay there.

Dwight and Tammi discuss nearby bars and clubs for the next leg of their celebration while Lia and Pixie try to take selfies in the dark.

"So, Izzie ditched again?" Jordie asks, quietly sidling over to me and nudging my elbow with his.

I nod until I realize he can't see me in the dark, so I say, "Yeah. She wasn't feeling well or something."

"*Or something.*" Jordie's tone gives nothing away, but I know if I could see his face, his worry would be written all over it. "Everything okay with you two?"

"Of course! Why wouldn't it be?" I rush the words from my lips, like the faster I say them the truer they'll be. Besides, the last time Jordie and I talked about my relationship with Izzie he had more opinions than I wanted to hear.

"Fine. Okay. Don't tell me."

"There's nothing to tell!" But my chest tightens and my hands ball into fists by my side. I know it's a lie, but I don't know what the truth is, so it'll have to do.

Jordie stands beside me without speaking. I know this tactic—I've tried it on him a hundred times while GMing a game. People can't handle quiet, so they'll talk eventually if only to fill the silence. It's my favorite way to make them engage with character role-play. He can't use my own tricks against me and win, though. I'm the mighty Steph and I own this game.

Finally, Jordie cracks. "I can't tell if you're bullshitting me or not right now, so I'm gonna be straight with you."

I chuckle. "At Pride? That's homophobic."

"Haha, yes, wordplay," he deadpans. "But really, Steph. If you think everything's fine, you're not paying attention."

I groan. "I know. Izzie's just… She gets weird after we play. I guess she just needs time to wind down or something."

"I'm not talking about Izzie." Jordie presses his shoulder to mine and bends his head so only I can hear him. "I mean you."

"Me?" My eyebrows join forcefully at the center of my forehead, like they're making some business deal over my perceived mental state.

"Yes." Jordie lets out a long, exasperated breath. "Look, I'm not gonna pretend I *know you* on some kind of deep soul level, but it's pretty apparent to everyone that you've changed."

"Is this about Save Point? Oh my god, Jordie, it was just a job!"

"It's not about the job—it's about everything else. Steph, when was the last time you hung out with me and Ollie on purpose?"

I open my mouth, ready to list any number of events we've all attended together over the past few months, but he cuts me off.

"And your own gigs absolutely don't count. What about like we used to? It's been ages since we played *D&D* or had a movie night, and you're way behind on *Critical Role*—no, don't even try to pretend like you're not. If you were caught up, you'd know what I mean when I say 'Keyfish.'"

There's silence in the wake of that statement because… he's right. I have no idea what he's talking about.

"How long has it been since you've rolled a d20, Steph?"

"I… I've been busy, okay?"

"Look, I'm just saying… I miss my friend Steph."

I feel defensiveness crawling up my throat, but I shove it down, so when I say, "So am I just supposed to stay the same forever?" it comes out dry and a little tender like a wound.

"What? No! Steph, that's so not the point—"

But I don't let him finish. Maybe I should, but I just can't hear it right now. Because if Jordie misses who I used to be, then I'll have to acknowledge that I've changed. I'm not really sure who I used to be, but I'm not sure who I am now either and that scares me.

"Whatever. I'm out," I say.

"Steph, come on!" Jordie catches my arm. "I'm saying this because I care."

"Yeah right." I wrench my arm from his grasp and stalk away, but I can still hear him as he shouts after me in the dark.

"Lots of people love you, Steph. You just gotta let them."

Izzie's in the garage when I get home, headphones crowning her head. She's watching something on her phone, knees curled to her chest. She doesn't notice me at first, too engrossed in whatever she's watching. I pause in the doorway, remembering what Pixie said about Izzie needing alone time after gigs. I don't want to interrupt her wind-down, but I also don't want to lose my nerve.

Luckily, Izzie looks up from her phone after about a minute and pushes her headphones down.

"Hey. What time is it?" she asks.

I take a step into the garage and shrug. "Like eleven thirty, I think?"

"Oh—you didn't want to stay out longer?"

"Trying to get rid of me?" I mean it to sound lighthearted and teasing, but instead it comes out accusatory. I try to brush past it, crossing the room to look at her phone. "What are you watching?"

She turns the phone toward me. "Recording of our set."

Shaky footage shot from the audience plays on the screen— we're washed out by the lighting, and whoever's holding the phone is jumping up and down, but it's cool to see us up there on that stage, playing our music for so many people.

"This is rad!" I reach for the phone and she unplugs her headphones so I can hear the audio. It's distorted, but distinctly us. Nowhere near as clear as the studio stuff we recorded, but I can't help but smile as Izzie sings the chorus of 'Riot Pride.'

"Yeah," Izzie says, but her voice wobbles a bit. "I figured it would be good to have video to watch back—see how we can improve for next time."

My chest clenches and my throat goes dry. "God, Izzie. Really?" The words tear from me before I can stop them. "Can't you just… be happy that we played a good set and enjoy that?"

"We lost, Steph. I think it's fair to spend some time thinking about why." Izzie's face goes still and she looks down at the phone between us. "There's nothing wrong with wanting to learn from our mistakes. I'm just being practical."

"Practical?" I repeat, tossing the phone back to her. "Or critical? I swear, Izzie, it's like your brain just skips over all the good stuff."

"Well, that's not how I see it." Her voice is quiet, but her hands are jittery, fingers drumming against her phone case.

I let out a long sigh and pace along the garage. I want so

badly for her to see it my way, for her to see how amazing she is, how amazing we are, maybe even how amazing I am. Because if all Izzie can think about are the mistakes, if all she's looking at is the potential, then she's forgetting to see the progress. Even though we've been at this for a year now, I can't help but think about how she's been doing this so much longer than me, how she's this professional musician and I'm still just some girl who happened along with a ruined T-shirt and a dusty old drum kit.

"So, what, we didn't win and now you think we suck?" I ask, fully aware that's not what she's saying at all, but I kind of don't care. I'm still bristling from my fight with Jordie, and I can't seem to stop the antagonistic energy pouring from me. At this point, I just want to see how she responds, see if she bothers to argue back.

"I didn't say that."

"Yeah, but you're thinking it, right?"

Izzie turns away, bending to uncoil and recoil an amp cord.

"God, you really are thinking it! What the fuck, Izzie?"

Izzie lets the cord drop back to the floor and turns around. The moment she does, all the fight bleeds out of me. Her cheeks are damp with tears and her eyes are lidded and dim.

"Shit." I cross the room and grab for her hand. The pain in my chest doubles as she pulls it back. "Izzie, what's wrong?" And maybe it's a stupid question, because obviously the answer is that we lost, but there's something else going on here—there has to be.

"I…" Izzie's lip quivers, and she puts a hand over her mouth to hide it. "I messed up, okay?"

"What do you mean?"

She fixes me with a glare, but it's devoid of animosity—like it's not really meant for me. "I don't think *we* suck. You were great tonight—even behind the drum set, you have great stage presence."

"Thanks, I guess." I would feel better about the compliment if it didn't imply a 'but.'

"It's me," Izzie says in barely more than a whisper. "I was off my game tonight. I'm the reason we lost."

"Okay, well that's just not true." The truth is we lost because The High Seas were better than us. They deserve their win, and it feels wrong to imply we could've beaten them if only Izzie hadn't missed the final note. Maybe we could've, but I think it's more than likely we lost the second The High Seas finished their set. It didn't matter how good we were because they were better. But Izzie doesn't need to hear that—no amount of logic is going to dispel the negative thoughts mulling over in her mind. I roll my seat from behind the drum kit and plop down on it next to her. "Why d'you think that?"

"Because… I didn't do my best. I flubbed the last chorus of 'Compton Cafeteria' and I was all in my head because of fucking Astrid."

My head shoots up. "Astrid?"

"Yeah, she and the other girls—"

"When I saw you with them before the gig, you said they were being nice!"

"Yeah, well, I should've known better than to trust that, shouldn't I?"

I groan. "God I hate them. What'd they say?"

Izzie curls her toes against the cold floor and crosses her arms. "They didn't *say* anything." Then she passes me the phone again and points to the bottom half of the screen, where some of the audience can be seen dancing and cheering along with our song.

At first, I think she's pointing out Ollie and his big *Drugstore Makeup* sign, but then I see them—all three members of Vinyl Resting Place. They sneak into the crowd during the opening notes of our third song, and as they pass in front of the camera, I see it. All three of them are wearing full faces of makeup— caked on and sloppy. They look kind of like clowns.

"Okay, well they just look stupid—" but I don't finish the thought.

It's only for a second, but the camera catches a glimpse of the sign Astrid is holding up and I freeze. It's our logo with our band name scrawled across it, but in small letters, just below Drugstore Makeup, is written 'a cheap knockoff of the real thing.'

"Transphobic shit stains!" My neck and cheeks flush with anger.

"Yeah. I don't know if they meant it like that, but… it fucked me up when I saw it."

Izzie's voice, somehow calm and steady, pulls me back to her. My rage can wait. I reach for her again, and this time Izzie lets me pull her over and down onto my knee. I bury my face in her shoulder and breathe her in.

She sighs into me, body melting against mine. "I should've just ignored them, but it got to me, and I messed up the song, and we lost. So, we're not going on tour, and we're not getting free studio time, or a fresh paint job for the van."

"Don't forget the free ice cream for a year."

She laughs against my hair. "That too."

I exhale the rest of my anger, deflating like a popped balloon. Instead, all I can feel is the hurt in Izzie's heart beating against mine. I run my hands up her back and say, "I'm so sorry, Izzie."

She slides her fingers into my hair and leans her cheek on the top of my head. "You didn't do anything wrong."

It's the right thing to say—the call and response of an apology that isn't really mine to give—but it still feels false. I came here tonight with every intention of picking a fight because I was feeling… I don't know, neglected, ignored, unappreciated? Because I've been packing away pieces of myself to be the right girl for her and I don't think she's even noticed. Because even if she hasn't, my other friends definitely have. But none of that feels important right now.

"Hey," I say, tilting my face up so my chin rests on her shoulder. My gaze meets hers, and I hope with every fiber of my being that something I say will bring the light back to her eyes. "I have an idea."

"Yeah?" She wraps her arms around my shoulders, fingers dancing at the nape of my neck. "Whatcha got?"

I lift my mouth to hers, teasing a smile onto her lips with a kiss. "Izzie Margolis, will you go on tour with me?"

Twenty-One

The minute the words leave my lips, I know we have to do it. A tour is the perfect next step for us—we'll level up as a band and it will pull Izzie out of this doom spiral she's in. She needs this. But even more importantly, *we* need this. I can feel the fault lines in the foundation of our relationship. One good shake and it will all come tumbling down. But maybe a tour can help us piece things back together, remember why we're in it in the first place, give us something to work toward as a team.

"I don't know—would anyone even come see us?" Izzie stands up, and I feel the absence of her touch everywhere. "Like, I know we're not nobodies, but what venue outside of Seattle would host us?"

"You were all excited about the Battle of the Bands tour. How is this any different?"

"That was all-expenses-paid, Steph! We can't afford to go on an unsuccessful tour."

My eyes trace the outline of her nerves—the way her hand finds a loose thread on her pajama pants, the way she rolls her lip between her teeth, the way her gaze flickers down to her bare feet. She's right. We can't afford for this not to work. And I don't mean in terms of our bank accounts. We won't survive this going poorly, but maybe we won't survive anyway. The risk is worth it.

"Okay, well let's make sure it's successful." I stand up too, now, pulling my phone from my pocket and pulling up Google Maps. "And we'll go to places where we know people, so we don't have to pay for hotels and stuff. My grandma lives in Sacramento, so we should definitely do a show there—she'll let us crash with her. I can start contacting places in the morning. Plus we'll need flyers, posters, and stuff. And what about the van? Maybe we can take out the back seat to make room for some cool road-trip stuff. Make it so we can sleep in the back for the cities where we don't have friends."

"Like what?" Izzie gives me a perplexed look. "A waterbed and a mini fridge?"

"Mini fridge—that's a great idea!"

"Oh my god, I was kidding."

"I'm not!" A grin plays across my face. This is the energy we need—forward momentum, something to run toward. "When do you think we can go? Is fall too soon?"

"Slow down."

Izzie puts a hand on my shoulder, fingers biting into my bare skin. Her grip is like a heavy weight, dragging me back down to earth. Skepticism is written all over her face, and a little light of fury rises in me at the people who made her doubt that we can do this. I want to prove them wrong.

"Slow down? Why?!" It's almost midnight, but this is the most awake I've felt all day. My body hums with energy and I want her to feel it too. "Izzie, this is our chance! We have to take it!"

"We haven't even booked any shows yet."

"Yeah, but we will."

"Come to bed, Steph. We'll talk about it in the morning."

Izzie drags me toward bed and falls asleep almost as soon as her head hits the pillow. I lie awake, brain abuzz with possibility. I won't let her hesitance temper my enthusiasm. I *can't*.

*

I spend the next morning researching venues on the West Coast. Pixie gives me the names of some places The High Seas played on their last tour and I even post on Reddit, asking for recommendations.

That's when I discover something I didn't really believe until now: Drugstore Makeup is popular. There are already posts on Instagram with video clips from the Battle of the Bands. The clip of us kissing between songs has been shared a lot, and it's still racking up views. The comments are mostly positive with a few homophobic trolls in between. Lots of rainbow emojis and a few people saying they wished they lived closer to Seattle so they could've seen us.

It's not just fans, though. We've gotten some good press since releasing the EP. I scroll through the search results, finding our music on listicles like 'Seattle bands you should be listening to,' 'Queer punk anthems of the summer,' and 'Songs to listen to while you punch a Nazi.' I paste the links into an email to send Izzie—just in case she hasn't seen them—and then, for good measure, I send them to my dad, too.

My inbox chimes almost immediately after hitting send, and I'm sure I've gotten Dad's out-of-office or something, but no. It's a reply to my post on Reddit. I navigate back to the tab and read.

Hey Steph! We love Drugstore Makeup in SLC! If you're thinking about heading to Utah, a friend of mine runs a queer-friendly club called Atomic Decay. I can put you in touch for scheduling!

I grin, and by the time I've typed my reply, there are two more messages suggesting places in Denver and Reno. Before I know it, I have a tentative schedule in the works.

"Hey there, hot stuff," Izzie says, pushing up the garage door. "Literally—it's boiling in here. How are you not liquified?"

Honestly, I didn't notice, too engrossed in my research to turn on a fan. "Did you know that Drugstore Makeup is one of this year's most moshable bands?" I ask, holding up the laptop for Izzie to see the article I've just found.

"What the hell is *moshable*?"

"Like… mosh pit, I think. I don't know—whatever it is, we're it."

Izzie takes the laptop from me and points at the screen. "What's this?"

"That is a schedule of very real venues with very real audiences that have offered us very real show dates." I nudge her. "What do you say to a winter tour?" I tap the column where I've listed February and March dates.

"Well, it's—" Izzie begins, but I cut her off before she can shut me down.

"Look, I know you're disappointed about last night. I am, too. But we can't let assholes keep us from our dreams! Maybe your old bandmates hate us, but you know who doesn't? The thousands of listeners who've streamed our music! A lot of them want us to play in their cities, so… let's do this, okay?" I almost add 'please' to the end, but it feels too pathetic, too desperate. I want this—but even more than that, I want her to want it.

"You didn't let me finish!" Izzie cracks a smile and tugs on the belt loop of my shorts. "I was going to say it's a good thing the van's insulated." She pulls me forward toward the open garage door where the van is parked and pops the trunk to reveal an open space. The back seat is gone and in its place is a little battery-powered mini fridge. "It'll be a bit of a tight squeeze with the drums, but—"

"I love a tight squeeze." I wrap my arms around her middle and lift her up into the van.

Izzie giggles as we topple over, clumsily bumping into the mini fridge, but the sound barely escapes her before I capture her laugh with my lips. It's messy and imperfect, our hearts beating a discordant rhythm together, but it's also exactly what a summer kiss in the back of a van on a ninety-degree day should be.

Fall

Twenty-Two

It doesn't stay warm and sunny for long. The temperatures drop and so does my mood. I try to lose myself in tour planning, but our lineup is basically set—seven stops across seven states. We'll be on the road for a month, but we don't leave until February. It feels so far away, here in October.

I find myself refreshing the Reddit thread over and over, but nothing much changes other than some guy with the handle Gabsurdity93 who keeps asking us to come to a place called Haven Springs in Colorado. I write back, hoping the exclamation points I use in my message will translate over to enthusiasm in the real world.

Steph-Right-Up
We'll be in CO on March 8th at The Hermit Cave in Denver! Come see us!

He writes back a few seconds later.

Gabsurdity93
Swing through Haven Springs on the way! You can play the Black Lantern—they've got amazing fries in addition to fully functional outlets!

I roll my eyes, but type back.

Steph-Right-Up
Fully functional outlets—how can we possibly resist such amenities?

I roll onto my front on the living room couch, arms and head hanging off the side as my eyes glaze over. The sound of rain pelting the roof is tinny and constant. Even noise-canceling headphones aren't enough to keep the weather from affecting me. Usually I'd find a distraction at work—curating playlists for the day that would keep me upbeat and occupied—but without my coffee-shop job, there's too much time in the day for my thoughts to spin out of control.

My phone chimes with a text from Jordie.

> Hey—haven't seen you in a while. Idk if you're around, but the Critical Role finale is tomorrow and it would be cool if you came

I cringe. I know Jordie and I both regret how things went at Pride, but we haven't had a chance to talk about it. I want to. I want to say I'm sorry and I want to hear he's sorry, but part of me is afraid that he's right—I *have* changed.

> I'm still not caught up

> That's okay! We can give you a highlight reel!

> Ollie's making d20 shaped cookies

> And we're gonna play bingo

> I'll try to make it

Even as I type the words, I know it's a lie. I can barely move my limbs today, fused to the couch by some heaviness in my chest I can't seem to shake. Part of me wishes Izzie was home so I could curl up with her and let the press of our bodies wash away the ache in my heart. Another part of me is glad to be alone.

I know she needs me to be excited about the tour, to be positive in the face of her doubt. But I don't have it in me to be a source of light today.

As day turns to night and the cloudy sky goes dark, I hear the scrape of a key in the lock. I can't even be bothered to look up from my phone to see which of my housemates has returned, refreshing the Reddit page futilely once more. It's not until I feel a weight on the cushion beside me that I realize Izzie's been saying my name.

"Steph, are you even listening?"

"Sorry," I scramble to pull my headphones off. "What'd you say?"

"I want to show you something—maybe it'll cheer you up."

I swallow, blink, and summon every ounce of energy I have to turn my lips upward into a smile. It feels leaden and rusty. "I don't need cheering up! I'm cheered!"

Izzie gives me a skeptical look and holds out her hand. "Come on."

The feel of her fingers against mine is an acute shock to my system. I almost flinch at her touch, but she wraps my hand in hers and pulls me to my feet.

"I know it's still a few months away," she begins as she leads me outside.

I sink into the cold embrace of what promises to be a stormy night. Raindrops speckle my skin and a wind rustles the bushes along the driveway.

"Chilly," I say—it's all I can manage.

"Just a sec—I promise." Izzie runs her hands up and down my arms, and guides me toward the van parked in the driveway. "Okay, ta-da!"

She flings the doors open, and light spills out onto the pavement, soft and gentle, generated by a strand of fairy lights taped around the windows. The bed area has a mattress with blankets and pillows piled on top, and in the center is a cardboard pizza box.

"Thought we could have a slumber party in the van. Give it a test run. Pretend like we're on tour."

It's so sweet I could cry, and as Izzie drags me out of the rain and into the van, I realize I *am* crying. Izzie doesn't ask me about it, though, just pats the space on the mattress beside her and pulls the lid off the pizza box to reveal a Hawaiian with herbed crust.

We eat in silence, Izzie's hand resting on my knee the whole time like she's afraid if she stops touching me, I'll drift away. I'm glad. For the first time all day, I feel like I actually want to be where I am.

"I wish Mom could've met you." I don't actually realize it's true until the words are tumbling from my lips.

Izzie pauses mid-bite, cheese hanging like a limp spiderweb between her mouth and the slice of pizza. "Yeah?"

I nod, words stuck in my throat.

"I don't know if you know this, but I'm very cool." She smiles and brings her other hand to the small of my back. "I'm a big hit with parents."

I shift to lie down on the mattress, curling my knees up against my chest. The thing they don't tell you about losing someone is that it's not just the memories of them that haunt you. It's the future you never get to have together. My imagination spills forth, concocting for me a false reality in which I bring Izzie home to meet her.

Mom answers the door in her floral apron, hands dusted with flour. She's been baking in preparation for our visit. She fusses over Izzie as we take our shoes off. She calls her beautiful. She scolds me for not warning her. Throughout the visit, she tries to feed us everything in the pantry. She worries we're not eating enough. She worries about a lot of things. In the end, she welcomes Izzie to the family—like it's a label that's hers to give away, not mine.

Even the version of her in my imagination still finds ways to make decisions for me. When I was younger, I learned to rely on it. It's how I survived the unhappy years before the divorce. Now, at almost twenty-four, I still look to her for my cues.

"Do you think she'd like me?" Izzie asks as she settles down beside me, tucking her chin against my spine.

"Yeah," I choke out. I don't have the energy to tell her the rest. I wouldn't know how to say it even if I did—how I think, on some level, she'd like Izzie even more than I do, how that scares me more than almost anything else. Instead, I just say, "She'd hate your taste in pizza, though."

Izzie's laugh wraps me up like a blanket, but even in her arms, cuddled up as we are, I'm still cold.

Twenty-Three

When I wake up, I'm in motion. I'm still in the van, curled in a ball on the mattress, but Izzie's not next to me anymore. Her absence is a whisper of cold against my back, and I shiver. There's a low rumbling sound—the engine—and every so often there's a bump, jostling me: the road.

"Izzie?" I say, scrambling to my knees, only to be promptly knocked back down by another bump in the road. "Izzie, what's going on?"

"Ah, you're awake." Her voice comes from the front of the van, a little muffled. "Just in time. We're almost there."

"Almost *where*?" I manage to get to my feet and stumble up to the front seat.

We're driving down a scrap of freeway I don't recognize, the signs obscured by morning fog. At least it's not raining anymore.

"You'll see!" Izzie says cheerily, turning onto a narrow lane lined by a thin smattering of trees.

I yawn and settle into the seat, tucking my legs up against my chest. "How long have we been driving?"

"Couple hours." She pulls into what can only be called a parking spot in the loosest possible terms and cuts the engine. "I woke up early."

"That's an understatement."

"I just… I know things have been rough for you lately, and I had an idea for how to cheer you up."

"Did that idea involve a plan to procure caffeine?" I rub my eyes, still groggy.

"We can pick some up on the way back?" Izzie pops the door open and hops down. "Come on."

Instead of pavement, my feet hit something soft and I stumble over loose dirt and rock. There's a rushing in my ears and a familiar smell in the air I can't quite place—pine and salt and *cold*.

Izzie loops around the side of the van and takes my hand, stabilizing me. "Let's go." She leads the way along the path as it gets narrower and narrower until we have to adjust to go single file down a steep decline.

"Here we are," Izzie says, gesturing at the view.

My heart leaps into my throat so violently I almost choke on it and my lungs falter, tripping over breath after breath. Because Izzie has brought me to the one place I don't want to be.

The coast.

We don't have beaches in the Pacific Northwest. Not in the way that California or Florida do. We don't have fluffy white sand and warm ocean waves and colorful drinks with umbrellas to sip on while we sunbathe. We have rocky shores and ocean spray and bonfires. The coast is cold and brutal most of the year, but today it nearly rips me to shreds.

The wind makes a mess of the tears on my face, obscuring my vision. I dip down to my knees, unable to stay upright as the world seems to bend and break before me. It isn't Arcadia Bay, but it may as well be, with the way my body recoils and rejects this place where sand meets sea.

"Steph?" Izzie's voice is far away, as though from another plane of existence entirely. "Steph, are you okay?"

The question is so absurd to me it's almost laughable. Am I okay? I haven't been okay for a long time, and I can't believe it took someone driving me to the coast for me to realize it.

I push off the sand, damp circles pressed into the knees of my jeans, and come to standing. With a shaky breath, I look to the horizon and say, "No."

And then I sprint down the shore.

I don't know how long I run, but eventually I come to a large, craggy rock with a lighthouse perched atop it, reaching up into cotton-candy clouds, and I have to turn around. The beach lightens and the fog clears as the sun inches over the horizon, but I can't see Izzie anywhere in the distance. Maybe she's waiting for me back at the van. Maybe she's given up and left me behind like some kind of wildlife drop-off. That's it, leave the feral beast in her natural habitat—near the ocean, where grief is as likely to get her as the ocean waves.

I kick the sand with the toe of my white Vans as I begin the trek back. This time, I don't run. I walk slowly, weaving backward and forward across the beach, eyes skipping over stones and shells and kelp left behind by the tide. I pick up a whole sand dollar and a bit of sea-weathered glass, smooth and green.

Eventually, the trailhead comes back into view, but I'm not ready yet, so I carve myself a little seat in the sand. I feel like I'll never be ready. Part of me will always be stuck here at the edge of land and sea. The seam between the two vacillates as the tide creeps in and out, leaving little bits of foam in its wake. I want to take all my feelings and throw them into the wind, let the ocean spirit them away to weird and wondrous depths. But I don't know how to loosen my grip on these emotions. How do you let go of someone you already lost? How do you do it without losing them again?

"There you are." Izzie's voice is coarse and clotted. "Fucking hell, Steph."

I immediately tense, my muscles matching her tone.

"What is going on with you?" She plops down next to me in the sand. "I know things are rough right now, but… I really thought a change of scenery would help."

I meet her with a hard gaze and words dripping with sarcasm. "You did, did you? What a genius idea — take the girl with coastal-town trauma to the coast."

"Coastal-town trauma?" Izzie shakes her head, hair sticking to her face, wet with wind. "What are you talking about? I thought this was about your mom."

I've told Izzie more than almost anyone — anyone who wasn't there to witness it themselves, like Mikey or Chloe. But I haven't mentioned it since that night a year ago when I told her about my mom, so how is she supposed to remember? How is she supposed to know how I feel when *I* don't really know how I feel? I've only rarely said the words out loud, given name to the place that still holds so much of my fractured heart.

Arcadia Bay.

The words are on the tip of my tongue, an endless scroll of stories I could tell. I could tell her about winters spent curled up by the fire watching movies with my dad, springs spent on the lawn of Blackwell Academy playing tabletop RPGs with Mikey, Chloe, and Rachel, summers spent collecting enough seashells to decorate the sandcastles we built. But mostly I should tell her about fall. About one fall in particular.

I should *really* tell her — more than just the basics. I should tell her about the wind and the rain, about the wreckage, about the final phone call with my mom, about our last words to each other over a static connection. I should tell her about how I still can't look at the ocean without the grief welling up inside me, how I can't bring myself to text Chloe or Mikey anymore because it reminds me too much of the time before my life came crashing down. I should tell her she's the first new person I've said *I love you* to, about how I'm still waiting for the words to ruin her the way they ruined Mom.

I can sense the precarious cliff we stand on, toes curled around the ledge, on the precipice of falling. And Izzie's right here, hand outstretched. Maybe she's here to save me, pull me away from the edge. Or maybe she'll take my hand and we'll jump together.

I stare unseeing at the shoreline, waiting… for what, I can't say. Because I know how this will go. I will tear myself apart, pulling at this emotional thread until I unravel before her eyes just so I can hand her this little piece of myself. And she will take it in her hands, ready to shelter it from the wind and rain, but it's the rest of me that will be in ruin.

Opening my mouth, I turn to begin the process of unmaking myself before her, of shedding myself layer by layer so she can see the truth of the girl she loves. In her eyes is a desperate longing. She wants this. She wants me. If I tell her everything, it will make her feel closer, it will make her feel better.

But it will only make me feel weary and raw.

"It doesn't matter," I say, nearly choking on the words. "None of it matters."

"Steph, talk to me." She grabs for my hand.

I let her hold it. I won't let her have anything else.

"I don't want to talk about it, okay? Just… can we go home?" I sigh and add a tired, "Please?"

Izzie stands, helping me to my feet, and we march back to the van in silence. She finally lets go of my hand when she starts it up. The heat from the vents blows directly on my arms, warming my skin. Neither of us speaks as she sets up her GPS, but before she puts the van in reverse, she glances my way, tracing the curves of my face with her eyes. I wonder if she ever gets tired of it, looking at me.

Self-conscious, I find my reflection in the mirror on the back of the sun visor. I look exhausted. I look aged. I feel both. I flip the visor back up. The only thing worse than the judgment of her eyes on me is my own.

As we pull away from the beach, it's finally light enough to see the sign and I almost laugh.

Cape Disappointment State Park.

Twenty-Four

October turns into November and November turns into December with little fanfare. I barely notice until I see Izzie's put up Hanukkah decorations—a menorah on the kitchen table perched precariously on my Pride sign, a few wooden dreidels in a bowl beside it, a string of blue and white lights taped around the living room window.

"First night?" I ask, finally wandering out of the garage around noon.

Izzie nods and chews her lip.

"Looks nice." I cross to the fridge to look for something to munch on. It's been a while since I've bought groceries, and Bruce and Saturn both went home to visit their families for the holidays, so I'm surprised to find it totally stocked.

"I got easy stuff," Izzie says quietly. "Like yogurt and string cheese and carrot sticks—stuff you don't have to cook."

"Cool." I grab a string cheese and tear open the plastic. "Why?"

Her eyes roam over my pajamas and messy hair. There's no judgment there, but a blistering concern that makes me flinch a little.

"I'm going to drive up to Bellingham to visit my parents for a couple of days—do Hanukkah with them and stuff. But I'll be back in time for your birthday, okay?" She says it quietly, cautiously, like I'm a child about to throw a tantrum.

"Oh." My fingers pick at the cheese stick in my hand. "Right. Yeah. I'll be fine."

"Will you? You seem… not fine."

It hurts that she's noticed—almost as much as it would if she didn't.

I shrug and angle away from her, like I can somehow hide the parts of me that are already so invisible. "It's just the season. It's a bad time for me. You know that. I'll get over it."

"Depression isn't like a cold, Steph. You can't just wait it out with soup and tissues."

I flinch, the word 'depression' sinking deep into my skin. "You don't know that," I grunt. "You don't know anything about it."

Izzie audibly exhales. "I don't know what it's like to lose a parent, you're right. But… you do know you're not the first person to go through depression, right? You're not even the only person in this room!"

I feel like a fool. Of course I'm not the only one. "Maybe it'll go away by the time you get back," I say gruffly. "It always does eventually."

Izzie's hand floats up to hover just above my shoulder, fingertips grazing the corner of my sleep T-shirt. "Yeah… maybe…" She lets her hand fall. "Look, I know it's not the same for everyone and what worked for me might not work for you, but just… depression is a jerk. It kicked my ass a few years ago, and I was really lucky to have a therapist to help me through it."

"A therapist?"

"Yeah…" Izzie's face twists into a wince. "It's like… basically a requirement to get any kind of gender-affirming care as a trans person."

"Right… and it helped?" I'm making an absolute mess of this string cheese now, more like mush cheese as I squeeze it between my fingers.

"With the depression, yeah. It helped with some of the gender stuff, too. Mostly it was a hoop to jump through at the time, but I'm glad I had the option." She grabs a piece of paper from the counter and hands it to me. "I wrote down a website for you to check out. There's some info on here and the names of some therapists who are taking patients if you decide you want to try that."

"I'll just… I'll get it together. You'll see."

"Okay." Izzie frowns and puts the paper back on the counter. "But you're allowed to need help, Steph."

"No, it's fine. I can do this. It's my hill to climb."

"I get that, but… you know it isn't cheating, right? Asking for a map and getting the right shoes first doesn't mean you didn't climb the hill yourself." She crosses to me and cups my elbow in her palm. "All I'm saying is you don't have to do this alone."

But as Izzie packs her things and takes off in the van, all I feel is alone.

It takes me two days to finally take Izzie's advice. I've watched something like thirty hours of *Critical Role* on 2x speed and I'm officially past the acceptable level of stinky. I feel rotten, like someone who has eaten an entire pack of string cheese in one sitting. Which, of course, is exactly what I've done.

I pull out my phone and type a text to Jordie.

> Okay I get the Keyfish thing now

I hit backspace instead of sending it. I can't just text him like nothing happened, like I didn't totally flake on our friendship. I try again.

> Hey, so I fucked things up, huh?

And that's no good either.

> Could you just talk to me? I'm really fucking lonely

I throw my phone down on the couch and groan, pressing the heels of my hands to my eyes. Maybe Jordie's just the wrong person to text. I grab my phone again and pull up my text thread with Izzie.

> How are the parents?

Oh, you know, overwhelming

Dad tried to bake gluten free challah

> Is that as gross as it sounds?

Grosser.

How are you? Everything okay?

A sigh rips through me. I know if I'm honest it'll only make her feel guilty for leaving. She'll get back in her van and drive all the way home without stopping, and I won't even have to ask her. But there's a part of me that isn't sure being sad with her would be any better than being sad alone. Because it's not Izzie I miss; it's Mom.

> Rootin tootin

> Literally

> I've been experimenting with dairy

> Did you know that string cheese makes a great improvised spoon for yogurt?

Is this a cry for help?

I am an innovator!

Okay well innovate your way to a Tums
or something so you don't get sick

I put the phone down, pick it up, put it down, and then pick it up once more.

Izzie will be home in a couple days, and I can't still be wallowing like this by the time she does. I can shower and I can cook and I can put a smile on my face, but all that will just be a costume. Maybe she's right. Maybe I don't have to do this by myself.

I heave myself off the couch and find the note she left me on the counter. Scrawled in her loopy handwriting is a website, so I type it into my phone's browser. It's some health site with information about depression and therapists in the Seattle area. The text is a jarring shade of blue that makes me want to close the window immediately, but I keep scrolling.

A bold heading sticks out like a thorn.

Seasonal Affective Disorder.

I try the words on my tongue, sounding them out to see how they feel—familiar. I read on, wondering if what I have really counts. It's not like I've always been this way, so is it really seasonal affective disorder, or is it just trauma? My brain sort of trips and falls on that thought, like it's a rock in my shoe and I can't keep going until I deal with it.

But trauma isn't as simple as tipping your shoe upside down to see what falls out. It's the blister that won't heal, and the world is the shoe that will never quite fit, irritating the sore every time the seasons change. So maybe it doesn't really matter if it's trauma or not. I still feel like crap either way.

I leave the website and type the phrase into a Reddit search instead. I'm way more interested in other people's experiences than in a paragraph lifted from some medical textbook. I scroll through a couple of threads—some people talk about getting UV lamps or taking vitamin D supplements. Others say the only thing that helped was medication. Maybe this thing that knocks me out every fall isn't an immovable object. Maybe I can actually do something about it.

The second I think it, guilt climbs in my throat—hot and suffocating, like my body is rejecting the idea entirely. Because yeah, I could get a special lamp or a therapist or a prescription, and maybe I'll stop feeling so wretched. But if I stop feeling this, if I stop missing Mom, then isn't that just like another death?

I feel the sob rise in me, raw and ragged. It drags up my throat like sandpaper. I think about texting Izzie and asking her to come home. I think about texting Dad or Jordie or Lia. Hell, I even think about texting Chloe. It's been years, but she was *there* when the storm hit, so maybe she'll get it.

Before I can begin to make any conscious decision, a notification pops up in the Reddit app. It's a new message from Gabsurdity93, the user who's been steadily campaigning for a tour stop in their town. I tap the icon and open the message.

Gabsurdity93
Heya! Have you given any more thought to coming to Haven Springs?

Steph-Right-Up
Can't say that I have

Steph-Right-Up
Isn't it just a little mining town? Would anyone even show up?

Gabsurdity93
Absolutely! Haven Springs might be small, but we're mighty!

Gabsurdity93
And loud!

Gabsurdity93
And we love Drugstore Makeup!

I sink down into a chair at the kitchen table. I want to be able to tell this person yes, I want to be able to make someone happy today, even if it's just a random stranger in a random town.

Gabsurdity93
I'm Gabe, by the way

Steph-Right-Up
Steph. But I guess you knew that already

Gabsurdity93
Nice to meet you, Steph

Steph-Right-Up
So what's the deal, Gabe? Why so into getting us to play?

Steph-Right-Up
You some kind of superfan or something?

Gabsurdity93
I mean, sure. I'm a fan!

Gabsurdity93
But really I just love music

Gabsurdity93
We don't get a lot of live music out here and I guess I thought it would be neat

Steph-Right-Up
Neat?

Gabsurdity93
Hah. Yeah, guess I sound like an old fogey. But I don't know. My sister and I used to have the best time listening to records together, and I think it would be cool to make that kind of moment for this town I love

Steph-Right-Up
That's actually very sweet

Gabsurdity93
So you'll do it?

I lean back and stare at the ceiling as I listen to the patter of rain against the roof, against the windows, against the concrete outside. Eventually, I look back at my phone and the empty message bar, and I type.

Steph-Right-Up
Hey Gabe

Steph-Right-Up
Is it raining right now in Haven Springs?

Gabsurdity93
Nope

Gabsurdity93
Why?

Steph-Right-Up
Just think I could use some clear skies

Gabsurdity93
Does that mean what I think it means?

Steph-Right-Up
Doesn't mean anything

Steph-Right-Up
Yet

And I know I have to talk it over with Izzie, convince her we should do it, but me? I've already made up my mind.

Winter

Twenty-Five

2017 comes to an end, not with a bang, but with a frenzy of last-minute planning. Our tour is a little over a month away, and there's so much more to do than I expected. It's a good thing, really. It keeps me too occupied to focus on the weather. I try vitamin D and the lamp thing, and I get on a waiting list for a therapist, but none of that helps me nearly as much as having the tour to look forward to.

Izzie and I finish setting up the van and, after a couple of tries, figure out how to fit everything without blocking visibility. There's a decent chance of decapitation by cymbal if we crash, but that's just a risk we'll have to take.

I design flyers and T-shirts we can sell at each gig with a giant pair of red-and-white painted lips and our band name in big letters against a black background. They end up looking pretty rad. I set aside a couple for Dad and Renee. They continue to be our least likely but somehow biggest supporters.

I glance down at the box of neatly folded T-shirts, thinking about all the fans we'll meet who will go home with a sweet new shirt and some memories. But all those strangers wearing our merch and loving our songs pales in comparison to the image that lights behind my eyes—Jordie, Ollie, Lia… all standing in the front row, hands raised toward the stage, rocking out along with us. I wonder if they'll even come to our kickoff gig on February 13th.

Then I decide to stop wondering. I rifle through the T-shirts and grab a medium for Jordie and an extra large for Ollie. It's not exactly an olive branch, but it's what I've got.

It doesn't take long to get to Jordie's apartment, which is a pity because I could use more time to sort through what I'm going to say. I pause outside before deciding to do another lap around the block and really get my thoughts in order. So I turn around and—*wham!*—smack directly into the one and only Jordie Abdullah.

"Okay, well, *ow*," he says, rubbing his shoulder where it hit my jaw. "Steph?"

"Hey, hi." I clutch the shirts to my chest and avert my eyes. "Fancy, uh, seeing you here?"

"This is my apartment, Steph."

"So it is."

Jordie furrows his brow and eyes me with a searching gaze. "Did you... want to come up? Or just passing by?"

I nod. "Yeah. If you'll have me."

"You weirdo." Jordie slings an arm around my shoulder and drags me toward the door.

After we climb the three flights of stairs to his apartment, he takes off his shoes and makes for the kitchen, leaving me alone in the living room. I've been here what feels like a hundred times, and it wasn't that long ago that it felt like a second home. Now, I feel like a trespasser, like I don't really deserve to feel comfortable in a space that isn't mine.

"So, what's up, Steph?" Jordie plops a bowl of chips between us—barbecue, his favorite flavor—and settles down on the floor.

He has a perfectly good couch, but Jordie's always been a floor sitter. Maybe it's because he's usually hosting a handful of people and all the couch spots are taken up, so it's become a habit, but I think he just likes to stretch out his legs.

"I owe you a massive apology," I say in a rush as I join him on the throw rug.

Jordie shrugs. "I don't know about *massive*, but go on."

"I totally ghosted on our friendship, and I don't really have a good reason. I wasn't even busy—just sad and a little fucked up." As far as apologies go, this isn't one for the books and I know it. "I should've told you what was going on and trusted our friendship. I really care about you, and I know you care, well, at least you *did* care about me, and I should have just been honest, I guess."

"Okay, well first of all, you're not like… obliged to tell me stuff. You know that, right? Like our friendship doesn't hinge on your willingness to tell me every little thing about your life." He takes a chip and turns it over in his hands, spreading barbecue dust across his fingers. "But you *can* tell me stuff. If something's going on with you, I want to know—but not in a weird pressure-y way."

"So you're… *not* mad at me?"

"I mean I'm not *not* mad. It sucks that you bailed." He leans back and tips his head against the sofa cushion. "It felt like you ditched me for your girlfriend, basically."

I want to argue with him, tell him that's not how it is. Izzie's not just my girlfriend, she's also my bandmate and my roommate and… well, that's exactly how it is, I guess.

"Sometimes it feels like as an ace person I'm like a waypoint for my friends, a rest stop to hang out in until they find their person. It's like I'm a benchwarmer until you find someone better. I know that's not how you meant it to feel, but that's just how it goes for me. All through college I was just that friend people had until they found a partner, and then I'd get left behind."

"Oh man. That sucks, and you're right, that's not how I meant to make you feel, but that doesn't really fix it."

Jordie shrugs. "You're one of my best friends, Steph, and I like having you in my life. Just 'cause you have Izzie and I have Ollie doesn't mean we aren't still us, you know? And, yeah, I've got other friends, but you're one of a kind."

"Aw, wholesome!" I nudge his arm with mine.

He turns and the smile on his face looks genuine. "I guess

I'm not really *mad* and more just kind of hurt. Like… maybe you stopped wanting me around."

My chest tightens and I bring my knees up closer to my body so I can rest my chin in the divot between them. "More like the opposite."

"How so?"

I knew I'd have to say it eventually, but I just thought when I did it would feel… scarier. And maybe it's because it's Jordie, not Izzie, who's asking. Yeah, he's known me for years, but for some reason it just feels like less pressure, probably because I don't live with him. He's removed from the situation in a way that Izzie can't be.

"Have you heard of seasonal affective disorder?"

"SAD? Yeah, my cousin Jamal has that—he moved to California as soon as he turned eighteen so he wouldn't have to deal with it."

And suddenly I feel so much lighter. There's a person like me, a person with a name, a person Jordie knows. "Okay yeah, so I get in a funk every fall and whether or not it's true, I start to feel like I'm a bummer to be around. Sometimes I push through it and sometimes… well, you get the idea."

"Oof, okay."

"Yeah. I still don't really know what to do about it—or how much of it is actually SAD and how much of it is just…" I trail off, unable to give voice to all my baggage. It still feels so heavy, so overwhelming to unpack.

"I get it." Jordie lets his knee knock against mine. "Whatever it is, you know you're never a bummer to me, right?"

"Even when I'm grumpy?"

"Even when you're grumpy."

"Even if I suck at talking about my feelings?"

"Even then."

"Even if I… eat this whole bowl of chips and don't leave you any?"

Jordie gasps. "Diabolical!"

I stretch my legs beneath the coffee table and pick up the T-shirts sitting beside me. "I don't know if you and Ollie are available but… Izzie and I are kicking off our tour with a Seattle show. It would be neat if you could come."

"Oh my god, Steph! Did you design these?" He holds one up against his chest and makes a Blue Steel model face. "How do I look?"

"Like you've got chip on your face."

He wipes his mouth, getting even more chip dust on his chin, and says, "Want to hang out for a while? *Critical Role* started their new campaign last week and this one's got lesbians!"

"Say no more. I am *in*!"

Jordie grabs his laptop. I settle in beside him for an afternoon of adventure, and finally my smile feels like it fits.

There's one more apology I need to make, so on my way home I dip into a grocery store and grab a bouquet of pink and yellow flowers and a bottle of wine. Izzie spent her birthday with her parents, so we didn't really do anything. I don't think she expected much, since we've been spending almost every waking hour prepping for the tour, but that will hopefully make this an extra surprise.

When I get home, the sun has already set, and Izzie is curled up on the couch with a copy of *Milk and Honey* by Rupi Kaur propped open on her chest. Her eyes are closed and the lightest of snores blows her bangs up and out every few seconds. As I stand in the doorway, I'm struck by how very Izzie this picture is. It almost breaks my heart to ruin it.

"Hey, Iz." I sink onto the couch and sweep her feet up into my lap.

She doesn't wake up immediately, just nuzzles deeper into the couch cushions, so I climb up next to her and brush the flowers beneath her nose. She lets out a little contented sigh, and it's so cute I just want to stay in this moment right here for as long as we can—before I can fuck it up with feelings.

Unfortunately, I don't have dominion over time, and Izzie's eyes flutter open. "Hey," she says groggily, covering her mouth as she yawns. "Guess I took a nap."

"You deserve it!" I put the flowers down on the coffee table and turn to face her. "You deserve a lot of things."

She shifts up to a sitting position and fixes me with a strange look. Her eyes are shadowed, like a wall is going up behind her gaze.

"Like… an apology?" I say it quietly, my inflection going up at the end like it's a question. And maybe it is. I wonder if Izzie even wants an apology or if the tension is all that's keeping our relationship standing. "If you're… okay with that, I mean. I know things have been *off* lately, and I just… I want this tour to be fun. I want us to have fun again."

Izzie lets out a long exhale, her entire body seeming to melt with it. "Oh my god, Steph. I thought for a second you were like… breaking up with me or something."

"Breaking up with you?" I recoil at the thought. "What? Why would I…" I hold up my peace offering. "What kind of person would dump someone with flowers and wine?"

"You are exactly the kind of person who would do that. Like… Here's some emotional devastation, but you can get drunk on Two Buck Chuck afterward."

"Excuse me, this bottle cost me nine whole dollars."

"Okay, so not exactly bottom shelf." She swings her feet down to the floor and pads over to the kitchen to retrieve the bottle opener and a couple of glasses. "This tour *is* going to be fun, Steph."

I swallow, staring down at my hands and wishing I was the one who'd gotten up for the glasses, if only so I'd have something to do other than sit here. "How do you know?"

"How do I know?" Izzie reappears in the archway between living room and kitchen and surveys me from across the room. "Because it's our tour! Because we've been working toward this for months and, honestly, if it's not fun, then I significantly fucked up."

"Right," I mutter. "Of course."

She crosses over to the couch and sets the glasses down with a clink. "I just think this is an opportunity for us to really reset. I know that the coast trip was a bad idea, but I do think a change of pace will help us get out of the rut we're in. New towns, new people, kind of... refresh our passion. Also, you'll be there with me. And no matter what, everything is always better with you."

My insides do a somersault and I am overwhelmed by the need to hold her in my arms right this second, so I launch myself across the couch and throw myself around her.

"Steph!" She shrieks my name as I bury my nose in her hair.

I breathe her in, lips finding the apex of her jaw and throat. She smells like apples and vanilla. I make my way across her collarbone toward her sternum, pressing a kiss to her skin for each tour stop on our trip.

"Seattle, Salem, Sacramento," I say, and she tips her head back in a laugh. "Reno, Salt Lake, Haven Springs, Denver, Omaha, then back home." I circle up and rest my lips against hers, a slow, lazy kiss.

But Izzie pulls back, turning her face so my nose bumps against her cheek.

"What was that?" she asks.

"What... is my breath bad or something?" I breathe into my palm and try to sniff. "I ate a ton of barbecue chips at Jordie's."

"No—your breath is fine, although, yeah, barbecuey. I mean what was that extra city? Haven something?"

I sit back on my heels. "Haven Springs?"

"Yeah. That's not in the lineup. I thought we were going straight from Salt Lake to Denver?"

"Oh, uh, yeah. I was thinking of adding it," I say, averting my eyes. "We've got a pretty dedicated fan base there, actually, and since we have like almost two weeks between Salt Lake and Denver, I figured it wouldn't hurt to slot in another show."

"Huh. I guess that makes sense." Izzie pulls her hair back and away from her face, then lets it all drop again, fluffy and soft. "Wish you'd told me about it."

"Sorry, I… thought I had." The lie slips from my lips as easily as a kiss.

"It's just… I think we should stick to the big cities. You know, the places that will really draw a crowd."

I shrug, still keeping my eyes glued to the floor. "Oh. Yeah. Okay."

I don't have it in me to fight this fight. I know Izzie's in this for the exposure, for the prestige, for the industry people we'll meet along the way. And me? I'm in it for Izzie.

But I thought, maybe, I could have this one little thing that was just for me. This one guy, Gabe, who likes his town so much, he practically begged us to go there so they can experience our music. It feels like a weird thing me and Chloe might have done when we were kids back in Arcadia Bay. The kind of thing that would have meant a lot to us.

"It's probably too late to cancel," I say, hoping she won't call my bluff. I haven't even confirmed the gig yet.

"Well, maybe it'll be fun anyway. We can try out some of our more experimental stuff on them—maybe I'll even write a new song while we're on tour!"

"Yeah?" I ask, hope a bubble in my throat. It's been months since Izzie's written anything new, and it occurs to me that maybe my moods are impacting her, too. That maybe the trip to the coast wasn't really about cheering me up, but cheering *her* up. Guilt piles up in my stomach, hot and angry, but before I can do anything with it, Izzie leans into me, fingers curling around the fabric of my flannel as she tugs me closer.

I come crashing down toward her and, as she rolls me over to flip our positions, my foot snags on the coffee table, sending it and everything on it toppling to the ground.

"Ah!" Izzie lunges forward, but it's too late. The sound of glass breaking wrecks the moment as the wine glasses shatter against the ground. "Fuck!"

I sit up, snaking my arm around Izzie's waist. "Oops."

"Guess we'll have to drink our wine out of mugs."

"Or straight from the bottle."

"Steph!" She nudges me, but her smile is wide and bright.

It's a welcome sight. Between the two of us, there hasn't been much in the way of smiling lately, and I can't help but lean forward to kiss it.

When Izzie pulls back, she slowly traces the outline of my face, tucking a few strands of hair behind my ear. "Hey, I love you," she says.

And when I say it back, the words are honest in a way that wrecks me just a little, because I'm beginning to worry that maybe love just isn't enough.

Twenty-Six

In the hours before our Seattle kickoff gig, I finally drag my suitcase out from storage. It's dusty and full of stuff I barely recognize: a box of mismatched dice, a T-shirt with a zombie on the front and the phrase 'When it brains it pours,' and a loose-knit blue beanie.

"You almost ready?" Izzie calls out to me in the garage.

"Yeah, give me a minute."

"Need help?"

"Nah, I got it." I frantically pull pants and jackets from the dresser to haphazardly shove into the purple suitcase.

"Okay, just hurry up! I want to get the van packed."

I hear the click of the garage door and exhale into the wall. It took Izzie hours to decide which outfits to bring on tour. She showed me every combination, trying to narrow things down to the best possible looks for the stage. And I loved every second of her twirling around the living room, her energy shifting slightly depending on how comfortable she was in the clothes. Everything about this process has been meticulous for her, from our set lists to our driving schedule to her wardrobe.

"Come on!" Izzie grabs my suitcase from me before it's zipped all the way closed and throws it in the back of the van along with hers. "Phew! That's it!"

"That's it," I echo. It's weird—I thought I would feel more energized and nervous, but I just feel normal. Like this is any other day and not the start of something great.

Izzie bumps my shoulder with hers. "We're doing the thing, Steph. We are *doing the thing*."

Her smile is infectious, bright and blistering. I can't help but smile back. "Yeah. We are."

She squeezes my hand and takes the driver's side. As we pull away from the house that we share, I can't help but hope we're not just leaving the bed and the couch and the kitchen table behind, but also the energy that's plagued us for the past few months.

I've never been a superstitious type, but I hold my breath over every bridge and through every tunnel. It feels like the kind of day where a little extra luck would go a long way. Tonight sets the tone for the next month, and I really need for it to go well.

When we pull up to the Dotted Quarter, I take a deep breath and exhale all the tension I'm holding. There's no point in carrying it with me. I jump down from the van and march around the back to where Izzie's unloading our instruments.

I snake my arms around her waist and lean in from behind to kiss her cheek.

"Want to get a photo with our poster?" I ask, pointing at the front doors where a Drugstore Makeup flyer is proudly posted in the window.

Izzie glances down at her clothes—a baggy sweatshirt and plaid pajama pants. "Maybe after we get ready?"

"Oh, come on." I grab her hand between both of mine and pull her forward.

"Steph! It'll look so much better on social media if we do it later." She gestures to her clean face. "Plus, isn't it weird—we're called Drugstore Makeup, not Makeup Remover."

"Okay, putting aside that Makeup Remover would be a terrible band name, who says this has to be for social media?" I take out my phone and set it up on the hood of the van so it's balancing. "This is just for us."

"Okay, okay!" Izzie ambles over to the front door and poses, fingers pointing up at the sign and a look of excited awe on her face.

I set the timer and join her, trying to let the moment really sink in. We're going on tour! Me and Izzie! People are going to hear our songs, maybe even connect to them in really powerful ways. And really, is there anything better than playing for people who love your music?

The light blinks and Izzie breaks her pose, striding back over to the van. "Come help me with the drums," she calls over her shoulder.

"Sure." I cross over to the van and snatch up my phone. The photo is clear and crisp—Izzie and I stand before the poster, smiling and pointing at this accomplishment between us. It's a happy moment. It should look like one, too. But Izzie's smile is forced, her posture uncomfortable, her eyes not quite meeting the lens of the camera. If I didn't know better, I'd wonder if we were strangers.

By showtime, the Dotted Quarter is packed to the brim. Everyone we know is there, it seems. My chest unclenches painfully when Jordie and Ollie walk through the doors an hour early, wearing the T-shirts I brought them, and The High Seas show up with a gaggle of friends from the Seattle music scene. I even spot Bruce chatting with Jerry in the corner.

The big surprise of the night is Izzie's parents. They arrive just in time to wish us luck before we take the stage, swooping in to kiss Izzie's cheeks like the world's most aggressive sandwich.

Ben and Donna Margolis are the epitome of cheer, smiley and supportive well beyond the call of duty. Izzie's mom is short with dark curly hair and kind brown eyes just like Izzie's, while her dad is a string bean of a man with round spectacles balanced on large ears. I am immediately consumed by warmth when their attention falls on me.

"You must be Steph!" Her mom pulls me into a hug, then holds me at arm's length. "Oh, aren't you adorable!"

"Let her breathe, Donna." Izzie's dad leans over his wife's shoulder and surveys me with sincere curiosity. "We've heard a lot about you—our Izzie's steady rhythm section."

"That's me!" I point to my chest with both thumbs.

If I'd known I'd be meeting the parents tonight I might have… I don't know, practiced looking like a responsible adult person they can feel confident about trusting with their daughter. But maybe it's better that they're getting me as I am, nervous and uncertain, dressed in a black jean jacket with alternating leather and lace chokers around my neck that Izzie picked out for me.

"We're just so proud of you," Donna says, stroking Izzie's hair.

"Mom!" She swats her away and grabs her guitar. "We have to go on in a minute."

"Okay, okay!" Her mom holds up her hands in surrender. "Let me just get one photo."

Izzie's dad places a hand on her mom's arm, but she shakes him off.

"Oh, leave it, Ben. Let me have this, at least."

Izzie groans, but beckons me over to pose. She slings her arm around my waist and says cheese when prompted. I do my best to match her energy, but by the time I've positioned the smile on my face, it's over and Izzie is pulling away toward the stage door.

I turn to follow, but my attention is pulled back by a light tapping on my shoulder. I turn to see Izzie's dad standing behind me, shoulders rounded, hands in his pockets.

"Uh, hi," I say, awkward as can be.

Luckily, Izzie's dad doesn't seem to notice, pretty damn awkward himself. He glances down at his shoes, then up at my face, and says, "Thanks, Steph."

I furrow my brow. "For what?"

"For being what she needs." His lips thin and nearly disappear into a smile. "It means a lot to see her so happy."

I open my mouth—*is* Izzie happy? Am I? Happiness feels like this thing we keep narrowly missing, like an exit on the freeway even though we're following all the signs.

Luckily, Izzie's mom saves me the trouble by saying with a gasp, "Aw, how sweet!"

She holds up her phone with the picture she just took, and I peer at the image. The difference is night and day, compared with the one I took this morning. Izzie looks radiant. She practically glows with energy and exuberance, her smile so bright it could light the whole stage. Beside her, I look small and uncertain, like an old accessory that doesn't quite match her outfit.

"Come on, Steph!" Izzie tugs me toward the door and we spill out onto the stage to the sound of our names over the speakers.

The lights hit my eyes as I find my way over to the drum set, squinting and feeling for the seat. But even though I can't see the audience, I can see something else.

Two pictures. Two girls. Two lives.

And it dawns on me that maybe there's a reason we don't look like we belong in each other's.

Twenty-Seven

It's a breezy four-hour drive from Seattle to Salem. Izzie seems content to drive the whole way. She turns on the radio, since the van was built sometime between the era of tape decks and aux ports, and flips channels until we finally find something gay to listen to. The new Hayley Kiyoko song blares from the speakers, and we sing along to 'Curious' as loud as we can. As far as road trips go, I can't really ask for much more.

Green landscapes zoom across my passenger window. Forests and fields and the occasional train. It's peaceful, in a way, but as we cross the border between Washington and Oregon, I put my hand on Izzie's knee and squeeze.

"Hungry?" I ask.

She jams her thumb over her shoulder and says, "Snacks in the back."

"Right... do you want to stop, though?"

"I'm good!" Her voice is cheerful and unbothered, eyes trained on the road.

"Okay, but Portland could be fun, and we don't have to be at the venue 'til evening." I glance at her, trying to read her face, but it's blank. "Come on, bet we'll see something weird!"

Izzie worries her lip and checks the clock. "I guess—but only for a little bit, okay? I don't want to hit traffic."

I let my eyes drift to the clock as well—12:05. I resist the urge to tease her. There's no way we'll hit traffic this early.

Whipping out my phone, I pull up my maps app. "Get ready for a Portland adventure!"

I may not be an Oregonian anymore, but I still feel like an ambassador, taking Izzie around to all the Portland sights. We only have a couple hours before we need to be back on the road, so I narrow down to the essentials.

First on the agenda is a trip to Voodoo Doughnut. I went there once with Chloe after Portland Pride, and we laughed until we cried over the doughnut names, ranging from clever to crude. On the drive back, we invented our own flavors. Mine was vanilla glaze dipped in rainbow nerds, and Chloe's creation was an everything doughnut—"You know, like everything bagel, but sweet."

I approach the bubblegum-pink building with a skip in my step, holding open the door for Izzie. "After you, milady," I say with a short bow.

I get the Bacon Maple Bar and Izzie gets the Grape Ape at the recommendation of the guy behind the counter. We hold hands as we lean against the van, eating our doughnuts.

"So?" I ask after she's taken a few bites.

"Surprisingly not cough-syrupy." She inspects her doughnut with all the care of a lab technician. "It shouldn't work, but it does. I get the hype."

"Hah!" I pump my fist triumphantly. "Score one for Steph!"

Izzie squeezes my hand, then goes to open the driver's-side door. "Okay, back to the road?"

"Absolutely not!" I say through a mouthful of doughnut. "We've barely just begun!"

I direct her over the Burnside Bridge to Powell's, and I know I've hit a home run when her jaw drops open as we enter. As far as bookstores go, this one's pretty much the holy grail. Taking up a full city block, Powell's is full of tomes from floor to ceiling. They don't call it the 'City of Books' for nothing.

We lose ourselves among the shelves. Izzie peruses poetry while I familiarize myself with the slope of her neck and the muscle that pops from beneath her racer-back tank top every time she reaches for a higher shelf. I plant my hands on her waist and cozy up behind her to watch her absorb the world around her.

An hour later, my arms are full of books, and Izzie is all smiles.

"You realize we have to fit these in the van, right?" I ask.

"It'll be fine!" Izzie waves me off as she pays the cashier.

"Oh it will, will it? Where are you going to put them? Inside the bass drum?"

"No, I already put my sweaters in there."

"Oh my god, I was kidding, but okay."

In the end, we manage to cram them in the glove compartment and wedged between Izzie's amp and her suitcase before we get back on the freeway and drive south.

When I check my phone, I've got a text from Jordie.

> How's the tour, rock star?

> Stopped in Portland

> Izzie bought us a portable library at Powell's

> Cute!!

> Not cute!! There's barely room to think in here!

"Well, shit." Izzie slumps back against the seat as the car slows. "So much for beating the traffic."

I look up from my phone to see three lanes of cars stopped ahead. There are curves upon curves of them, so it's hard to see what's caused a traffic jam at two in the afternoon. I navigate over to Maps. There's a red line tracing the freeway for… well… miles. "Looks like it's gonna be a while."

Izzie slams her palms against the steering wheel and her jaw tightens. "I knew we shouldn't have stopped. Total waste of time."

I stiffen. "Waste of time? I had to practically drag you out of Powell's."

"Whatever. It doesn't matter." She exhales hard. "We're probably going to be late now, thanks to your side trip."

"Okay, you know what? No." I turn to face her, seat belt painfully digging into my throat. "You were having a good time. You liked the doughnut. You liked the bookstore. You don't get to blame me for something neither of us could have seen coming."

"I would've just kept driving if it was up to me. We stopped *for you*."

"Wow, okay." I grit my teeth as I stare down at the red outline of the Terwilliger curves on my phone. My stomach churns, an angry sea, and I'm reminded of another ill-fated road trip in recent history.

Was this how Izzie felt when she took me to the coast, only for me to pop like a blister? She was trying to do something nice, just like I'm trying to do today. But no amount of trying can prevent failing, I guess. Dad would absolutely quote Yoda to me in this moment and it would be supremely unhelpful, but there's another dad-tactic I can use.

With a few swipes on my phone, I pull up an alternate route.

"Take this exit," I say with as much authority as I can muster. "We'll take the back roads." Maybe I did the wrong thing today, and maybe I didn't, but either way, I can still fix it.

Izzie doesn't argue, just follows my directions as I navigate us over to highway 99 instead. We get stuck behind a tractor going thirty miles an hour for a long stretch, but we still make it to Salem with plenty of time to spare.

When we finally climb out of the van, Izzie groans and stretches her muscles, but otherwise doesn't speak to me as we unload our instruments. We dress in silence, but minutes before we're set to go on, Izzie crosses over to me with a red makeup pencil in hand.

"Here," she says, and leans over me to draw a heart on my cheek. "Let's rock, okay?"

A tingle starts in my belly and spreads warmth up to my chest as I look at the little red heart on my skin in the mirror. It's like an apology, like forgiveness. Maybe marking me like this is Izzie's way of saying we'll be okay.

Or maybe, as I realize when we walk out onstage to see a plethora of pink and red streamers, it's just because it's Valentine's Day.

Twenty-Eight

It takes us two days to get to Sacramento, and when we do, I couldn't be more thrilled to get out of the van and be somewhere Izzie isn't. The van is littered with water bottles and chip bags, and it's beginning to smell distinctly road-trippy. After a night spent in a campground near Ashland, sleeping back-to-back in the van and barely communicating beyond directions, I'm ready for a change of scenery *and* company.

Gran meets us in the driveway, her white puffball hair like a beacon as she waves us toward the front door of their two-story townhouse. It's painted bright turquoise—despite protests from the homeowners' association, as she'll tell anyone who asks—with a rainbow progress flag posted above the door next to an American flag of the same size.

"Oh, Steph, sweetie!" She scoops me into her arms and hugs me tight. "It's been too long."

She's not wrong. In the years between my early childhood spent in Sacramento and now, she's changed almost as much as I have. Her skin is looser, her wrinkles are deeper, but so is her smile. Suddenly it hits me that I haven't seen her since Mom's funeral, and even then I was too emotionally wrung out to really pay attention to anything other than my grief. It wasn't even her own flesh and blood—just her ex-daughter-in-law—but still, she came and sought me out and let me cry into her blouse.

"It's black—no one will notice any tearstains," she'd said.

"That's the trick to surviving what life throws at you, you know. Sensible clothing, especially shoes."

I smile at the memory, at how resolutely I have adopted her advice into my life. I squeeze her to my chest and whisper, "I have to pee so badly!"

Gran barks a laugh and points to the door. "You know where to go!"

I take off at a half-skip-half-run, chased by the sound of Izzie introducing herself to Gran. I know I should facilitate that sort of thing, but… they're both adults. They can handle a little social awkwardness to save my poor unattended bladder.

By the time I return, snaking my way through Gran's house by memory, I find them in the living room sipping Arnold Palmers.

"Steph! Join us." Gran pats the magenta and yellow sofa next to her.

I cross the room, decorated in brilliant gem tones, all screaming together in the world's most intense visual harmony, and accept the offered glass with little ice cubes shaped like skulls floating in the liquid. Gran's always had eccentric taste, and I see that hasn't ebbed at all in the years since Grandpa died. If anything, she's become more flamboyant. I spot a new addition to her decor—a taxidermy weasel by the fireplace to which she has affixed a sparkly unicorn horn.

"Izzie was just telling me about your tour! How *exciting*! This is a much bigger deal than you led me to believe, young lady." She waggles her finger at me.

I raise my eyebrows at Izzie, who catches my gaze above her drink. "Well, we *are* rock stars, I guess."

"I was just explaining that there are a couple of talent scouts coming to our Sac and Reno gigs," Izzie says. "You remember, I told you about them."

I definitely don't remember, but that doesn't mean I shouldn't, so I just shrug. "Hopefully they'll like us."

"Oh, what happens if they do?" Gran turns to face Izzie,

elbows propped on her knees to form a shelf for her chin. "Tell me everything!"

A smile inches across Izzie's face as she describes the kind of success we could find along the road, the big break that might be awaiting us at any one of the shows we'll play—record deals, endorsements, the connections we'll make. She lights up as she speaks, and I want to share her hope, but the longer she goes on, the more I wither and dim.

Eventually, I make my escape to begin unpacking our essentials from the van. It's good to move my legs, to use my muscles for something other than bracing for the next fight we'll have. I text Jordie, just so I can tell *someone* how I'm feeling.

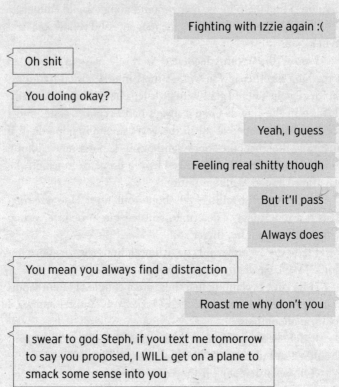

> Fighting with Izzie again :(

Oh shit

You doing okay?

> Yeah, I guess

> Feeling real shitty though

> But it'll pass

> Always does

You mean you always find a distraction

> Roast me why don't you

I swear to god Steph, if you text me tomorrow to say you proposed, I WILL get on a plane to smack some sense into you

Ow

Too roasty toasty

I know Jordie's joking, but the familiar prickling of his accusation rises to the surface. This pattern that Izzie and I have slipped into—where we fight and make up, then fight and make up, without ever actually resolving anything—is precarious at best. I keep hoping it will get better, keep hoping we'll find a way to fix whatever's broken. I know I'm trying. I know she's trying. But for some reason, it doesn't feel like we're really trying *together*, and maybe that's it—that's what's broken.

Before I can get too deep in my feelings, Gran reappears on the doorstep, barefoot and showing off a tarnished toe ring. "Izzie's gone upstairs to take a little nap. Poor thing—you really should offer to drive part of the way."

I sigh and sink down onto the lawn—a wild patch of clover next to her neighbor's perfectly manicured grass. "She won't let me, Gran. Izzie likes to be behind the wheel."

"Ah, I see." Gran joins me, settling beside a statue of a gnome in a strawberry hat. She pats the gnome on the head as if in greeting, then says, "Would you say she's… driven?"

The joke comes out of nowhere and I bark a laugh. "Gran!"

"Well, someone had to say it, and Tobias isn't around anymore."

Grandpa's name spills so effortlessly from her lips, and my shoulders tense a little.

"It's okay," she says. "He's been gone a long time."

Longer than Mom is what she doesn't say. But still, not by that much. I feel so small beside her, this woman who can laugh and joke in the face of loss. And maybe we're actually similar that way, because that's what I do most of the time. Optimism is how I've made it as far as I have. But sometimes it feels real and sometimes it feels more like a mask.

"How do you do it?" I ask after a short pause. "How do you carry on after?"

"Practice, sweetie. It's all practice." She gives me a smile so bright I almost miss the sadness layered underneath. "When your grandpa died, I was a lot younger than I thought I'd be. A bit like you with your mom. It's hard to lose people before we're ready, and we're rarely ever *ready*. But it gets easier with time."

I nod, a tightness rising in my throat. "Don't you worry about… losing their memory? Like if you let go of grief, you'll let go of them too?"

"No! Not at all!" Gran reaches for my hand and lays it palm up between both of hers, like a little hand sandwich. "Learning how to love someone who's gone is like learning how to ride a bike. It's all a balancing act, and if you try to hop on and pedal right after, you'll wipe out on the pavement. Grief is kind of like training wheels. At first, you can't even think about those you've lost without the grief. You need it, because you have to process the loss. But eventually, you'll be able to think about them and miss them and honor them without it."

"Yeah?" I choke out the word, unable to reach for more with my voice.

"Yeah." She nods. "Of course, it helps to have an absolutely sterling sense of humor like I do."

"Of course." A chuckle ripples through my chest painfully. "You ever tried stand-up?"

"Please, with my bad hip? More like sit-down." She lets go of my hand and instead wraps an arm around my shoulder. "It also helps to have people you love around you."

I wince. "Wish we lived closer sometimes."

"Oh, I don't mean to make you feel guilty. Really, I've got people here."

"You sure? I mean, you have more than just like bridge club or whatever, right?"

"Bridge club? What do you take me for?" Gran fixes me

with a dead-eyed stare. "Me and the girls are far more interesting than that—Lois organized a ballroom dancing night for us last week, and every Tuesday we get together to call our elected representatives about whatever new poppycock that idiot-in-chief is saying."

"Gran!" I lean back and survey her through new eyes.

"What, you thought I wasn't *cool*?"

I have to laugh at that. "No way. With lawn decor like this, how could you be anything but?" I point to a couple of plastic flamingos dressed in handmade cowboy hats and fringed vests.

"That's right!" She jabs a thumb into her chest. "We're going to be the most punk-rock grannies at your show!"

I don't point out that she and her friends will probably be the *only* grannies there. Instead, I lean my head on her shoulder and take a deep breath, letting her energy fill my lungs.

"I'm glad you've got her," Gran says.

It takes me a minute to realize who she means. "Who, Izzie?"

"She's a lovely girl… Focused, lots of energy and passion." Gran nods as though agreeing with herself. "Yes, you found a good one. I like her." She holds out her hands and beckons me. "Now, help an old lady get back up. My back's not what it used to be."

I scramble to my feet and help her stand. It's not lost on me that she was there for me when I was just a toddle-thing, probably helping me back up time and time again. She's not Mom, but she's family, and it's nice that she likes Izzie.

As we make our way inside, Dad's words echo in my head. *It's a lot more important that you like her.* And I don't know, maybe it's just exhaustion from the road trip or fatigue from our fight, but while I'm pretty sure I love Izzie, I'm not sure if I like her anymore, and that would be a lot easier to swallow if Gran didn't either.

*

We say goodbye to Gran and her quirky California home in the early morning after our show at the Junkyard Music Hall. I barely have time to wipe the smudged eyeliner from my face before Izzie's handing me a power bar and an iced coffee for the road.

It was a good show. I can tell because Izzie is all smiles as we pull out of the driveway, despite the lack of sleep. She chatters about some guy named Gray who, I gather, is a talent agent or something. It's the happiest I've seen her in a while, and so I resolve to be happy, too.

It's easier said than done, though, as our show in Reno is packed to the brim with strangers. It's not the first time we've played for a crowd of people we don't know, but it's disorienting to be onstage with no face in the audience to ground me. My eyes keep flickering to Izzie, who never once catches my gaze.

She stands, centered onstage, under purple and white lights like some kind of punk fairy princess in a metallic blue dress. I'm reminded so strongly of the first time I saw her play—her overpowering stage presence that entranced me so effortlessly. Back then, I was just some girl in the crowd. Now, I'm onstage behind her, laying down a rhythm for her melody. But somehow, this is the most I've ever felt like a spectator.

It feels like only minutes pass between leaving the stage at Sam's Saloon in Reno to climbing up behind the drums again at Atomic Decay in Salt Lake City. It's the longest drive we've had yet, but I can't really remember much of it except flashes of landscape and billboards. Izzie's voice blends into the vibration of the van against pavement as she talks herself in circles about the order of songs in our set and whether we should open or end with 'Riot Pride' at the next stop.

I focus on the music instead, looping through our songs in my head as we drive. I want to play a good show for all the people who will come out to see us. I want to play a good show for *Izzie*, the one constant whose opinion I really care about.

We take the stage to an uproar of applause that never seems to cease throughout our set. I see rainbow flags everywhere, like it's Pride all over again. The energy of the crowd is hypnotic as Izzie tells jokes and shares anecdotes about each song. I chime in like we practiced, but even our onstage banter feels more performance than playful.

After 'Riot Pride,' cheering engulfs us. It's our last song, and judging from the Pride flags thrust into the air, I can tell the crowd really love it.

"Thank you so much, Reno!" I shout into my mic.

There's a dip in the applause, and Izzie laughs awkwardly, the sound reverberating through the venue. "She means Salt Lake City."

All my muscles go taut as I look out at the room, so similar to the last we played I can barely tell the difference. Salem, Sacramento, Reno, Salt Lake City… same songs, different towns.

"Tour life, right?" I say nervously. "Can you tell we haven't been sleeping much?"

There's an uncomfortable silence after I speak in which I contemplate what the punishment is for musicians who shout out the wrong city.

There's a whoop from the back of the crowd, and someone yells, "Love wins!"

The tension releases in ripples as people laugh and wolf-whistle. And even though they've incorrectly pinpointed the reason for my insomnia, Izzie seems to relax a little, too.

"At least she always gets *my* name right, and that's really what counts," she says with a chuckle.

But as we leave the stage, the light in her eyes goes out and all that's left is a dull annoyance.

"Good save," I murmur under my breath.

"Yeah. Could've been worse." Izzie unhooks the strap and hands her guitar to me. "If you're that tired, maybe you should get some sleep while I meet with the record-label guys on my own."

I shrug and watch her disappear into the crowd, but my stomach does a complicated twisty dive, the kind that makes me almost seasick to watch during the Olympics. Because… yeah, I don't really want to meet with the record-label guys. That's way more Izzie's realm than mine. Still, I don't feel like going back to the van on my own.

I finish dismantling my drum kit on my own instead. It's not exactly easy work, but it's soothing in a way. Gives my hands something to do while my mind spins. By the time I'm done, there's still a decent crowd dancing to a pre-selected playlist that's a mix of Top 40 and classic rock. I scan the room for Izzie, but I don't see her, so I make my way to the bar and order a cider.

The bartender slides my drink to me without a word, and I glance at the people around me. There's a couple in low conversation to my right, and a group of older women in artfully ripped T-shirts and bandanas. Everyone is chatting and laughing and dancing. I feel so small and slow, like I'm falling through thick honey.

When I can see the bottom of my glass, I hesitate. I could order another. The rhythm from the speakers lures me into a comfortable disassociation and I kind of like sitting here in the dark where no one is looking at me, where no one is expecting a performance. But when the bartender asks me if I'd like a refill, I shake my head. I'm surrounded by people, but I've never felt more alone. This is how we always do things after a show— separately—but I usually have Jordie and Ollie around, or The High Seas to keep me company. Now, all I have is this cider that tastes more bitter than sweet on my tongue.

I pay for my drink and make my way through the crowd. I cast a cursory glance around for Izzie and spot her at a corner table with a couple of people—they must be the people from the label. I don't want to bug her, especially not while she's working so hard for our future, so I slip out the side door, silent as a shadow.

Outside, the Salt Lake City night is sharp with cold. I climb into the back of the van and fumble for a sweatshirt in the dark. My hand passes over a sticky candy wrapper and a pile of dirty laundry before I find the soft fabric of one of Izzie's cardigans. I stick my arms through the holes, barely caring that I've put it on upside down. Even though it's freezing, I can't bring myself to stay inside. The scent of leftover drive-thru food mingles in the air with my own sweat and I feel like I'm in the world's worst-smelling hotbox.

I'm sitting on the cold concrete curb, staring up at the stars, when Izzie finally leaves the club. She's all smiles and excitement.

"I think this is going to be really good!" she says, climbing into the back of the van. "They've got a couple other people they're sending to our Denver show, but I think it's basically in the bag. They really like our sound, but even more they really like *us*. Isn't that cool? Steph?"

I blink and nod. "Yeah—cool."

"I knew this tour was going to be good for us."

I don't say what I'm thinking, which is that she didn't even think the tour was a good idea in the first place. I don't say that what's good for the band might not always be good for the relationship. I don't say anything at all.

Izzie reaches for my hand to pull me up into the van, but I resist. I'm not quite ready yet.

"Wanna look at the stars for a bit?" I ask, pointing up at the night sky, full of twinkling lights. "I can tell you what shapes I see and then you can tell me what constellations they actually are?"

"No way. It's freezing out there!" Izzie shivers and scoots further into the van. "Besides, gotta get some sleep before we head out tomorrow."

"Sure. Right. Of course." I pull my arms around my body, but I don't follow. "I'll just be a few more minutes."

The van door clicks shut and I'm alone again. I don't know how long I sit there, but eventually I'm roused from my reverie

by a buzzing in my pocket. I pull out my phone to see a new
message on Reddit, and I smile when I see who it's from.

Gabsurdity93
Next stop Haven Springs! Can't wait!!

My chest fills with air. It feels like the first full breath I've
taken in days.

Twenty-Nine

Haven Springs is nestled in a close embrace of the Rocky Mountains and a glittering blue lake. We take a winding road through the mountains, and the eagle-eye view of town from above is straight off a gift-shop postcard. My jaw hangs open, and I very nearly forget to watch the road as we make our way into town.

"Steph! Pay attention!" Izzie smacks my arm lightly and groans, sinking deeper into the passenger seat.

"Sorry! Sorry!" I grapple the steering wheel and train my eyes forward just in time to narrowly miss hitting a deer, casually strolling across the highway.

After a couple hours of the windy climb over the Rockies, Izzie's stomach revolted and she finally let me drive.

"We're almost there," I say, glancing at her ashen complexion. She looks worse now than when we stopped to switch seats. There's visible sweat on her brow, and her lips are pursed like she's just eaten sour candy.

Izzie reaches for her water bottle and empties the rest into her mouth. "We're getting ginger ale as soon as we stop."

"Absolutely. And some fresh air." I speed up just a little, narrowing my focus to the road.

When I pull up outside the Black Lantern, I hop from the van and rush around the other side to help Izzie. She plants her feet on the pavement and breaths heavily with her hands on her knees.

"You okay?" I ask, placing my hand at the center of Izzie's back. "Need a barf bag?"

Izzie shakes her head, then winces at the motion. "Nah, just need to lie down or something."

"Hey there!" A jolly voice greets us, and I look up into the smiling, bearded face of a guy about my age.

"Uh, hi," I say. "Sorry, my girlfriend's just a little sick. We can move our van in a sec."

"Huh?" He looks at me quizzically. "No—no you don't have to. This is fine. Sorry. I'm Gabe. Gabe Chen. We've been talking on Reddit." He points his thumb back at his chest. "You're Steph, right?"

"Gabe! Oh good, I was like… worried we parked in a tow zone or something."

"I mean, you definitely did." He looks over my shoulder at the street behind us. "I don't know how you even managed to get down here. You're not supposed to drive on Main Street. But it's totally fine. We'll get your instruments unloaded and then find you a real parking spot."

"Hey—violently ill person here. Can I sit down?" Izzie looks paler than before, if possible. "Feel like I'm gonna faint or something."

"Altitude sickness got you, huh?" Gabe winces. "It happened to me when I first got here, too. Come on, my place is upstairs. You can lie down there for a bit."

I tighten my grip around her waist and let her lean into me as we follow Gabe inside.

"What no, paparazzi?" A gruff voice greets us as a bell chimes overhead at our entrance. Behind the bar stands a tall man sporting an impressive mustache and wearing green flannel. "These are the rock stars, right?"

"Not exactly that kind of rock star," I say, but then tack on, "Yet."

"Hah! That's the spirit." The man wipes his hands on a rag

and circles around the bar. "The name's Jed."

"This is Steph and Izzie," Gabe says, pointing to each of us in turn. "Jed owns this place—plus he's a local hero."

Jed waves a hand in dismissal. "Oh, please. No need to bring that up. Ancient history."

"Well, you're my personal hero, too." Gabe just shrugs, like it's not a total cheeseball line. He turns toward me and says, "Jed gave me a job here when I first came to Haven *and* a room upstairs. It's not every boss who'd be that generous. This guy— he's a good one. Haven wouldn't be the same without him."

"Flattery will get you nowhere with me, son. Now go on, I've got work to do so you can have your big rock concert." He shoos us toward the stairs.

Gabe takes the lead and Izzie follows, but I just turn slowly on the spot, taking the place in.

The Black Lantern is empty except for the four of us, but I've never been in a room that feels so full. The walls are decorated with plaques and photographs. There's an enormous red chandelier above the bar and neon signs everywhere, lighting up the otherwise dark space. My eyes bounce around the room, from a jukebox in the corner to old-looking maps on the walls to a huge taxidermy bear by the pool table. I've never been anywhere like it, and yet it feels so familiar, so homey, so… lived in.

"Kind of small," Izzie mutters as she eases herself up the staircase.

I stiffen a little. She's not wrong. This place is definitely more pub than concert venue. But it's far from the first thing I noticed. It's not like we haven't played our fair share of bars, though, and it *is* a small town.

Gabe leads us upstairs to the loft and a warm feeling spreads from my chest out to my limbs. It's one room, but it feels so much bigger, with a high ceiling and big windows.

"Sweet space!" I eye a The Torchheads poster above a corkboard full of flyers and ticket stubs.

"Welcome to my crib," Gabe says with a flourish.

Izzie staggers over to the couch and flops face first onto it. "Uhggg," she says, eloquent as always.

My gaze lingers on her for a moment before my attention does a hop, skip, and a jump across the TV, a record player, and— "Oh my god, foosball? No way!" I dash over to an old foosball table and give one of the handles a good spin.

"You play?" Gabe asks, joining me.

"Not even a little bit, but I bet I could kick your ass."

"Is that a challenge?"

Izzie lets out another unintelligible sound. "Can I request that any ass-kicking occurs after I stop feeling like an inflated slug?"

"Right, right." I give Gabe an apologetic look.

To his credit, Gabe doesn't look put out at all. Instead, he crosses over to the kitchen and fills a glass with water. From a lower cabinet, he grabs a packet of crackers and a straw before setting it all down on the coffee table.

"Altitude sickness can really suck, so take it easy. Hydrate and try to eat something with salt to keep your body functional. If you start to feel better, help yourself to anything in the fridge." He pats the arm of the sofa and stands up. "We'll get out of your hair, let you nap. What do you say, Steph? How about a Haven Springs tour from an expert?"

"Ah yes, but where will we find an expert?" I ask, contorting my lips into a goofy grin.

He nudges my shoulder as he passes me and opens the door. "Ha ha, very funny."

And the thing is… it's not very funny, but we both still laugh anyway. It's like something about this place has let me finally exhale a breath I didn't know I was holding. Even this high up in the mountains, where the oxygen levels are enough to lay Izzie flat, it feels so good to really breathe again.

*

It turns out, aside from some residential areas, Haven Springs is just the one block, but somehow this tiny town holds my interest the way almost nothing else has in recent months. And maybe it's not so much the town as it is Gabe's love for it. He lights up as he walks me up and down the street, showing me all his favorite spots.

"This place is new—just opened a few weeks ago—but you gotta try the ice cream!" Gabe exclaims, pointing up at a sign with snowy mountain peaks that says Avalanche Ice Cream.

"In February?" It's not snowing or anything, but I still have my puffy blue coat over my flannel and my hands jammed in my pockets.

"Yes!" Gabe takes me by the shoulders. "It's the thrill of the chill!"

"Well, when you put it like that… my flavor is Rocky Road."

"Yeah… your flavor is whatever Sonny decides it is."

"Sonny?" I ask, peering inside the ice cream parlor to see a middle-aged man with bright eyes and a brighter smile beckoning us to come in.

"You're gonna love him." Gabe chuckles. "He's got a real talent for flavors that really shouldn't work, but somehow do. My favorite so far is Cereal Milk."

"Cereal Milk?" I ask as we push open the doors.

"Yeah, you'll see. It's a lawless land in there."

We leave a few minutes later with our ice cream cones— Gabe gets Strawberry Balsamic and I take his recommendation for Cereal Milk, which, lo and behold, tastes like the dregs of a bowl of Cheerios.

Our conversation halts as we lick our ice cream, leaving me time to really absorb the town.

Just like inside the Black Lantern, my eyes can't decide what to look at first. Tall lamps mark the brick pathway every few feet, spiral-pattern ribbons looped around the base like on a maypole. Little purple crocuses burst from the ground, and colorful murals cover the sides of buildings. It feels like a festival, even on a mostly empty street.

We meander down the street a bit to sit on a bench, and my gaze lands on a majestic statue of a deer in the middle of the street. The sculpture is hauntingly real, muscles sculpted in iron as if in motion.

"What's with the deer?" I ask.

Gabe shrugs. "Dunno. Guess we just… take deer pretty seriously in this town."

"Does it have a name?"

Gabe cocks his head, eyebrows joining at the center of his forehead. "You know, I don't know. Maybe we should name it."

"Deirdre," I suggest.

"I dunno, I think it's a boy, right? With the antlers?"

"Okay, well, gender is a construct, but I see your point." I roll my lip between my teeth. "Bucky."

Gabe chortles and shakes his head. "We've got a local named Ducky and I think people would get confused."

"Okay, well what would you name it?"

"Stagatha Christie."

"Ohhh, that's good! But what happened to it being a boy?"

Gabe shrugs. "You're right. Gender is a construct."

I take a lick of my ice cream, but I barely taste it. For some reason, I can't tear my eyes from this statue. "It looks so real… like the way its head is tipped up like it smells something delicious… Maybe it's the pine trees."

"Maybe it's the ice cream." Gabe raises his cone like he's making a toast, but clips the side of his face so the ice cream smashes against his nose and lips, leaving a perfect pink circle in the middle of his face.

"Rudolph? Is that you? I'm your biggest fan!" I cackle, but hand him one of the napkins wrapped around my cone.

"Gabe? I thought I heard your voice." The door to The Silver Dragon, a little dispensary a few doors down from the flower shop, opens and through it steps a black woman with gold jewelry and at least three layers of colorful cardigans. She looks, in a word, cozy, like she probably gives great hugs. "Ah—and you must be Drugstore Makeup!"

"Hey—yeah, I'm Steph. My other half is upstairs." I jab my thumb over my shoulder at the Black Lantern just up the street.

"This is my girlfriend, Charlotte," Gabe says. "Hopefully that's still true now that she's seen me with ice cream all over my face."

Charlotte purses her lips, failing to suppress a smile, and laces her fingers with his. "It'll take more than a little ice cream to send me packing."

My chest swells a little painfully at the look they give each other—the smile that tugs Gabe's lips to the left, the certainty in Charlotte's eyes. It's a quiet kind of love. The kind that doesn't have to prove itself.

"You coming to the show?" I ask.

"I wish!" Charlotte's eyes snap back to me. "I have to drop my son off with his father tonight, otherwise I'd be there. Ethan's really disappointed, too."

"Yeah, you're gonna miss all my sexiest dance moves."

"Oh yes, the fabled dance moves." Charlotte kisses Gabe on the cheek. "Maybe it's better for you if I *don't* see those."

"Your loss. I'm going to tear it up tonight!" Gabe quirks an eyebrow and swings his arms into an impressively bad robot.

Charlotte and I both burst into laughter.

"Oh, I can't wait to see more," I say when I catch my breath. "Izzie's gonna love that."

"I hope she feels better soon." Gabe's smile falters and he glances back at the Black Lantern. "She's missing out!"

I nod, but I can't help but think if she were here with us, we wouldn't be laughing half so much.

I stand straighter, refusing to let the moment crumble. "Come on, what else d'you have to show me, Mr. Haven Springs?"

"Under no circumstances will I be calling you Mr. Haven Springs," Charlotte deadpans, but she's smiling as she gives him a squeeze and retreats into the shop.

"You haven't seen the lake yet, have you?" Gabe points down the street toward a dock at the end, and we meander toward it. "This is my favorite part of town," he says. "Even when this place is bustling, it's always quiet down here."

I step onto the dock and immediately feel a shift. A weight lifts from my shoulders and my feet skim across the wooden boards as light as cappuccino foam. The lake spreads out beneath me, shimmering and still like glass. Mountains rise up from the opposite shore, snowy peaks reaching for the sky. I want to reach with them—so I do. I put my arms in the air and stretch, feeling all the tension in my body unspool.

From the end of the dock, I can see the sprawling expanse of a wooded park. Little fairy lights hang from some of the tree branches, and a spark ignites in me. I want to see this place at night. I want to see this place in spring, in summer, and even in fall. I want to see how it changes with the seasons.

I want to see how I might, too.

Thirty

As the sun sets over Haven Springs, the lights in the Black Lantern shine a beacon, recalling us before the show. I'm surprised to see Izzie downstairs setting up her amp in a corner. Her hair is pulled back into a loose ponytail and I can see the color has returned to her cheeks.

"The patient lives!" Gabe exclaims as we enter.

Izzie stands and there's a smile on her face—small, but it counts. "I will never again disparage the healing properties of saltines."

I bounce over to her and plant a kiss on her cheek. "You look so much better!"

She just raises an eyebrow, as if to say, *So do you.*

And she wouldn't be wrong. There's an energy around us that wasn't there before, and I don't know if it's the air, the place, the people... Whatever it is, I'm grateful. It feels like a rising bubble of hope, like there's still joy to be found along this trip and we're about to unearth a whole lot of it.

I wrap my arms around Izzie's waist and lift her up. "This place is so cool—I can't wait to play for the people here."

"Well, I'll get out of your hair." Jed crosses over from the bar and claps Gabe on the shoulder.

"You sure you don't want to stay?" Gabe asks.

"Nah—don't want to be in the way. You young folks have fun. Don't forget to lock up after. Ducky's whiskey is on the shelf if he asks for it, but make sure he pays you this time."

"Hah. Right." Gabe points to us and winks. "Rock stars drink for free though."

"Perks!" I sweep Izzie toward the bar. "How will you ever make a profit like this?"

Gabe laughs, filling glasses with foaming golden beer. "Don't worry about that. We have plenty of paying customers."

But it turns out Gabe's wrong about that. Seven o'clock comes, but no one else does. The door to the Black Lantern stays resolutely shut all night.

"This is so embarrassing." Gabe checks out the window for what seems like the twentieth time in as many minutes. "I swear, I did actually tell people about it. I put up flyers and everything."

"We believe you! It's okay!" I say, but I glance at Izzie to see how okay it actually is.

She shrugs and plays a chord that reverberates through the room. The acoustics, it has to be said, do not suck in the Black Lantern. Something about the shape of the room or something really amplifies our sound in a cool way.

"I'm going to call Ryan again. He gets off work in like an hour and I'm sure he'll show." Gabe grabs his phone and starts dialing.

"Don't worry about it." Izzie's voice is lazy and languid. A smile spreads across her face and she picks out a few more notes on her guitar—the opening melody of 'Beanie Babe.' It sends a little ripple through me, my spine caving toward her, bowing like a willow in the wind. "Music doesn't need an audience to be great."

I don't need any more invitation than that. I swipe my drumsticks off the floor tom and raise them high above my head to count us off.

"One, two, three, four!"

Gabe's dance moves are as horrendous as advertised, but Izzie and I don't care. He jumps out from behind the bar, waving his arms in the air and twisting his hips. He applauds and cheers our name at the end of every song, more enthusiastic than even the most packed shows we've played. And yeah, it's just one guy, but it's also us—me and Izzie—playing for each other.

Here in this room, there are no talent scouts, no lofty expectations. We play our songs out of order, not caring about the flow of energy. Instead, we take requests from Gabe—some songs from our record, some covers we know and love—and we even throw a few new ones at him, songs we haven't polished to perfection for the tour circuit. After we run through our set, repeating a couple songs at Gabe's insistence, Izzie runs upstairs to grab her notebook and plays a new song even I haven't heard yet.

The lyrics paint a picture of a house made of books. The roof, the doors, the tables, the chairs. She sings about pages of history and fiction sitting side by side, sisters in arms. I can see the seed of inspiration, planted when we were at Powell's in Portland. A place I showed her.

But when she hits the chorus, I realize the song isn't about books. It's about walls. It's about holding back and giving your all. It's about her and me. It's about what has been and what could be.

> *"I don't know the secrets you keep*
> *But I'm asking you to take the leap.*
> *They're just three words.*
> *Read 'em and weep."*

I follow along as best I can on the drums, messing up here and there. Even Izzie plays a couple wrong notes on her guitar, but she smiles through all the mistakes.

> *"I wonder when you've gone to sleep*
> *If you dream of something deep.*
> *With you and me,*
> *We sow what we reap."*

I falter a little at the honesty in her song. It's not an attack and it's not an apology, just an acknowledgment of past blunders, of the bumps in the road. I have to hope she sees a steady course ahead, because I still feel so lost.

And as the chorus bleeds into the bridge, she sings about the unknown, the gentle romance of mystery, the way love isn't always what we expect.

> *"But looks*
> *Can be deceiving.*
> *So I'll climb the shelves*
> *And read of us in storybooks."*

It's not exactly a love song, but it's not *not* one either. I feel splintered and whole all at once after, like maybe I'm not the only one who's noticed this distance between us. Like maybe it isn't mine to cross alone.

Gabe applauds us, but the sound is so distant I barely hear it. This feels less like a gig and more like that first time Izzie and I played together in the greenroom at Bar-None, after Vinyl Resting Place booted her from the band. It feels brand-new, like we can do anything we want. The world is our oyster. Nothing is off-limits. And it also feels heavy and waterlogged like we've been standing out in the rain all this time and only just noticed.

I reach for her across the hi-hat, fingers tangling with hers, and I squeeze. I'm not a wordsmith like her, putting feelings to music, but I hope she understands through my touch what I'm trying to say.

I'm here. Don't let go.

It's almost midnight by the time we finish playing. I'm not tired at all, but Gabe says we might get in trouble if we go on too late—there's some kind of noise ordinance—so Izzie and

I pack away our instruments and head upstairs while Gabe cleans up. The bar looks pretty much spotless to me, but I'm not about to argue, especially not with Izzie tugging me up toward the roof.

The night air is blisteringly cold, but Izzie wraps me up in her arms and nuzzles her nose into the crook of my neck. It's a moment I want to savor, but there's something sour in my throat that I just can't seem to swallow.

"So, Haven Springs is kind of magical, huh?" I stare off at the dark horizon. The mountain peaks carve a jagged smile in a starry sky and the twinkle lights in the park are finally lit up.

"I guess," Izzie says into my shoulder. "I'm just glad I don't feel so sick anymore."

"Me too." And… I am glad. But there's a tiny part of me that feels protective of this place I'm just growing to love and "I guess" really isn't good enough. "I want to show you around tomorrow. Gabe took me to all the cool places and I think you'll really love it."

"All the cool places?" She scoffs. "It's like one street."

I unspool from her grip and beckon her toward the edge so we can look down at the town. "You have to try the ice cream, for sure, and there's a dispensary!"

Izzie follows me, but drags her feet. "We have all that stuff back home, Steph."

I'm barely listening. "There's a flower shop and a record store, and there's a totally cute bookstore, too!"

"I already bought too many books this trip."

"Oh, and Gabe's girlfriend is so nice! You'll like her, I think."

"We need to get on the road."

I open my mouth, ready to form more words, but my voice just… stops. My mind is an echo chamber of her words.

Back home. This trip. On the road.

And something slams into place, so obvious, it's like the final puzzle piece after everything else has been fitted together.

I don't want to leave.

This is the best I've felt in weeks, maybe months. Haven is familiar and new all at once, like all the best parts of Arcadia Bay rolled into the mountains. It's something special, even in all the ways it is mundane, and I think... I think I want to stay.

I don't know how to say the words, so I skirt around them.

"I grew up in a small town," I say quietly, my voice soft with rounded edges, afraid anything sharper will puncture the moment. "On the coast, obviously, but still. I think I'd like to live in one again someday."

"Really? I can't see you in a place like this. You'd get so bored!" Izzie guffaws. "Yeah, like, what would you even do on a Friday night around here? Go for an evening showing of the... moon rising? Even the Black Lantern didn't have a single customer tonight. What a joke."

Her words are a knife, like her laughter is at me, not the town. "I don't think it's a joke."

"You'd last like three days in this place before your brain would start to melt. Trust me, I know you."

I stand up straighter, my shoulders clicking as I roll them back. Izzie reaches for me, her fingers glancing off my arm before I flinch away. "No, Izzie. You don't."

"Okay, sorry..." Izzie sighs, long and dramatic. "Actually, no. I'm not sorry. I've been busting my ass trying to make this tour what you want it to be, trying to make you happy, and you just... It's like you're determined not to be or something."

I pull back, staring at her with a pinched brow. "What the fuck are you talking about?"

"I'm not an idiot, Steph. I know we've got problems. But I thought this tour would fix things. Like, if we could make Drugstore Makeup into something successful, that would... I don't know... make everything okay."

My stomach bottoms out at her words. I almost want to laugh—we've been doing the exact same thing, and still we've managed to somehow fuck it up. But... it's not funny. It's just kind of sad.

"There's a lot more wrong than a tour can fix, huh," I say quietly, eyes traveling back out to look at the mountains.

"Yeah, well, I can't fix it if you don't want talk about it. You have to stop expecting me to just *get* everything about you without you telling me. I know you have this thing with your hometown, but if you won't talk about it, then how am I supposed to understand?"

I shove my hands in my pockets and turn to face her. "This isn't about Arcadia Bay." It's easy to lie to Izzie—I've made a habit of it when it comes to my hometown—but it's much harder to lie to myself because everything is about Arcadia Bay. Everything is always about Arcadia Bay. On some level, I've been in a holding pattern since the storm, since Mom died. I put myself in some kind of emotional cryo-chamber, waiting for the day it doesn't hurt anymore to emerge. But that's not really living.

Living is about making choices, taking action, doing things that will make me happy. It's about getting in the driver's seat and finding the path that will lead me where I'm supposed to go. Instead, I've been letting Izzie steer all this time, pursuing her dreams, fighting for her joy, living for Izzie's dreams so I don't have to figure out what mine are.

"Izzie..." I trail off, no idea where to begin. But I do know one thing. I know what I want right now. "I... love it here. This town, this place." I gesture at the mountains above us, the stars twinkling in the sky—each one like a wink specifically for me, letting me know this is right. "I think I want to stay."

"What, like, until our next show? I guess I could go on ahead and you could take a bus or something."

"No, I mean for longer. Like... this probably sounds wild, but I might want to live here." A little laugh escapes my lips as I trip over the joy in those words, the truth in them.

"When you... retire...?"

"No, *now*, Izzie!" I can't keep the grin off my face. "I feel like I've just been treading water all this time, you know? And this town feels right. It feels special."

I glance at Izzie, searching for the same spark of inspiration I feel under these stars, surrounded by mountains and trees, but it's not there. Her face goes slack and her gaze falls to her shoes.

"Well, fuck," she says softly. "You're just going to, what, leave Seattle on a whim? You're going to leave the band? You're going to leave *me*?"

The pain in her voice is almost enough to make me change my mind. I could say, *No, of course not. I'd never leave you.* And we'd be back on track, heading for Denver, heading for fame, heading for whatever adventure Izzie dreams up next. But that's not what I say.

"You could stay here too. I wouldn't try to stop you." And it's there, in the space between my words, the hollow core of what I'm asking without asking. *You don't have to leave me. Hold on. Don't let go.*

I've stayed by her side all this time, followed her through every turn. Maybe it was passive, maybe it was lazy, but it was still a choice every time. It was a choice not to change things, even as our relationship soured. And now it's a choice I offer her, one I hope she takes… or maybe I hope she doesn't. But it's not up to me, it's up to her.

"Yeah. Good." A sad laugh breaks through her words as she speaks. "I'll be the only trans person in a town with a population of like four. That sounds like a blast for me. Thanks for 'not trying' to stop me."

My words thrown back at me sound raw and bitter and final. "I'm sorry, Izzie," I say, and I am. I am *so* sorry. I'm sorry for what this will mean for her dreams. I'm sorry for letting this feeling fester inside me for so long. I'm sorry for not realizing what I wanted sooner. But I'm not sorry enough to change my mind. "It's not you. And it's not the band. I fucking love that shit. But I need to try this. It's just… time for something new."

"I knew it. I knew this would happen eventually." Izzie's words tear from her throat, and I am reminded of what she once told me about relationships, about being the right fit.

People always leave, one way or another… I guess I was just waiting for it to happen with you, too.

I swallow, my throat tight. I don't want to be just another person who leaves her, who makes her feel like she isn't enough. But the truth is that we're both not enough, or maybe we're both too much. Either way, this relationship has been heading down the wrong path for a long time now, and I can't fix it, not when we want such different things.

Reaching for Izzie, my fingers find her wrist, but she tugs free and gives me a long look. Maybe if I was more of a songwriter like her, I'd be able to read deeper, see all the layers of emotion hidden in the depths of her brown irises. Instead all I see there is regret.

"Fucking… See you around, Steph." Her voice cracks as a single tear streams down her face, smearing her makeup, and then she's opening the door and heading for the stairs.

Thirty-One

They say when you die, your life flashes before your eyes. Well, the same thing happens with a breakup, only it's all the moments you had together. In the wake of Izzie, I am rocked by a hundred memories: the first day we met, when we played music together for the first time, our first kiss, our first gig, our first fight. A relationship is just a series of firsts until it ends in a first breakup.

But it does end, and even though I wish I could have said more and I wish I could have said less, it's over and what's done is done.

I send Gabe a text.

> Think you could put me up for a few days?

< Uh. Don't you have more tour dates?

His response comes almost immediately. He's probably finished cleaning up the bar. Maybe he's in his loft, chilling, and I could just go downstairs and talk to him, but I'm not really in the mood to talk. I'm not really in the mood for anything.

Another text comes in after a few minutes.

< Shit did something happen?

Part of me wants to just spill everything to him, but Gabe's

basically a stranger. He's just some guy who likes my music—
music that will never be played by me and Izzie again. How do
I tell him that the band he brought here to Haven is no more
when I can't even bring myself to say the words myself? There
are a dozen people I should tell first. Like Jordie or Ollie or Lia.
Or Dad.

But the only person I really want to tell is Mom.

That's impossible, though, so instead I type another text.

> No not really

> I was just thinking maybe I'd stick around Haven
for a little longer than we originally planned.

But not both of you?

> Look man can I crash with you or not?

Yeah yeah of course

If you need to talk, hmu

With that settled, I lean over the railing and look down at the
town. My eyes find Izzie's van, still parked illegally. The light's
on. She's probably curled up on our mattress, reading one of her
new books or writing a song about how much I suck. I think about
joining her, about holding her, about kissing her one last time.

But instead I just watch from above until she turns off the
light before heading downstairs to Gabe's place.

I find him sitting on the couch, a beer in one hand and brick
of cheese in the other, which he's eating like some kind of feral
mouse.

"I see you started the after-party without me," I say, flopping
down next to him.

"Steph?" He jumps a little, eyes wide. "Hey, uh… you okay?"

"I will be if you're into sharing that cheese. Nothing soothes a broken heart like dairy."

"You're not lactose intolerant are you?" Gabe asks, horror flashing across his face as he hands me the brick and stands up to head to the kitchen.

"Why, do you have a farting policy?"

"Nah, the circulation in here is great. Just wanted to make sure I wasn't contributing to some kind of self-destructive behavior." He returns with a plate and a knife. "Let me know if you do want something stronger. I've got beer, gummies…"

As Gabe rattles off the various amenities he has to offer, my brain trips, falls, comes to a screeching halt. I don't want to bury my feelings in a substance—not even cheddar cheese. It surprises even me as I realize it, but what I actually want right now is to tell someone how I'm feeling. I've spent all this time locking down my emotions, keeping them to myself out of some kind of fear that sharing them would make them worse or make them spread. But emotions aren't an infectious disease, they're part of me.

"Broke up with Izzie." I brace myself for the plunging feeling in my stomach, the dread, the regret, the anguish. But none of it comes. Instead, I just feel sort of empty.

"Yeah, I kind of figured." Gabe turns to look at me, eyes full of concern. "You okay? Sorry, that's a stupid thing to ask after a breakup, isn't it?"

"Actually… I think I *am* okay." I exhale, long and slow, clutching the block of cheese to my chest like a stuffed animal. "For the first time in a while, I feel… pretty good."

"Well, that's promising."

Gabe doesn't ask me what happened, he doesn't ask me why. And maybe that's what makes me want to share. He's not acting like my vulnerability is a condition of our friendship. We haven't really known each other long enough to *be* friends. But I think I'd like us to be.

So I tell him. I tell him about me and Izzie, the making of and the breaking of. I tell him about Arcadia Bay and the memories that pull me under every fall. I tell him about how frozen I've been feeling and how Haven Springs somehow thawed me out, even in winter.

And then I tell him about my mom.

"I think part of me stopped living when she died. I thought it was the only way to remember her, to stop moving, and because I couldn't stay in Arcadia Bay, I stayed in the grief."

"I get that. Death is weird and it can really fuck with you," he says. His hands are clasped at his chest and he stares up at the ceiling with unblinking eyes. "When my mom died, I felt like I had to be strong about it all. My dad totally flaked after, and my sister, Alex, was still a kid, so it was like it was all on me to keep us afloat. Sometimes I wonder if we'd all still be together if I'd actually let myself feel things instead of pushing it down."

"Where are they now?" I ask.

Regret flashes through Gabe's eyes as he sighs. "No idea. Alex and I bounced around the foster system for a while and I lost track of her. Dad just… kind of vanished. I've been trying to find them both, actually, but I just keep hitting dead ends."

"Ohhh, a mystery!" I sit up a little.

"Yeah, that's how I ended up here, actually. Dad came to Haven Springs years ago and I thought I might find more clues, but nope. The trail ends here."

"I'm sorry." I cringe as the words land awkward and wrong. "That's, uh, well that sucks."

"Yeah, it does. I mean, he wasn't a good dad. I don't think he was even that good a man." He scratches his chin and contorts his face. "I don't know. People change. Or maybe they don't. I guess I thought if I could find him, maybe I'd have a chance to see for myself."

I nod, unsure what to say to that. Maybe like with the thing about my mom, the right thing to do is just listen.

"It's not all bad, though. Maybe I didn't find my dad, but I did find a family here in Haven Springs. Haven's done a lot for me. Makes me wonder if this place might've helped him, too."

"I get that. Haven feels like it has the power to really change people—or maybe it's the people that change it. I don't know." I let silence fall between us, comfortable and soft like a blanket. Then I say what's been on my mind since I took my first step out of the van into this town. "I really love it here. I just feel like I can be myself in Haven, if that makes sense."

"Totally. Haven Springs is pretty special—like it's made by the people instead of the other way around, you know?" Gabe pulls his legs up under him and turns so his whole body is facing me. "Haven is all about the community. Eleanor Lethe—she owns the flower shop—she's lived here for like thirty years. She's always coming up with ways to decorate the town. You should really see it in springtime when everything is in bloom. And Jed! I wasn't kidding when I said he's a hero. He's modest about it, but he saved a ton of people during a mining accident about a decade ago. Plus he's been really good to me. And you've gotta meet Ryan. That's Jed's son. He's the best—seriously, a good guy."

"What is this, a sales pitch?" I laugh as I slide down the couch and prop my feet up on the coffee table.

Gabe stares at me for a beat, then shrugs. "Yeah, I guess. Maybe it's stupid, but I think Haven is great."

"It's not stupid."

"Yeah?" A grin spreads across his face. "Yeah! I'm right. Haven *is* great. Everyone should live here."

"Well, maybe not *everyone*," I say. "That would defeat the purpose of a small town."

"Good point. Not *everyone* should move here." Gabe nudges my shoulder. "But I think maybe you should."

I set the block of cheese down on the coffee table and my eyes flick up to meet Gabe's. His expression is hopeful, brow taut, smile tentative. My lips curve and a laugh bubbles up in me because even though it feels totally wild, it's exactly what I think, too.

Thirty-Two

I get the best sleep of my life on Gabe's lumpy couch, curled under a scratchy yellow blanket with my toes tucked in between the cushions. I crash hard and by the time I wake up, there's sunlight pouring in through the windows. I stretch my arms up and let a yawn consume me for a few seconds before checking my phone for the time.

It's 1:54 p.m.

And I don't have a single text from Izzie.

It hits me harder than I expect. It's not like I thought she'd change her mind, but maybe I kind of hoped she would.

My eyes drift to the coffee table, where there's a teal sticky note with a message scribbled on it.

> Working today. Come down when you're
> awake—breakfast is on the house.
> —Gabe

Hoping that offer extends to a late lunch, I push myself off the couch and make a pit stop at the bathroom before shoving my feet back in my shoes and descending the stairs to the Black Lantern.

The place isn't exactly bustling, but compared to last night, it's a pretty good showing. There's an older guy with long gray hair tucked into a booth, and a pretty white girl with a daisy woven into the end of her auburn braid sits in the back room, poring over a textbook, while a couple of guys play pool nearby.

"Good morning!" Gabe waves me over from behind the bar. "Or afternoon, I guess. Whatever."

I ease onto a bar stool and give him my best smile. "It's morning somewhere, right?"

"That's the spirit. You doing okay?"

"I'm fine." And maybe that was the truth when I first woke up, but the longer I go with no message from Izzie, the more anxiety churns in my stomach. "Maybe a little hungover." It's not true—I only had a couple drinks—but I still feel increasingly nauseated the longer I'm awake. "Can you get hungover from cheese?"

"I'd believe it." Gabe pushes a menu toward me. "Lucky for you, we have the best hangover food in town."

My eyes dip to the menu, but I can't seem to absorb the words. "Dealer's choice," I say, pushing it back.

"Oh, that's dangerous. Gabe has very weird taste."

I turn to see the girl with the flower in her hair smiling behind me. She has a book bag slung over her shoulder and a thick pink sweater in her arms.

Gabe just shrugs and slides a glass of water across the bar. "No take-backs."

"I'm Riley." The girl—Riley—gives me a little wave.

"Steph," I say.

"Are you visiting?" Riley takes a seat beside me and brushes her hair back behind her ear. "We don't see a lot of tourists in Haven."

For a second, I think maybe she's flirting with me. And even though she's not really my vibe, it's weird how much I don't hate the idea of being flirted with by someone new. So weird, in fact, that I interrupt Gabe as he's explaining my presence here to ask, "Have you seen Izzie yet?"

"Izzie?" Gabe repeats her name, blinking. "Uh… yeah. Sorry, Steph, I figured you knew. She left this morning."

I swallow with difficulty, my throat tight and sandpapery. "Oh."

"She gave me your bag."

Gabe dips below the counter and retrieves my purple suitcase. I just stare as he hoists it up onto the bar. And I guess maybe I should be grateful that she had the presence of mind to leave me with more than just the clothes on my back and my phone, but my mind circles over the only part that really matters.

She left.

"I have to—" I break off, pushing off my stool with a dissonant scraping sound and barreling for the door.

Momentum carries me out onto the street, and then I can't stop running. My feet pound against brick, my breath crashing through me in waves. I bump somebody's shoulder without apology and nearly trip over a dog. Nothing stops me until I cross the bridge and reach the main road out of town. It's deserted.

I don't know what I expected—Izzie left hours ago—but some part of me thought maybe if I ran hard enough, she'd be here waiting. That maybe we could talk. That maybe she'd change her mind. That maybe I'd change mine.

A sob rips through me and I feel myself falling before my knees hit the ground, gravel digging painfully into my jeans.

"Hey, you okay?"

I almost don't want to look up, and just let myself melt into this new kind of grief I'm only just discovering, but instead I wipe my cheeks and try to slow my breathing.

"Not really," I say, and turn to see a guy about my age with light brown hair and a concerned expression. "Sorry, I know that's not really the ideal answer to that question."

"Nah, that's okay. All that matters is if it's true." He sinks down to sit cross-legged beside me. "So... what are we dealing with, on a scale of 'I missed the bus' to 'I just found out the apocalypse is today'?"

I don't even know this guy, but I already feel grounded in his presence, like his humor is a tether. My breathing slows and I hiccup around my words. "Somewhere in the middle, I guess."

"Okay, okay, middle's good."

"Is it?" I raise my eyebrows.

He just shrugs. "I mean, better than the apocalypse thing. I ate all of my emergency canned food last time it snowed, 'cause I didn't feel like walking to the store and I'm sadly not in possession of a time machine."

"Bummer. I really could've used one of those."

I'm joking, but my mind fills with all the moments I could change with that kind of power. I could go back to last night and redo my conversation with Izzie, introduce this town to her when she was in a better mood, let her really see its magic for herself. Or I could go back to before the tour and never accept Gabe's invitation to play the Black Lantern. Or I could go even further and actually tell Izzie about Arcadia Bay and my mom—all of it, not just the surface stuff.

But I can't rewind the clock, and even if I could, I don't know that any of those things would save us.

"You're Steph, right?"

The guy saying my own name jars me from my thoughts, and I must give him a weird look because he hurries to explain.

"I swear I'm not a weird stalker. I'm Ryan—You know Gabe? Gabe Chen? We're friends. He showed me your music and I recognized you from some of the videos." He lets out a long breath. "That doesn't make me sound any less stalkerish, does it?"

"I don't think I have any room to judge. I just ran out here to try to catch my girlfriend before she left me forever." I trip over the world 'girlfriend' and an ache spreads through my chest.

"Oof. Okay. I take it you didn't make it in time?"

"What gave it away?" I deadpan.

Ryan nods slowly, eyes trained on the road before us. "Do you know where she's headed?"

"Denver, probably."

"Okay, well, there's a bus that runs through here you could take and try to catch up with her."

My heart leaps into my throat. "A bus?" But the second the words leave my lips I feel shattered, because even if I did get on a bus to Denver, I'd be doing it because I'm scared, not because I really want Izzie back. Exhaustion weighs heavy on me at the very thought. She deserves better and so do I.

"Yeah, you can probably get a ticket still, but—"

I shake my head. "No, never mind. It was a stupid idea," I say, pushing up to standing. "Sorry, I'm kind of fucked up today."

"Already? It's only like two in the afternoon."

"Huh?" It takes me a minute to realize he thinks I'm drunk or something. To be fair, he did just witness me collapse in tears next to the road, so it's not like he's without evidence to back up that assumption. "No, no, not like that," I say, waving my hand. "I haven't even eaten anything yet."

"Okay, well we should definitely fix that." He beckons me back toward the bridge and Main Street. "Some food will help you straighten out your thoughts."

I don't quite have it in me to smile just yet, but I can't help but take the bait. "As a lesbian, I've never had a straight thought in my life."

Gabe and Ryan form quite the cheer-up committee. For two guys who barely know me or my situation, they really are genuinely great about it. Gabe provides me with a never-ending supply of onion rings from the kitchen and Ryan plays a couple rounds of pool with me to keep my mind off Izzie. Neither of them asks me about her.

Charlotte stops by around dinnertime, and Gabe disappears to a corner table with her.

"Date night," Ryan says by way of explanation. "Sorry—was that too much? I know something's up with your girlfriend and I don't want to—"

"Breathe, dude." I clap a hand down on his shoulder. "It's

fine. I promise hearing about someone else's happy relationship isn't going to send me into a spiral."

"Cool, cool, okay." Ryan's eyes stay on Gabe and Charlotte for a couple beats before he drags his gaze away, back to the pool table.

I don't quite catch his expression, and maybe it's nothing, but I can't help but ask, "What about you?"

"What about me?" He chalks the end of his pool cue. "Oh, no, I'm single," he says, seeming to catch my drift after a moment. "Happily," he adds.

"Happily?" I cock my head, eyeing him with curiosity. It's been almost two years since I've been single, and though I remember my college years and even some of my high school years fondly, I don't know that I'd attribute any of my happiness to singledom. The pursuit of love, even before I was ready to feel it again after Mom died, has always guided my steps in some way or other.

Ryan shrugs. "Yeah, I guess. I mean, I've dated before. Semi-successfully."

"Semi?"

"Okay, so I'm not great at it. I'm not exactly the smoothest of players."

A laugh bursts from my chest. "Holy shit, say 'players' again."

"Absolutely not." Ryan reaches out to straighten the triangle of billiard balls, setting off a chain reaction as he nudges one a little too hard and they all scatter. "Fuck."

We scramble to collect the balls, and once we have them mostly contained, I say, "So what's your secret? To being happy?"

Ryan runs a hand over his beard and quirks his lips. "I don't know that it's really a secret, just how I approach life. Romance is cool and maybe I'll find it one day, but it's not the only thing that matters. It's not the only kind of *love* that matters." His eyes flick over to Gabe and Charlotte, who are holding hands across the table.

"He's a good friend, huh?" I ask, following his gaze.

I thought at first maybe it was jealousy—for what they have, or maybe for one of them being with the other—but now I can see as clear as the night sky here in Haven that the look in Ryan's eyes before was just uncomplicated affection. And maybe he's right—that kind of love matters. It's that kind of love that brings people together. It's that kind of love that makes a town like Haven so special.

"The best." Ryan nods and turns back to me. "I know you haven't known Gabe long, but if you let him, I think he'd be a good friend to you, too."

If ever there was a place to heal a broken heart, I think Haven is probably it.

After several rounds of pool with Ryan and coming to a stalemate, I take myself for a walk through the park. The sun is beginning to fall behind the trees, sending dappled light across the grass. It feels uniquely precious, like some kind of natural marvel that should be protected. The Parks Service would probably put up signs warning tourists not to take it home, if it was the kind of thing you could pick up and slip into your pocket like rocks or pine cones.

"Do you like it?"

A melodious voice breaks through my thoughts and startles me into a leap backward. An older woman with short gray hair and glasses stands at the head of the trail, a brown apron worn over a thick purple sweater.

"Oh, sorry dear—I thought you were someone else." She extends a smile and a hand to me. "I'm Eleanor."

"Steph." I shake her hand.

"Nice to meet you." She pauses, surveying me carefully. "I don't suppose I could bother you for your opinion?"

"Well, it definitely wouldn't be a bother. I'm full of opinions."

Eleanor points to a nearby lamppost adorned with bright

pink and purple flowers. "I'm trying to get the spring decorations just right and I can't decide—baby's breath or no baby's breath?" She holds out some white lacy-looking flowers from a bucket full of different blooms.

I take them and run my fingers along the little buds. I'm reminded of Renee and her floral arrangements—the way they're always a little ragged around the edges but personal, the charm in the mistakes.

"I think yes to the baby's breath, but it's still missing something." I glance down at the bucket by her feet. There are white daisies and yellow daffodils, but they're all too bright or too big to add to the arrangement without overshadowing the delicate beauty of what she's already designed.

"Yes, it's just not quite right." Eleanor frowns, lines around her mouth deepening.

"The color balance is off. It's too soft—you need a contrast. What about something green? Like some leaves or something?"

Eleanor snaps her fingers. "Yes! You're absolutely right." She dips into the bucket and comes up with some fern leaves. "These will do nicely."

"Perfect!"

She fits the leaves and baby's breath into the arrangement, then steps back to admire her work. "Perfect, indeed! Thank you, Steph."

"No problem at all—it's really beautiful." I smile and wave before carrying on with my walk, but my heart beats a dull bruise against my chest as I think about how special this could have been to share with Izzie. I slip my phone out of my pocket and open and close my text thread with Izzie multiple times. I want to tell her *something*, but I don't know what. I guess in the end there's really nothing new for me to say.

Instead, I click on Jordie's name and tap out a text.

> So shit hit the fan

With me and Izzie

Fuck

You okay?

Yeah

I guess

Don't really want to talk about it

Okay

When you do, I'm here

Thanks

I'm gonna chill in Colorado for a bit

Figure out my next move

You need anything?

I take a deep breath. I'm not good at asking for help. I'm even worse at recognizing when I need it. But right now, Jordie's offering, and there *is* something tangible he can do for me.

Yeah if you don't mind

When Izzie gets back to Seattle, could you pick up my stuff?

Yeah of course

Maybe just give it to my dad until I get back

Do you know when that will be?

I stare down at my phone, at the question blinking up at me from the screen. I told Izzie I wanted to stay here. Maybe forever. As I look up at the nature surrounding me, at the town cast in the shadow of sunset, I think maybe I could be happy here. But… who just moves to a small town they hadn't heard of until a few months ago? Izzie was right about one thing, it would be on a whim, and it's been a while since I let something as flimsy as that decide things for me.

I switch over to the browser, where I pulled up the bus schedule for Haven, then type a response to Jordie.

In a few weeks

Maybe

I hover my finger over the button to purchase a ticket to Denver. I can catch a flight back to Seattle from there. I know it's the smart thing to do. Probably even the *right* thing to do. So, I click it.

Thirty-Three

The next few days are rough. On Thursday, I lose spectacularly at pool to Charlotte. On Friday, I get a spider bite that swells to the size of a quail egg on my ankle. And on Saturday, Izzie blocks my number.

Izzie: Hey

Home safe

I think it would be best if I blocked your number

It's not personal I just feel like the temptation to text you would be too much

And I want to let you get on with whatever it is you're doing out there.

So

Bye

And fuck if it doesn't *feel* personal. But I guess that's how breakups go. I text Jordie to let him know Izzie's back, and then send my dad an email.

Hey Dad,

Tour was fun—I'm hanging around Colorado for a bit. This place is dope! I don't know why, but Colorado trees and Pacific Northwest trees have different vibes. I bet Renee can explain it.

Anyway, I don't want to get into it, but Izzie and I aren't together anymore. Jordie's going to bring over some of my stuff for you to hang on to until I figure out what I'm doing.

xoxo
Steph

I sit around in a funk all day after that and order way too many ice creams from Avalanche. Gabe and Ryan take pity on me, and Ryan offers to bring me to some of the trails around Haven.

"What part of all this," I say, gesturing to entire self, "made you think I was the kind of person who likes hiking?"

"Hah!" Gabe shouts. "I told you!"

Ryan rolls his eyes. "Knock it all you want, but you haven't really seen Haven until you've seen it from above."

"Spoken like a true park ranger," Gabe says.

"Just trust me on this. It's not even that bad of a hike." Ryan glances down at my Vans. "Do you, uh, own any other shoes?"

I raise an eyebrow. "Oh yeah, my suitcase is full of footwear. I've got everything from stilettos to Crocs."

"Okay, so… I'll take that as a no…"

Gabe pulls out his phone and sets it on the bar. "What's your shoe size? Maybe Charlotte can loan you some boots."

She does, luckily. I don't think I would have survived the hike in my shoes. Ryan vastly underestimated my level of fitness, and by the time we reach the top, I'm thoroughly winded.

"Not that bad, my ass!" I wheeze, dragging my feet to follow Ryan out of the trees and toward a grassy point.

"Sometimes I forget not everyone's used to the altitude." Ryan offers me his arm to lean on.

It takes me a minute to catch my breath, but when I do, my eyes widen. The view is stunning. From here, I can see the entire town—the lake, the bridge, the park. We're pretty high up, but I still feel so much a part of this place. There are deer grazing down by the river and a flock of geese flies overhead in the shape of an arrow. All around us, the trees rustle in the wind as if whispering some juicy secret.

"Whoa!" I say, stepping forward.

"Careful. Don't get too close to the edge." Ryan grabs the back of my flannel.

"You can really see *everything*."

"Told you!" Ryan points down at the town. "There's the roof of the Black Lantern."

I nod, eyes sweeping over familiar landmarks.

"Hah, and you can see the statue of my dad from here."

"They really love Jed in Haven, huh?" Gabe showed me the statue a few days ago and, honestly, it's just as strange from up here as it was up close. I can't imagine having a statue of someone I know where I live, let alone my own dad. "Is it weird?" I ask. "Your dad being a local hero, and everything?"

"Kind of. I don't know." Ryan shrugs. "It happened when I was a kid, and it was definitely weird when I was growing up. But now I'm just kind of proud. He acts humble, but I know it means a lot to him to know how much the town loves him, especially after my mom died."

My throat closes over my words and I have to fight to say them. "You too, huh?"

Ryan gives me a quizzical look and I sort of wish I hadn't said anything, but it's too late for that.

"You're in the club?" he asks.

I nod and turn my eyes back to the view, blinking away tears. "It's a shitty club."

"Yeah, it sucks." Ryan lets out a long sigh, then says, "I'm glad I get to live in a place she loved, though."

"Really?" I say over the lump in my throat. "I don't think I could ever go back to my hometown, not after…" I trail off. "Too many memories," I say instead.

"I don't know. I don't think there's such a thing as too many memories." He gestures down at Haven, eyes glowing with all the warmth of a hug. "Haven means a lot to me, and not just 'cause I was born and raised here. It's special in a way few places are. I don't think I could ever leave."

I nod, throat too sticky for words, and my fingers find the bus ticket in my pocket. It's only paper, but it feels as heavy as lead.

As the days pass, my indentation in Gabe's couch deepens until there's a Steph-shaped pile of blankets and beer bottles and laundry. The date of my bus trip to Denver looms closer, but I haven't even begun to pack up what remains of my stuff. I know I can't keep relying on Gabe to put me up—he's done enough already—but there's not much waiting for me in Denver besides a flight back to Seattle. Leaving should feel more like moving on. Instead, it just feels like a backslide, like an inescapable gravity pulling me to repeat the past.

Increasingly, I find myself sitting on the roof of the Black Lantern, staring down at Haven with longing, or wandering aimlessly through the park like a forlorn lover in a period drama.

Gabe pulls me from my reverie with a text as I make yet another lap of the park's well-worn path.

> So I think I can get you a job in town if you're interested

> So you can stop couch surfing and get your own place

Guilt pulls at my stomach and I cringe. He doesn't know about the bus ticket yet, and I don't know how to tell him. It's not like he knows what I told Izzie on this very rooftop about wanting to stay here. He can't read my thoughts to know I want it so bad, my bones actually ache at the thought of leaving. But here he is anyway with an offer far above and beyond. Ryan was right—Gabe *is* a good friend.

> Dude maybe we ought to talk about that

I look up, finding myself back at the park's entrance in the shadow of the statue of Jed Lucan. I glance back at the path and go for another round. I'm not quite ready to put everything on the table with Gabe. Not yet.

> Crack open some beers, I'll be there in ten

I'm still not totally ready by the time I complete my walk, but oh well. I climb the stairs to Gabe's place and find him in the kitchen, cold beers in hand.

"Hey!" He holds one out for me to take. "Okay, before you say anything, I kinda feel like this is fate."

"Fate?" I swipe the bottle from his hand and take a swig, letting the tangy liquid spark against my tongue. "I don't believe in fate."

Gabe furrows his brow and gives me a dead-eyed stare. "Come on, Steph."

"Oh, that's rich, coming from the guy who doesn't believe in avocado toast," I say, leaning against the back of the couch.

"It doesn't make any sense! Why would you put avocado on hot bread?"

"Because it's delicious!" I throw my hands in the air, spilling a little beer on the floor.

"Yeah, but riddle me this, Gingrich—how am I supposed to

afford a house someday if I blow all my cash on avocados?"

"Yeah, I don't think it's the avocados, dude."

"Whatever." Gabe shakes his head and crosses over to his desk, where he grabs a napkin with a note scribbled on it. "Listen, you know the record store? They're looking for a new manager— for the store and the radio station. Perfect, right?"

His smile is so bright, I kind of have to return it, but I know my own is weak by comparison. "Yeah... perfect."

"I got the info here—Beatrice is the one you'll want to contact. I hyped you up pretty hard when she came into the Black Lantern today, so the job's pretty much yours as long as you show up to the interview with a pulse."

"Ah, no can do. The terrible secret I've been hiding all this time is that I'm actually undead."

Gabe rolls his eyes. "Come on, this is totally up your alley!"

I shrug. "I don't know... kind of thought I might move on."

"From music?"

"From Haven." I slip into my pocket and withdraw the bus ticket. It's dated for tomorrow. "I know I've overstayed my welcome on your couch, and I can't just hang out here forever. I have to get on with things eventually."

Gabe's face falls immediately. "No. Nope. Absolutely not."

"What are you, a thesaurus?" I raise my brows and sigh. "Come on, be realistic. I don't really fit in here, do I?"

"What are you talking about?" Gabe crosses over to me and gives me a light punch on the arm. "You're practically a townie by now. Everyone loves you."

"*Everyone?* Gabe, you know you only count as one person, right?"

"Me, Ryan, Charlotte." He ticks off the names on his fingers. "Jed's a fan—said your jukebox choices were great—and Eleanor told me she thinks you're 'a darling.'"

"Yeah, okay, but like... wouldn't it be weird for me to just move here on a whim?" I don't realize until I say it that I'm echoing Izzie's words. I'm the one speaking, but it's her doubts that worm their way under my skin and make me so uncertain.

Gabe shrugs. "I don't think it matters if it's impulsive or not. You should do what makes you happy."

"What makes me happy..." My eyes slide unfocused across the room.

It's weird, the way happiness feels so intangible to me. It's not because I haven't been happy. I can point to a hundred memories over the past couple of years where I've been happy—ecstatic, even. It's just that chasing happiness has always felt a little bit like a wild ride. Back in Seattle, it felt like I was floating along a river full of twists and bends and rapids. I was lost in the current, too tired from trying to stay afloat to really look for joy and hold on to it. Arcadia Bay was more like the sea—a push and pull of a steady tide. But the ocean is still dangerous: sometimes it's a sneaker wave that gets you; sometimes, a storm.

Haven is more like a lake, quiet and still with a reflective surface like glass. Here, I can settle. I can actually hear myself think. And, yeah, that's a little discomforting, but it's also refreshing. I've really filled my life with as much noise as possible so I can avoid it, but maybe what I really need is to actually just sit with myself and figure *me* out.

"I'll play you for it," Gabe says, breaking me from my focus. He points to the foosball table, a lopsided smile on his face. "If I win, you stay in Haven."

"And if *I* win?" I ask.

Gabe just shrugs. "Then you do whatever you want."

My heart leaps into my throat—a little yeasty after the beer—but I can't help but grin back. It means a lot that he's willing to fight so hard for this. It's not like I haven't had good friends before—Jordie and Ollie and Lia are all amazing—but this is next-level.

"You're on!" I veer to the left and give one of the handles a spin. The little soccer dudes in white and blue go head over heels—just like me for this town.

Whatever I want.

I don't know if Gabe already knows it, but as he places the ball in the center of the field, I realize that, win or lose, I'm staying.

Spring

Thirty-Four

I've never been so happy to lose a bet. Gabe absolutely crushes me at foosball, but I don't care. I rip the bus ticket in half as he celebrates his victory with yet another dance he should never debut in public. He wakes Ryan up with a phone call just to tell him the good news, and I hide my smile behind my hands.

I collapse onto his couch for my first sleep as an official Haven Springs resident, and he says, "You're not gonna regret this, I promise."

And I don't. Not once over the next few days do I question if I've made the right decision. Not at the interview for the radio-station job, which I do in fact land with ease. Not on my first day, when I realize how totally underqualified I am for the gig. Not even when I sign the lease for my very own apartment. Through it all, I feel one thing: certainty.

"Incoming!" Gabe shouts as he and Charlotte come barreling through the door of my new place with a queen-size mattress.

Charlotte lets Gabe push it into a corner and crosses over to me. "Congrats, girl! This is a great space!"

I shrug. "Thanks, I guess. I've never actually had my own place before."

It's not much—a one-bedroom with a decent-sized living room and in-unit laundry, which is honestly more luxurious to me than a whole castle. The wallpaper is a sort of faded green color and the bathroom has the ugliest checkered orange tile

I've seen in my life, but I don't really care.

"Hey, where do you want the desk?" Ryan asks, carrying a large Ikea box over the threshold.

"I have no idea." I look around at the room, still mostly empty but for a few boxes Dad sent me. "I don't really know what to do with the space, to be honest."

I blink, and realize I'm waiting for someone to tell me what *they* think I should do. I'm waiting for *Izzie* to tell me what to do. As I turn slowly on the spot, taking in the space before me, I imagine it the way Izzie would—the purple plush rug, the bookshelf full of poetry... But this isn't Izzie's room. It isn't Izzie's life.

It's mine.

So I roll my shoulders back and lift my chin. "I don't know, but I'm going to figure it out." I point to a corner of the room. "Maybe over there. If it doesn't work, I can always move it."

"Cool." Ryan and Gabe get to work on putting it together. The instructions are lost somewhere under a box almost immediately as they squabble over the pieces like children building a Lego palace.

Charlotte nudges me and says, "Got you a little house-warming thing."

"What? Oh, you really didn't have to." I turn to see her holding out something thin and rectangular, wrapped in brown butcher paper.

"It's not a big deal—just something I painted. Gabe told me you really liked that deer statue, so I—"

"Stagatha Christie?" I exclaim as I tear the paper off a beautiful oil painting. The colors pop off the canvas, depicting a street view of Haven. It's almost exactly the same as my first glimpse of the town—the brick street, the little flowers bursting from the earth, the snowcapped mountains in the backdrop. And there at the center is that weird deer, looking like it owns the place. "I love it! Holy shit, you painted this?"

Charlotte beams. "Yeah, I work The Silver Dragon by day,

but this is my real passion. I love making art for people who will really appreciate it, you know?"

And I do know. There was a time when I would have responded by talking about my music—and music is still part of me, always will be—and it's been months since I've picked up a pencil to draw. But here I am, in a new town, with new people, trying to be myself, so I gather my bravery and I say, "I *do* appreciate it. I'm actually an artist, too."

Charlotte's eyes brighten. "Oh, that's great!"

"I don't paint, but I draw comics and stuff. I did a zine in college for a while, actually."

"No way!" Gabe chimes in.

Behind him, Ryan is furiously trying to fit a screw into the wrong piece, eyebrows pinched in laser focus.

"Ethan is super into comics, too." Gabe takes the screw from Ryan and points to the correct piece. "He'll be so excited to have someone to talk to about it!"

"That's rad! I'd love to geek out about comics with him." I've met Ethan a couple times, now. I kind of always thought kids weren't my thing, but Charlotte's son is actually pretty cool—and apparently we have more in common than I thought.

"When he gets back from his dad's, let's set something up," Charlotte says. "In the meantime..." She pulls a bottle of wine from her bag. "I realize you don't have a TV yet, so we can't do a movie night, but how about a *moving* night?"

"Fancy!" I hop over to the kitchen, where I've already begun organizing the cutlery and dishes I managed to scrounge together. Between a couple of estate sales and the generous donations from folks around town, I may not have the most aesthetic dining set-up, but I kind of prefer it this way. All my cutlery is old, tarnished silver, and each mismatched plate and bowl feels like this town—storied and unique.

Charlotte pours the wine into four mugs and hands them out to Gabe and Ryan.

"Cheers," she says, clinking ours together. "To your new life in Haven Springs!"

We drink. And we laugh. And slowly this place begins to feel like home, not just because of the stuff I hang on the walls or the books I put on the shelves, but because of the memories I build within these walls and the people I share them with.

Haven Springs is not Arcadia Bay, but I don't need it to be. It's different in so many ways; and it's the same in just as many. But then, so am I. I'm not the same girl I was at nineteen. I'm not the same girl from before the storm. Arcadia Bay is gone, but home isn't. Because home isn't a single place. And it's not a person. It's something I hold inside myself, and it's up to me to put down roots and try to grow.

After Gabe, Charlotte, and Ryan head out, I turn to survey this place I've chosen for myself, and I catch sight of my purple suitcase pushed up against the wall. It's the only thing left. I cross the room and flip open the lid.

And, finally, I unpack.

Acknowledgments

No book is ever written truly alone, and I have been lucky enough to have an incredible team behind me for *Steph's Story*.

An enormous thank you to my rockstar agent, Saba Sulaiman, who has not once wavered in her support of me and my books. I cannot believe my fortune to have ended up in this business with someone as genuine, talented, and brilliant as you. May there be many more to come!

To the team at Titan who have ushered this book into being, my eternal thanks. Michael Beale, editor extraordinaire—I'd say I'm sorry for all the puns, but I don't think you'd believe me. Many thanks to Julia Lloyd, Lisa Morris, Dan Coxon, Kerry Lewis, William Robinson, George Sandison, Katherine Carroll, Kabriya Coghlan, Elora Hartway, and Jenny Boyce.

This book would not exist without the brilliant minds behind *Life is Strange*. Thank you to Raoul Barbet, Jean-Luc Cano, Michel Koch, and the team at DON'T NOD, for creating the original story and characters of *Life is Strange*—and to the entire team at Deck Nine Games for deepening the universe in *Life is Strange: Before the Storm* and *Life is Strange: True Colors*, and, most importantly, bringing us Steph! Thank you for building such wonderful characters and allowing me to play a small part in telling the monumental story that is *Life is Strange*.

Thanks also to the team at Square Enix, in particular Jon M. Brooke and Andrew James. If I could go back in time and tell teenage-Rosiee that I would one day get to work with the publisher of some of her favorite games, I think she'd probably spontaneously combust on the spot. Special thanks to the other storytellers in the *Life is Strange* universe—Emma Vieceli, Claudia Leonardi, and Andrea Izzo—who originated the crew of *The High Seas* in such vibrant color in the comics. And, of course, a massive thank you to Steph herself, Katy Bentz, whose performance has brought so much more than a voice to the character we all love.

My author friends and writing community have sustained me throughout this process. Thanks to Eric Smith and M.K. England, whose generosity with advice is unmatched. You're both the absolute best. RoAnna Sylver, you know what you did. I cannot begin to thank you enough. Thanks also to Kat, Emily, Jenny, Emma, Rory, Kalyn, Michelle, and Linsey.

Thank you to my family and friends: Mom and Dad—I *told* you playing video games would pay off someday; my D&D group—Faye, Stephen, Amanda, and Joel—who gave me infinite inspiration for the TTRPG scenes; Claire and Colleen who patiently let me ramble about this book despite knowing absolutely nothing about *Life is Strange* and almost certainly are responsible for some of the puns, though I can't remember which ones; and of course my dog Tess, who sat by my side the whole way through this process, and my cats Jane and Petra, who staunchly refused to do the same.

Finally, thank you to the entire *Life is Strange* community. The fans of this series are some of the most passionate and creative I've encountered and I'm honored to count myself among you.

About the Author

Rosiee Thor began her career as a storyteller by demanding to tell her mother bedtime stories instead of the other way around. She spent her childhood reading by flashlight in the closet until she came out as queer. She lives in Oregon with a dog, two cats, and an abundance of plants. She is the author of *Tarnished Are The Stars*, *Fire Becomes Her*, and *The Meaning of Pride*.

For more fantastic fiction, author events,
exclusive excerpts, competitions, limited editions and more

VISIT OUR WEBSITE
titanbooks.com

LIKE US ON FACEBOOK
facebook.com/titanbooks

FOLLOW US ON TWITTER AND INSTAGRAM
@TitanBooks

EMAIL US
readerfeedback@titanemail.com